DIAMONDS, DECEPTION & DESTINY

THE STARLIGHT SERIES

SAND, SEQUINS & SILICONE

DIAMONDS, DECEPTION & DESTINY

DIAMONDS, DECEPTION & DESTINY

PIA MIA

W FRAYED
wattpad books **PAGES**

Copyright © 2025 Pia Mia. All rights reserved.

Content warning: attempted date rape, attempted sexual assault, alcohol abuse

Published in Canada by Wattpad WEBTOON Book Group, a division of Wattpad WEBTOON Studios, Inc.

36 Wellington Street E., Toronto, ON M5E 1C7

www.wattpad.com

No portion of this publication may be reproduced or transmitted, in any form or by any means, without the express written permission of the copyright holders.

First Frayed Pages x Wattpad Books edition: July 2025

www.frayedpagesmedia.com

ISBN 978-1-99834-117-7 (Trade Paperback)
ISBN 978-1-99834-161-0 (eBook)

Names, characters, places, and incidents featured in this publication are either the product of the author's imagination or are used fictitiously. Any resemblance to actual persons (living or dead), events, institutions, or locales, without satiric intent, is coincidental.

Wattpad Books, W by Wattpad Books, Wattpad WEBTOON Book Group, and associated logos are trademarks and/or registered trademarks of Wattpad WEBTOON Studios, Inc. and/or its affiliates. Wattpad and associated logos are trademarks and/or registered trademarks of Wattpad Corp.

Frayed Pages and associated logos are trademarks and/or registered trademarks of Frayed Pages, Inc.

Library and Archives Canada Cataloguing in Publication and U.S. Library of Congress Cataloging in Publication information is available upon request.

Printed and bound in Canada

1 3 5 7 9 10 8 6 4 2

Cover design by Emily Wittig
Author Photo © Pia Mia
Cover image © yuyanga, © whitehoune, © Studio Images,
© LeMusique via iStock; © tomertu via Adobe Stock
Typesetting by Delaney Anderson

To anyone who has a dream but might not have found the courage to go for it yet. This is your sign. Destiny is waiting.

1

One week before the events of Sand, Sequins & Silicone . . .

I must have been under the influence when I agreed to this because . . . how am I on a blind date? Not remotely my style. When the car pulls up to the curb, I do a quick mirror check before stepping out. Santa Monica Boulevard is busy with cars zooming by, with people pouring out of Ubers all loud, smiling and chatting, and dressed up to enjoy their night.

That used to be me. Heartache takes a lot out of you. Since John and I broke up three weeks ago, I haven't wanted to do much. The betrayal. The constant feeling of not being able to trust him. How he put his own selfish success over what we were building. Going behind my back and then lying about Riley. I should hate him, but the heart doesn't work that way. Love just doesn't disappear overnight.

Some days, I don't even get out of bed unless I absolutely must. My record release is a week away so there is plenty to keep me busy, but I haven't been in the mood to go dancing or hang out. I am definitely not feeling up to dating. Still, my girls, Maya and Valerie, had other ideas. And it's hard to say no to them when they get an idea in their heads.

"Trust us. This is exactly what you need!" Maya said the other day when she was organizing everything.

"But a blind date?"

"You need to get out of your head for a night. Take a break from working and wallowing. Have a real meal and sit across from a gorgeous man who's going to remind you there is soooo much more out there. That there is life beyond John."

Earlier today, they both insisted on coming over to the condo armed with miniskirts and matching tops for me to try on. Of course, they made the whole time fun. Blasting music, drinking cocktails, gossiping about the latest trashy reality TV episodes. For once in far too long, I was able to forget my troubles and didn't think about all the drama with John or Riley. The girls worked their makeup and glam magic with Jessie on FaceTime giving her final approval before loading me into the waiting black car.

You can do this. I took a deep breath to calm my nerves. I put my hand on the door handle waiting for the courage to reach my fingertips. *Just have fun.*

Pushing my shoulders back, I walk into the restaurant, stopping inside the door. Dan Tana's is a very popular Italian restaurant and usually hard to get a table. I was expecting it to be lively and packed but it's completely empty. Did I come on the wrong night? Popping open the text window on my phone, I'm about to ping Maya when the hostess appears.

"Princess." She smiles, and I wonder how she knows my name. My face must look confused because the hostess giggles. "We've been waiting for you. If you'd like to follow me, please."

I try to take everything in—roses and candles lining the bar, jazz music playing softly in the background—and I can't decide if I feel nervous or just excited. The whole night is feeling so mysterious. It's been forever since I went on a date and never a blind date. I'm used to meeting new people and putting myself out there—it's part of my job as a musician—but when it comes to dating, I've always been very reserved. Even more so after John and I crashed and burned, and then crashed again. *No,* I insist, *I'm not letting my past ruin my future.*

This dark empty restaurant feels quite intimate. Suddenly, I'm clutching my purse tightly. Maybe I am more nervous than I thought. Maybe I should've taken that shot on my way out the door of my condo. Damn it.

There's a man sitting at a table in the corner, but I can't see him because my view is blocked by a giant bouquet of flowers. When he stands up, it takes a few seconds for my brain to process who I'm seeing, and then I'm the one laughing.

Win walks around the table to greet me. He puts a hand on my upper arm and kisses my cheek. My heart skips a beat. The surprise of seeing him. And that he smells so goddamn good. Win comes from money—well, his family has money—but he's also a hard-working, astute businessman with great style and innate charm. He oozes the kind of confidence that simply can't be bought or made.

My eyes linger on him a moment too long trying to get a read on him. I'm so confused. How is Win my blind date? Did he know I was the one who'd be showing up?

"You're my blind date?"

"Looks like it." Win smiles and pulls out a chair for me. "And these are for you."

He gestures to the bouquet as we sit down. It's filled with what must be a hundred pink and white roses, my favorite, and I wonder how he knew.

"Knights used to wear red roses . . ."

". . . for their ladies after battle," we both say. Random facts sticking in my head was a quirk I hadn't outgrown since childhood.

Win raises an eyebrow and gives me a half-smile. He sits in the chair next to me and leans back. He always looks so comfortable and relaxed, which instantly makes me feel the same. He makes me feel safe. From the day we first met, while he seemed hard-shelled to some people, he was soft with me, always protecting me.

"Someone's been studying."

"I always do my research."

When I lean in to smell the flowers, something catches my eye. It's a flash of light, a glimmer. There's a necklace attached to the ribbon. It's a gold heart with small and perfectly cut stones. Are those diamonds? My cheeks flush. I am not used to being given gifts, especially not ones with diamonds on them.

"Win, this is gorgeous." When I turn the necklace over in my hand, there is a single music note engraved on the back. His generosity is overwhelming, but so is how much thought he put into tonight. "I'm so glad you're my blind date. I was feeling beyond anxious about coming here."

"Did you think your friends would set you up with someone terrible?"

"No." I laugh. "I trust them. They would never do that to me."

The waiter arrives with a bottle of wine. Win tastes the golden liquid and then nods to the waiter to pour it into our glasses.

"So, why nervous then?"

I didn't know how much to say. Win puts me so at ease that I am tempted to tell him everything. About me and John. How he was my first and, I thought, last love. How we made this record together and

I'm so proud of it, but he lied to me one too many times. How it had only been a few weeks since I called it off and I was still drowning in the heartache. That my single is dropping soon and I'm dreading all the questions I'll get about John and the status of our now-dead relationship. That I need to "get back out there" but I don't know if I'm ready to risk my heart being torn apart again. Deciding to keep it light I say, "It's a lot of things, really."

After taking a sip of wine, an orgasmic moan slips out of me. My eyes shoot to Win to see if he noticed but he's swirling his glass effortlessly with the stem perfectly placed between his fingers. Nice.

Once again, Win's taste is perfect.

"But also, I've never been on a blind date before. I'm not quite sure how they work," I say.

Win laughs. We've known each other for a few years now but I realize I haven't seen him laugh often. Truth? I like making him laugh. He's always been helpful and offers lots of career advice, but he's also a serious man. Win is one of the top angel investors in town, everyone knows him, and everyone wants to work with him. He's funded many apps and tech companies that we use on the daily and he's starting now to do a lot of business in the entertainment world. His family's interests are in fashion, which sparks his interest in the creative and entertainment world. We met back when one of his family's clothing brands came to me to collaborate for a music video. He decided to stop by the set to check things out. There was something special about our connection; I could tell the moment we met. There was an instant feeling of history even though we had none. We were drawn to each other and stayed in touch, went to dinners, called to check in every now and then. Win quickly became someone I leaned on for business advice. He's very busy so I'm grateful for the time he gives me. This date is the first time I've seen him in a more relaxed setting, and it's very attractive, which means I'm now teetering off a steep edge of lust in ways that I find quite surprising.

"It's like any other date. We talk. We ask questions. Get to know each other," Win says.

"Okay, then." I rest my elbows on the table and lean forward. "Why have you been set up on a date with me? I imagine you have no trouble getting dates all on your own."

He laughs and my heart skips a beat again. It feels too good making Win laugh.

"I lost a bet."

My heart sinks a little. "Oh. Should I be insulted?"

"No, no. It's a long story." He waves a hand to dismiss my comment. "I lost a bet but not the prize. I am happy to be here with you, Princess. Glad we finally have a chance to talk."

"Me too."

Up until now, we've only interacted in professional settings—an event, an office meeting, an official fitting. And if the meeting happened to take place over dinner, there was still that underlying feeling of it being work and only work. Did I think he was handsome? Sure. Did I savor the smell of his cologne every now and then? Maybe. You can't blame me for that though—Win's sex appeal oozes out of him. Regardless, Win is someone I respect, admire, and want in my life in any capacity.

"Tell me something about you that I don't already know." Win leans across the table to top off my wine first before refilling his own glass.

"Like what?"

"How about singing? How did you get started? And not the press package notes, the full story."

"Back home in Guam, I would sing for my parents. Put on little shows for them around the house. They constantly encouraged me. One day I got into a school musical of *Cinderella*. I never considered singing in front of anyone outside my family until then. I got completely obsessed. I worked hard to learn my lines, be the absolute best. Sang until I was hoarse. Even though I was just a kid, it was the first time I felt I had a purpose."

I don't mean to blurt it all out like that but as soon as I start talking it's hard to stop. For a second, I wonder if I should be embarrassed, or if I am boring Win with too much detail, but he doesn't look bored at all.

"*Cinderella*? Wow. I can totally see you as the leading lady." Win leans forward in his chair, bringing his wine glass to his mouth. Damn, he has nice lips. He puts his elbows on the table to match my posture.

"Once I knew what I wanted, I became very focused." We are sitting so close together that I can see the candlelight flickering in his eyes. "To be honest, it got a bit lonely at times. Which was hard for me to navigate, being so young. I took lessons when I could. Practiced constantly. Tried out for every play. Sang at weddings and events."

"You were ambitious even then."

"I'm very passionate about the things—and people—I love. I don't come from money and we didn't have any connections. I knew it would take hard work. And I wasn't going to waste any time." I put my hands over my face and laugh. "I've had to make sacrifices over the years, but I truly believe music is my destiny. Then I got to Hollywood and the work quadrupled. Once I figured out how things operated here, I was clearer on what I wanted. And I had very strong moral guide rails. Little did I know how much more difficult that would make things." I raise my eyebrows. "It's what I was meant to do. And performing is where I feel the most like myself. I sound insane! I promise, I don't have a giant ego."

"Anyone who knows you wouldn't think that about you, Princess."

When I look up at Win, I expect to see him laugh but his face is stone and serious. He's staring at me like he's trying to take me all in.

"You know, meeting you gave me such a sense of relief. Of course I had my team, and friends and family but it felt like you saw me in a different light. Maybe in a deeper way. I don't know if you believe in stuff like past lives but I do. If I had to guess, I'd bet money we were close in another life and I'm really happy we found each other again." *Seems like I can't stop talking.* "It's so funny being surrounded by so many people but still feeling alone. The business can be so cutthroat; it's easy to get swallowed up and lost in the crowd but you never let me feel that way. I felt seen."

"How could people not see you?" His voice is so low I wonder if he's whispering. I can almost feel it rumble against my chest. He leans towards me, our faces so close together I can feel his warmth. "You shine brighter than any of these wannabe stars. You light up rooms. You outshine every diamond handed to those rich kids."

"That's very sweet of you. But unfortunately, in my experience, it seems not everyone is so encouraging of others that shine bright." My laugh comes out a touch awkward and it's clear we both understand who we're really talking about: Riley.

"You sing like an angel, you're smart, hardworking, and kind. It's natural for people to be jealous and competitive. They pretend to not look when they can't stop staring." Win pulls back and smiles, locks his eyes on me. "So, let them all live in the dark. I don't care about them but I do care about you."

The waiter is suddenly at the table clearing his throat to get our attention. We both push back into our seats and smile up as he lists the specials, but I have trouble concentrating because I'm still thinking about everything Win said.

When I was new to Hollywood and didn't really know anyone, operating in this world couldn't have been more different than the laid-back nature growing up in Guam. Hollywood was a long way away from barbequing on the beach and taking a sunset paddle board. I might not have been in the ocean . . . but I was absolutely swimming with the sharks.

My newfound friends, Riley and her crew, had played every game there was at the arcade and I was on a high from winning a few rounds of basketball, earning me what felt like respect from the girls. We were maybe a bit too old to be at the arcade, but it was good, solid fun—and the photos for everyone's socials were pretty cool. Riley's brand manager had set it all up, and I was thankful to be included. Shy growing up, I was proud to be killing it in a new group of friends. At the end of it, all the parents rounded us up to take a group photo and before I realized what was happening I ended up in the center. Big. Mistake.

"You don't belong there! You need to move over to the side," one team member said. She'd been snapping photos for Riley's social media all day. Setting up shots. Creating a "scene." Riley's influencer status was stratospheric at this point.

My cheeks instantly turned bright red and tears welled up in my eyes. *Is she talking to me?*

"Flannel shirt, I'm talking to you. Move." The woman stood there with her hand on her hip chomping on her gum with a nasty smirk across her lips. *Enjoying this.* Humiliating a *me*.

What did I do wrong? I didn't know what to do or where to go. No one had ever spoken to me like that before. I looked at my new friends, hoping one of them would help or stick up for me, but they all stayed silent and just stared right back, as if I had in fact done something wrong.

"You're not supposed to be in the center!" the woman spat at me.

Nerves ringing through my body head to toe, I bolted out of the photo as fast as I could and tried to play it cool. I tried to maintain a (not so) calm and collected front. A skill I quickly mastered.

It was humiliating. The entire day went from being a fun outing with friends to this embarrassing core memory of being told I didn't belong in the spotlight. I wasn't good enough. I hadn't earned my place. As painful as it was, it was my first lesson in learning how quickly things can turn in this town. It could change from fairy tale to nightmare in seconds and it was all out of your control. Things worked differently here and I was going to have to learn how to play the game. I hated it but the lesson burned into me. I'd never forget it.

There are people in the world who will tell you what you want to hear. There are people who will purposely not tell you what you need to hear, too. And then there are those who will tell you what you need to know. My girls are in the latter category but I had to go through some rough patches with Riley to figure that out. And then what happened with John. But sitting here, now, instinctively, I know Win has my back.

Win double checks what I like, getting it all right, and orders for both of us. The waiter fills our wine glasses before walking off.

"Okay, now it's my turn." I take another sip of wine. "I get to ask you something now."

"I'm all yours." Win raises his glass like he's going to make a toast and I softly giggle. "I'm an open book."

Somehow I don't think that's entirely true. I tilt my head to the side and narrow my eyes. Win laughs at my look of skepticism.

He raises his hand up as if he's about to take the stand in a courtroom. "I, Win, solemnly swear to you, Princess, to answer whatever questions you throw at me with utter honesty."

I squint my eyes harder at him. "Why did you reserve the entire restaurant? Is this something you always do on first dates?"

"I didn't want to share my time with you. Didn't want any distractions."

"It's not because you don't want anyone to see you out on a date?"

His eyebrow goes up again. "You think I don't want to be seen with you?"

"I've noticed some things."

"Like what?"

"Like you never bring anyone to events. I never see pictures of you with a girlfriend or hear any rumors about who you're dating."

Win keeps his hand on his glass. He spins it slowly on the table while holding my gaze. If he were anyone else it might have been unnerving, but like everything else with Win, it was comforting.

"I prefer to keep a firm boundary between business and pleasure."

I almost ask if this dinner was business or pleasure but decide to avoid that topic. And clearly, he's avoiding admitting how he knows I was his date tonight.

"Tell me about your family. Are you close to your parents?"

Win doesn't flinch but I can tell the question makes him uncomfortable.

"I love my family but it's complicated. My parents divorced when I was a teenager. Dad worked a lot—*works* a lot—and Mom did the best she could with me, but she had her own issues."

"Were you a wild teenager?"

"No. Not really." Win picks up his glass, stares at the wine as he swirls it around. "I may or may not have been shipped to boarding school for a stint." His eyes flick to mine. "I take after my dad, though."

I have so many questions but know this isn't the right time to ask. Or maybe it isn't my place to ask at all. The last month has been an avalanche of disaster I've been trying to dig myself out of. Caught up in my career and John and everything that happened with him choosing to work with Riley over saving our relationship—it feels like forever since I really got to know someone new. I need to remember that this isn't a real date. Win is a business relationship, a friend at most, and he isn't interested in me romantically. He's supportive and kind. I'm sure he has pity for my disaster of a love life he's seen bits and pieces of from the outside, and that must be why he agreed to this blind date. And whatever bet he lost.

"Tell me more about *your* mom." Win reaches over and puts a hand on my wrist making my body heat in response. "She sounds like she really has your back. Is she still in Guam?"

I'm eyeing his hand on my wrist, trying to contain how much I'm enjoying the little bursts of tingling energy it's sending throughout my entire body as I tell him all about my mom and Jessie, moving to Hollywood and starting my career. We talk about what I've done so far and what I want to do next. I admit how excited I am about my release party coming up in a week and how much I love the pink theme for the album and marketing. I remind him that he's invited to the party and he promises he wouldn't miss the celebration. I talk about my plans for the cosmetics line; he chimes in that he'll put me in touch with an amazing company to help me roll it out. Win asks questions. He laughs. Pokes fun at me now and then. Offers advice about contracts, contacts, and marketing. He listens and he understands. He respects me.

I'm so glad that we have this entire restaurant to ourselves, but I suspect that nothing in this moment could have distracted us from each other. Friends or more, if I know one thing it's this: Win and I are going to be in each other's lives for a very, very long time.

2

Present day

"Princess! Princess! Princess!"

The crowd roars over and over. I have about thirty seconds before it's my cue to take the stage for the Cirque au bord de l'eau show in Miami. The DJ plays the intro for my set loud, the sound pouring over the audience, the beat picking up speed and my heart matching its pace. I'm never nervous once I'm on stage . . . but waiting in the wings has my chest pounding so hard I feel like you could see it beat through my pink custom-beaded corset top. I might look the part of a perfect popstar living the dream, but reality couldn't be further from the truth. And I can't help but notice the little ache in the pit of my stomach, the aftermath of everything that's happened with John and Riley. Why can't everything be going well at once, why does it have to be one or the other . . . career up, love life in flames . . . ?

Standing up tall and taking a deep breath, I remind myself this is not the time nor the place to start this spiral. John chose Riley. He picked her, that manipulative, lying . . . No, I'm not going to go there. What's past is past.

DIAMONDS, DECEPTION & DESTINY

The room buzzes with activity as musicians and crew members run around, getting on and off stage. No matter how many shows I've played so far, I'm still not used to being in the midst of all this chaos or one of the people everyone is focused on. It's a bit ironic that I've spent years and years working to get to this point, but I still struggle a bit to understand how I fit into this world. Performing and writing music comes naturally for me but working the business angle and playing "the game" is something else entirely. Kimi and Wayne set up the dinner party to celebrate my song's success after this performance so that means more networking and being on for everyone in the room. I'm going to need a solid boost to get me there. Yet another reason to be grateful I have my girls at my side.

My glam team applies my final touches in the moments before I hit the stage. Angel swipes one more coat of my coconut lip gloss. Ray fluffs my roots and creates a cloud of hairspray. My girls, Maya and Val, squeeze each of my hands tight, signaling me good luck. It's time.

"Kill it, babe." Maya flashes me a smile.

"You got this, we'll be right at the front of the pit singing . . . no, *screaming* all the words," Val says.

When the girls are with me at my shows, they're my extra bit of good luck.

"Love you both. Sing now. Party later."

I blow them a kiss, push my bow-detailed in-ears in, turn up my mic pack, and grab my diamond microphone bespoke with a red heart. Deep breath, smile on, and . . . as the heel of my boot steps onto the stage, the light catching on the glitter, I exhale into hysteria.

Screams fill my ears. I smile wide, looking out at the sea of people, some holding signs that read "We love you PRINCESS" and others wearing tiaras. Moments like this feel too good to be true. Emotions flood into me: the adrenaline, the comfort, the power. I worked hard to get here, and so much has happened along the way, I want to enjoy every second of it.

There are probably a couple thousand people gathered in the audience. The flashes on their phones illuminate the crowd like a thousand stars, making it easier to see each and every person all the way to the back of the group. The May heat blows through my hair like a glam fan and I feel like a goddamn superstar. Gratitude pours out of my soul—this is what I am meant to be doing. I hit all my choreography perfectly, smiling across the stage at the dancers, everyone keeping up and hitting all their marks. The Miami heat is heavy on me and I can feel the sweat dripping down my back but I keep pushing. Fans scream the lyrics to all my songs, clapping along, clutching onto each other, making memories they'll remember forever. Scanning the audience I see familiar faces at the front of the stage. Maya and Val are in the VIP pit dancing and singing. They see me notice them and start waving madly. I might have made my fair share of mistakes, but I know I must be doing something right to have friends like them. Jessie too. We're a tight unit and support each other through everything. I don't know where I'd be without them.

I hit my pose hard—one hand on my hip, the other holding the mic to my mouth—as the next song drifts in. Scanning the crowd, there's a girl in the front row, pink cheeks glittering, tiara sitting perfectly on top of her head. They are the reason. My eyes keep drifting to the side of the stage, and they catch again, this time stopping on Win. Fire burns deep in my belly as questions swarm in my head. He's tuned in, drink in one hand, phone in the other, and *he's filming me*. I move my hips side to side trying to look as effortless yet sexy as possible because right now, he looks fucking proud. If that really is what he's feeling, I sure as hell want to give him something to be proud of.

We spent last night together and it couldn't have been more unexpected and perfect. Another memory to add to my list of magical moments I'll recount before I go to bed tonight. He said so many sweet things and made me feel so special, but it was late, and he'd been drinking, and it was in the heat of the moment. Doubt creeps into my mind that maybe he'll feel differently today. I quickly push the thought far away. We care about each other but I'm not sure what it all means.

Five . . . six . . . seven . . . eight . . . sounds low in my in ears. That's my cue to start making my way into our final formation—the show is almost over. The last song starts playing and it's the one the crowd has been waiting for. The one that's about Win that I couldn't bring myself to admit to him last night. About being done with John and his lies and betrayals. Finding someone who supports me and believes in me. I wanted to tell Win the truth, but it felt too risky, and I've been hurt so much lately. Sometimes it's so much easier saying how I really feel in song. He'll know. He gets me. I know it deep down.

Riley's there in the VIP section. This is a big event with a lot of media attention so it makes sense she'd show up. She's staring up at me but she isn't singing along or chanting my name with everyone else. In fact, for a second or two, it's obvious she's angry, like she's got a bad taste in her mouth. As soon as she realizes I've spotted her she turns away. It all happens so quickly I wonder if I imagined it. She's right back to being pseudo supporter and taking photos posing with other people in the VIP, not looking at the stage at all.

The crowd goes wild when the song ends. I take my in-ears out so I can be completely enveloped by screams burying me, vibrating through my body. I take a long bow, hand in hand with my dancers. The crowd keeps chanting *Princess!* and *We love you!*, while we signal to the band. Maya and Val are cheering and clapping, leading the group around them to backstage. I stand for a moment longer waving at the audience. Do I really deserve this? I don't want it to end but I walk off stage with a new wave of adrenaline hitting me as my team rushes over.

"Incredible!" Kimi hugs me. "That was an amazing show. You blew them away, Princess."

"Thanks! Careful, I'm all sweaty." I laugh at Kimi's enthusiasm. There are few things more comforting in this business than really knowing that my management is in my corner. "It felt great to me too."

"We'll make sure the record label hears all about it." Wayne throws an arm over my shoulder and gives me a quick squeeze. "They've got big plans for you and that last song, the single." He passes me a bottle of water and a fluffy white hand towel.

"That's good to hear." I'm slightly distracted looking for Win backstage. Spotted. Handsome, magnetic, and oh my god he's holding a bouquet of flowers. *Are those for me?* When he meets my eyes, he's grinning. He shrugs his shoulders. Code for, *I have a very dedicated assistant*. Win understands how this business works. Business, get a grip, Princess. Events like this can be hectic but knowing he's here, even if it's at a distance, makes the chaos a little more bearable.

"We need to start posting now." Kimi is on her phone scrolling for something. "You need something on your personal account too."

"I got off stage five seconds ago." I laugh again but also feel a twinge of irritation. I'm sweaty, a bit tired, want to get out of my stage clothes and see my friends. Noticing my tone I try to soften the slight blow. "Give me a few to catch my breath and I promise I'll get some posts up. Cool?"

"Of course." Kimi presses her lips into a thin smile and shoots a sharp look to Wayne.

"We can't lose this momentum." Wayne is so excited that he's almost shouting. "You're not the hot new thing anymore."

Okay, ouch. I'm not sure how to respond to that comment. The two of them are bantering back and forth about next steps and reach and strategy and even my backup dancers have made it to the green room.

Win raises his eyebrows and looks a bit concerned. Analyzing my face to see if I need rescuing. I give my head a discreet shake to tell him I'm okay. Trying to maintain my composure I turn my attention back to the managers.

"The label is already talking about plans for your next single." Kimi beams. She really loves creating clever ways to leverage marketing strategy with my other projects and seeing my label engaging. "We should make sure we coordinate with the cosmetic line launch. Double the marketing power."

Slight panic arises. I didn't realize we were switching to a new song so soon. Shouldn't we give this one a second to reach its full potential? A group of people pass by on their way to the stage and bump into me. I almost lose my balance but recover before I fall. I look at them, but they don't even notice. I can hear the crowd clapping, welcoming them to the stage but everything sounds far away now.

"Hey." Win steadies me.

Was it only a few hours ago that we were together? Was that me? I really hope it wasn't all a dream.

"I'm really happy you made it."

"I wouldn't miss it for the world." He gives me a wink and hands me a beautiful bouquet of different-colored roses. White, orange, red, and yellow, wrapped in brown paper and a perfect red bow. Win took the time to get me flowers . . . I don't think John had ever done that for me. *Stop comparing.*

"Win! Thank you." I hold them up to sniff and a sparkle catches my eye. It's a bracelet attached to the ribbon. Before I can really take a breath, Win slips the bracelet off the bouquet and onto my wrist. "It's so beautiful."

His warm scent is intoxicating to me. How is this guy real? "Nothing compared to you." He says easily.

There's that blush again. It is an incredible thing to have Win's eyes on me. He makes me feel powerful and strong.

"Looks like the managers are going full force."

"Yeah, they're on a mission. Want to join me in my dressing room? I have to get out of this bodysuit and change my lip color before talking to the press."

I'm finally in my dressing room—I did a quick change into my silky baby pink Alexander Wang tracksuit set and am in the middle of touching up my red lipstick when my phone buzzes.

Maya: Princess! That was so fucking good!

Val: You were amazing babe! You ARE amazing!

Val: Everyone knew all the words.

Maya: At one point I looked over at Valerie and she had TEARS in her eyes. TEARS!!!

Val: Oh shut up! I saw you blinking back your own rivulets.

Maya: HAHAHA

Val: Hurry up and come to the party. We have shots waiting for youuuu.

Princess: I'm so glad you could be here. It meant the world to me.

My eyes start to sting a bit. It's one thing to be loved, but they see me, all the broken parts, all the messy parts, and they have never once batted an eye.

I send one more text before tucking my phone into my arm.

Princess: Did you see Riley? She kind of had a weird look on her face but maybe I'm reading into it.

Maya: Ugh I cannot do a Riley Vega recap right now. Let's talk about her later and focus on the good shit.

Princess: Agreed.

Jessie jumps into the group chat asking what she missed. There is a lot of back and forth between the three of them talking about the show, sharing photos and videos. Giving updates on everyone they met in the VIP section.

I need a huddle with them ASAP. They don't know about me and Win yet and I'm not sure what to tell them. Guaranteed there'll be a million questions about what will happen next, but to be honest I don't have a clue. Truth is I want to enjoy this moment and not think about everything else. I want to just *be* for once before everything changes again. When I glance up at him, he's typing away on his phone only to look up and give me a thousand-watt smile, turning my insides upside down.

Val: Did you see John? I heard he's here but I haven't seen him.

Maya: No. But I bet he'll sneak his way over to Princess soon enough.

I'm not sure if I'm ready to see him. The last time we spoke it was so terrible. Losing your best friend and a first love—to each other—feels like having your heart ripped right out of your chest. I guess John didn't mean it when he said our love would be forever, whenever, and always? We broke up, for good this time because he chose to be with Riley. We still have work to do on the album and the planned upcoming singles—so I have to be a professional, and that's hard for anyone.

Princess: I can't avoid him entirely. So if we see him let's just all be civil please.

A warning the girls are familiar with when it comes to John. He's put me through hell but I love him . . . loved him? He's a part of me and I don't think I'll ever be able to fully let him go. So if friends is all we are, then let's be friends.

There's a knock on the door, and it snaps me out of my John thoughts, their endless loop.

"We've got to move." Kimi pops her head in and then doesn't look up from her phone. She's typing madly. "They need you in the media tent for interviews."

I wait a minute to see if she'll look at me but nothing. I try not to be bothered by it. She's doing her job and juggling a lot at once, but I'm feeling a little bit more like a product and less like a person right now.

"Sure. I'll be right there." I smile tightly. "Need a couple of minutes."

Kimi opens the door wide and strides in, holding it open for Wayne. Good thing I've got clothes on, as boundaries have apparently left the building. Both are on their phones and looking very preoccupied.

Princess: They're driving me crazy! Is that selfish? I get it. They want to make the most of the moment. It's all about content these days. Right now I hate that word.

Win's phone pings, I can hear it in the background as I continue getting ready for the media blitz. I get it, I do. But I'm also feeling rushed. Like this moment in time isn't quite good enough for either of them or the label. I give my head a quick shake. I'm being too harsh. They've been great managers to me. Why would that change now?

Win: Content is good for business. What if I found you some social media help? Also, that bracelet looks great on you. But it's also okay to pause and take a beat. Enjoy what happened on stage. They work for you. They're here to support you. We all are. But you are the one who wrote that song. You are the one that gives those incredible performances. The audience cheers for you, Princess. You're it. Make sure to live in the moment before rushing off into the next one.

Can he read my mind?

"Princess! We need to get moving." Wayne waves at me. "Everyone is waiting for you."

"Let me say goodbye to Win," I say. He looks up from his phone as I gather my bag. My team will make sure the rest of my gear gets packed up and sent back to LA. See, I'm lucky. "I'll see you at the dinner party?"

"I'll be there."

I want him to kiss me goodbye, but he only puts a hand on my arm, grazing my new bracelet, lets our eyes meet one more time, and then walks away.

After another deep breath, I turn to face Kimi and Wayne. "Ready to go. Do I look okay?"

"Fantastic," Kimi says, "Let's roll."

Win ducks out of the room ahead of us. *God*, he is sexy even from behind. Focus. Win is right. This is my day and I am going to make the most of every minute of it. Come at me press, I'm ready.

3

The adrenaline rush from my set has worn off and I'm both exhausted and elated. What I need is a double-shot cocktail. All the press interviews and meet and greets have me feeling drained. The afterparty's planned for ten p.m. at Komodo, a high-end restaurant right in the heart of Brickell, a trendy part of Miami. After two more interviews, I'm free. It's second nature at this point, answering their questions. *What was it like growing up in Guam? What's next for you? Have you always written your own songs? What would you say to the fans?*

My mind drifts with the last question, and I ask the journalist to repeat it, which makes Kimi purse her lips in a way that's deflating.

The press room at the venue is sterile, and while the event has tried to sparkle up the space, it's concrete on concrete behind the drapes of blue fabric they've set up behind the chairs.

"We're working out what my next single will be right now," I say. "There are two or three songs we love and can't wait for the fans to hear."

She nods her head, shifts her microphone, crosses and uncrosses her legs. "What was it like growing up in an island paradise?"

And we're back. The sound of my little cousins laughing and building sandcastles hangs in the air as I lie back on my beach towel in the warm sunshine. I explain how coming home and spending time on our family's beach is one of my favorite things in the world. My aunties and uncles are barbequing and I usually play the role of sous chef but today they insist I go to the shore and relax. I fall in and out of sleep as the ocean rolls up and down the sand. I love Los Angeles but it could never replace my island.

"Thanks so much," the reporter says. "You've been great." She turns to Kimi, "The interview will go live tomorrow a.m.—it'll be shared on our website and YouTube, and shorter clips will be shared across our different socials. Princess will support on her socials, yes?"

"Of course!" Kimi agrees. Once more, I've got more "content" to produce, hype, and post about. My mood dips, but remembering my girls are waiting for me and that Win is here sparks little fireworks. I'm anxious to get to Val and Maya. I'm sure they've already got the party started and I'm even more excited to continue my conversation with Win. We hardly got enough face time before I was peeled away for artist duties.

Security's there with the golf cart to take me back to the artist's area. "Green room?"

"Yes please, thank you, Mark."

Mark's been with me for the last few years; we met through Win. I noticed that Mark always gravitated to me, keeping an eye out whenever Win and I would have dinner and stop by a party or two. Eventually I asked Win if he'd be okay with me bringing him onto my team whenever I had shows or events. As always, Win helped me set everything up. We're nothing but professional but Mark has become like a brother to me. "I'm supposed to meet Val and . . ."

"I know where we're going. And then I'll make sure you get back to the hotel to get ready for dinner."

"What would I do without you, Mark?"

"Good thing you never have to find out."

It's a little funny to see such a huge, built man carrying my bouquet of roses from Win, but I didn't want to leave them behind. A little smile breaks across my lips. I'm scheduled to be here for forty-five minutes. More industry people. More smiling, hand shaking, and picture taking.

As I make my way through the crowd of people at the industry party, I try to pull myself together and push away the bubbling anxiety of what's next. Valerie and Maya are at the bar nearby, and I shout to get their attention.

"Shots, shots, shots," they chant and as they run over, placing a drink in my hand.

Servers circle the party, some with trays of champagne, some with mini sliders and fries but I refrain from partaking in the mouth-watering bites because we have our own dinner planned and I'm too focused on getting through networking tonight.

Kimi and Wayne are heads down, tucked away in a corner, still working. As I weave my way through the crowd, a pretty brunette puts a hand on my shoulder in passing to congratulate me on the show. Mark gives me a look asking if I want him to step in. I subtly nod. I smile back at her and quickly say thank you, wondering if we've ever met before the thought quickly fades from my mind as Mark ushers me along. I love performing and giving my fans my all but, damn, does it take a lot out of me.

Win: I'll have to meet you at dinner, superstar. Have a bit of business at the hotel. Can't be helped.

Princess: No worries. Can't wait to see you. We're at the industry party now. Leaving soon.

"Clearly the tea is *hot*." Maya and Valerie chuckle and share a smirk as I give them a cheeky eye roll.

"We need details." Val reaches for my arm and she and Maya inspect my bracelet.

"I'm going to need to sit down. The story that goes along with this must be something," Maya says.

I give Val a quick squeeze. "Our date went extremely well, and I'm going to give you all the gory details, I promise."

I'm distracted rereading Win's texts when I abruptly collide straight into Mark's back, Valerie collides into me, and Maya into her.

"My bad."

"Oopsies."

"Damn it, I spilled my drink."

We apologize to Mark. He shrugs *no big deal* and takes a step back, revealing none other than Riley Vega. Fuck.

"I don't believe it. What does she want?"

I follow Maya's gaze to see Riley walking towards us, smiling like we're the best of friends and the last few months and the photos of her and John making out in South Beach didn't just happen. I know she left her explanation of the situation with John ambiguous, but it doesn't hurt any less for her to spend time with me, pretending to be in solidarity with me against John, and the next thing I see are photos of her making out with John on a beach. Like, *fuck,* that is so annoying. It amazes me how Riley can slip in and out of friendship mode. I've learned the hard way that Riley can tell you one thing then do the opposite behind your back. It makes it hard to trust her and know when she is being genuine. I consider telling Maya and Val that I'll meet them at the bar, but I feel steadier having them nearby. Also, I'm not sure Maya would leave even if I asked.

Maya is the mama bear in our group. Gorgeous, glamorous, and gives no fucks. An in-demand model who travels all over the world for work, she's also the first one to stand up to defend her friends. Maya didn't need to go through all the same drama with Riley; what I experienced was enough for Maya to dislike her. If only John had that same level of loyalty. I give my head a quick shake.

This is neither hot nor something we can play off. Each of us straightens up as Riley makes her way around Mark to greet us, restraining a laugh. I tuck my phone away and prepare myself for God knows what is about to come out of her mouth.

"Princess." Riley looks like she might hug me but decides against it. Who knows, maybe Maya scowling beside me scared her off. "Stunning performance, babe. Really great stuff. You must be happy."

"Oh, hey. Thanks. Yeah, I feel great. The crowd was so energizing."

"I know what you mean." Riley smiles like everything is sunshine and roses and nothing bad ever happened between us. "There's nothing like having a crowd wrapped around your finger. It's a real energy surger."

Riley waves at someone walking past us, flashing her sparkling new veneers that honestly look pretty damn good. She really does have this networking thing down pat. It probably helps that she's been in the spotlight with her famous family all her life. Her career is so different from mine. Riley comes from money and influence. Basically every door was primed and open for her. And when her status as an influencer took off, everyone was casting around to find her the next opportunity. When she wanted to meet with producers and record executives, the meetings were guaranteed. She didn't have to fight for studio time or prove herself. Her spot was given to her, not earned. I've certainly had some help along the way, but those are connections I made with my blood, sweat, and tears. Doors didn't just open for me. I had to push them. Kick them down.

None of this bothered me when Riley and I were friends. At first, she was generous and offered advice. She helped me figure out how the world worked here. I felt so lucky having her on my side. I loved when she'd tag along to my studio sessions. I'm not sure when our relationship started to change—it took me too long to figure out that it had. She got away with a lot of bullshit because I wasn't on the ball. I didn't suspect a good friend would undermine me until it was too late.

"I didn't mean it that way." I'm not trying to argue with her or trying to make her feel bad but I also don't want anyone to think I agree. "It's a real give and take with the audience. We feed off each other. That's what makes every show so special and unique."

For a brief second, Riley's eyes narrow but, instantly, she's back to smiling. Her face is locked in, like anyone would think she was having the best time. The photos in the gossip magazines would be captioned: "Ex-besties Riley + Princess will they/won't they friendship/hateship continues in Miami this weekend."

I used to believe I understood what Riley was thinking. Now I'm not sure if I ever really knew her at all. The only thing I do know is that I have a right to be suspicious of Riley's intentions so that's how I'll operate from now on. At least until she can prove to me that she is a friend. She's never hesitated to throw me under the bus if it means she'll get more likes.

"Wow, stunning!" Riley grabs a hold of my wrist. She pulls my arm closer to look at the bracelet. "Gorgeous. Is it new?"

"Yes," I admit. My first thought is to tell her it was a gift from Win but I quickly decide to stay silent—Riley tries to get a piece of everything I have and I can't let my guard down. Even though I am enjoying this interaction more than expected. "I just got it."

"Great taste." She smiles her approval. "Should we take a picture for the memories?" Riley moves in beside me and holds my arm up with the bracelet on full display. "Let's show this off."

I laugh because the whole thing is a bit strange and seeing Maya and Valerie's wide eyes is kind of hilarious. But really, why get a photo of my bracelet? What's the point of that? I'm swept up in the moment, though. Riley has a way of taking over any room or situation to her advantage. I might not be ready to share that Win gave me the bracelet, but it is beautiful. Plus, Riley clearly knows what she's doing. Only a few seconds after she posts the photo, I see her Instagram lighting up with notifications and comments about how beautiful it is. And maybe I wanted to keep it to myself, the feeling the gift gave me, how special it made me feel. Saying no would have been a bigger hassle—and now Riley has capitalized on a gift, a thoughtful gesture that was meant for me, and made it about her.

All she does is take.

And then something new and shiny grabs her attention and she moves on. In fact, Riley is so absorbed with reading everything that she barely gives us a *see you later* over her shoulder as she struts away.

"That was weird as hell." Val stands beside me with her arms crossed over her chest. "I'm shocked you rolled along with any of that."

"It doesn't seem worth it to fight," I reply. "Plus, Kimi will be happy we're in a post together. It's all about the publicity apparently." It's not worth my time to analyze it. "I'd rather focus more on us and making tonight one for the books."

We move deeper into the party and Maya nudges me with her elbow.

"Looks like you have one more distraction to deal with first," she says.

John. Leaning against the wall. Classic. There's no other reason for him to be there than waiting for me. He nods hello to Maya and Val, then smiles at me.

"Hey, Princess," he says, his voice gravelly, soft, sexy.

Pausing in front of him, I give him the opportunity to say more. Sure, I get why he came to the show—after all, he produced so much of my music—but I have no clue why he's *here*.

"Can we talk?" John looks like he's been losing sleep and I can't say I'm mad about that. When I don't reply right away his blue eyes shift from me to Valerie and back.

"You okay?" Val whispers and puts a hand on my arm so that I look at her. Maya eyes me closely. I nod a few times. "We're right over there if you need us."

Val and Maya make their way back towards the bar.

"What do you want?"

"Honestly, just to talk." John pushes himself off the wall. "Can you spare a minute?"

"Is that really a good idea?"

My emotions are too raw still to have a conversation. It's hard to be logical, or succinct, when your mind and heart still feel so broken.

"I get that you would prefer to avoid me, but I would really like a chance to explain myself."

It's so typical that John hurt me, betrayed me, then expects me to stand here and listen because *he* wants to explain himself so he can feel less guilty or convince both of us that he didn't do anything wrong, as usual. How is this about John when I'm the one who was hurt?

"Is this something I want to hear? I don't really see what you could possibly say. We've made mistakes before, John, but I'm not sure this is something we can come back from."

When he said he'd changed and learned his lesson with Riley, I took him back. But it was a repeat of the first time around with John. Sneaking behind my back to spend time and work with her because, at the end of the day, his career was the only thing that mattered. This time, though, they actually ended up together. It might have been a short fling but it was more than long enough for me.

"I'm not sure I want to try."

"I know, I know." He rubs his hands over his face. "I've been trying to find a way to put it all into words. I fucked up."

"Well, that's one way to put it." I let out a short almost-laugh. It's not funny but I'm frustrated.

John pushes himself off the wall and stands in front of me. He's close but I'm not going to back down or away.

"I should've listened to you." His voice is gentle and sounds sincere. "I thought I could handle it. Thought I could see through whatever games Riley might be playing. I was wrong and I should've had a better grip on my priorities. On you."

I roll my eyes. It feels like this is the thousandth time I've heard him make the same excuse.

"I told you over and over. Told you so many times that you acted like I was nagging you." I shouldn't have had to tell him more than once. John knew all the stunts Riley pulled and that should have been enough. I should have been enough. "How many more times was I supposed to tell you before you believed me? You willingly made the choice. You knew what you were doing."

"A few times more at least." John tries to soften the conversation with a small smile. "You know, to get it through my thick skull. I would never do anything to hurt you. I've grown a lot since then and I would love a chance to show you with my actions."

John and I started out as friends, and I mourned that relationship just as much as the romantic one. We bonded over music and making each other laugh. It's hard to say if romance will ever work out for us but I would hate if we had to lose our laughter too.

"We broke up." John stuffs his hands into his pockets. "I was vulnerable. Riley came in and before I knew it, I was in over my head."

Hearing her name off his tongue makes my blood boil.

"You were with her *before* we broke up!" I cock my head to look at him. Is this really the story he's going with? "Jessie literally saw you together. Kissing. On the front porch."

"That is not true!" John holds up a finger to make his point. "I get that Jessie might have got the wrong idea, but that was a hug. There was no kissing. We were saying goodbye."

"Sure. Because everyone's boyfriends don't come home at night and then get caught sharing long hugs with women who aren't their girlfriend."

"I made a mistake." John puts his hands on his hips and leans closer to me. "My headspace was all messed up. I was insecure. Riley and I were hanging out a lot, working a lot, and it was long hours. I was drunk at that Coachella party. And was manipulated. You get it. She's done the same thing to you."

"You did this, John. *You*," I say, my voice hushed so the whole party doesn't know what's going on between the two of us. "Don't blame

Riley for your decisions. She's not my favorite person but don't gaslight me and blame her. Plus, our stories with Riley are very different, John. And I tried to warn you. You refused to cut off contact even when we broke up. Instead, you went back for more."

"It was a mistake all around."

John shakes his head and takes a deep breath. For the first time in a long time, I see the man I fell in love with. Talented and funny and brave for all the world to see but also a layer of vulnerability that was available only for me. I loved seeing the real John and probably always will.

"We broke up and I thought working with Riley would keep my mind off things. She wanted to work on songs and was pushing for it really hard. Throwing myself into work is the best distraction. You understand that part."

I laugh again. Yes, I am all too familiar with using work as a buffer for the difficult subjects.

"Princess, I got carried away. Riley made it all seem so easy but then all this shit started happening with socials and paparazzi. I didn't realize it was all a setup until it was way too late."

Not wanting to kick him when he's down, and deep in regret, I don't say I told you so—again. If I could give Riley grace earlier, I could do the same for John now. I think about Riley posting the photo of my bracelet and the immediate fan response. It certainly seemed possible that it was part of a larger master plan, but how could posting a picture of my bracelet work to Riley's advantage?

"I hurt you." John keeps his hands on his hips but I can tell he wants to move them to my waist. I step a bit farther back, not wanting to invite the physical closeness. "It's killing me." He lets his head hang down. "I need you to know how sorry I am that I never listened to all your warnings. You were right."

It's strange but I understand what John is talking about. I've been there with Riley many times before. John isn't a bad guy, but he's ambitious. He cares about his career and music and he's had to push open every door too. Of course he wanted to work with Riley. Good music or not, the songs will get a lot of attention and that will help him. Get more jobs. Get into more rooms.

As much as I love him, John has to accept that it's his own fault the Riley experiment came crashing down around him. I've been duped by Riley more than once. It's hard watching someone you love be so upset and I can't deny that I love him—still—but I'm not sure how much that matters anymore. Real life happens and sometimes it's all about the choices we make.

"Princess, I've made many mistakes, but I've also learned so much. The person who did all that—that's not who I want to be. It's not who I am anymore."

"I really hope that's true. Everyone is waiting for me," I say. "And honestly, I'm tired of talking about this. I want to focus on myself and my friends right now."

"Sure. Of course." John steps back a few paces. "I'll see you later, though. At the dinner."

"Yes, I'll see you there."

"I'm not giving up on us, Princess," John backs away, smiling. "I've learned my lesson and I'm going to do it right this time."

I nod because I don't have anything to say in response. It would take me one second to let my guard down with John and fall right back in love with him. But I want to make better choices. I want someone who wants me. I want the love of my life, my happily ever after. Continuing to make the same bad decisions isn't going to get me there. Heartache can't have the spotlight right now. It's time to laugh with all my friends and get ready to take on the night, and leave all the turmoil behind me.

4

"No, the blue is better." Valerie nods to the rack of clothes. "It's a great match for your skin tone. Trust me, I got my color analysis done and I'm practically a pro."

We're back in the hotel room after schmoozing at the industry party. We've got about an hour before we need to be at dinner. The flowers that Win brought me are on the table in the middle of the suite. People are fussing all around us: stylists, makeup artists, hair stylists.

"Okay, fancy." I turn to see the back of my dress in the mirror. "Are you sure? I'm not sure I like the silhouette. This one fits better."

Spinning the other way to get the full view of my outfit, I see how the gold dress is skintight and curves over my hips and the neckline works perfectly with my necklace. My stylist Kaitlin arrived five minutes after we did with a dozen outfits and I've tried on every one. At least I can do this part without Kimi and Wayne.

I've always loved fashion and enjoyed dressing up for performances and events. There's a bit of make-believe to it. Kind of like a fairy tale.

I used to watch behind-the-scenes videos of other artists getting ready back when I was starting out and I love that it's my friends and I who get to do it now. I live for the glam.

"Val's right," Maya says, staring at me with hands on her hips, assessing me. "This dress is gorgeous, but the blue one is better. Gold says hot but the blue one says *fucking* hot."

"Honestly, babe, either way you can't go wrong," Kaitlin chimes in as I twirl around a bit more, considering all the opinions.

"You don't want to disappoint your *adoring crowd*." Val turns around so Kaitlin can lace up her '90s inspired 'Sunday dress' Vivienne Westwood bustier.

"Dinner tonight is inner circle and record company top brass." I stare at myself in the mirror. Lift my hair off my shoulders to see if I prefer that option. "This is a fan-free event."

"I didn't say fans. I said adoring crowd." Maya raises an eyebrow. "Win and his bouquet of flowers."

"And then John waiting for you at that party—god, he looked so out of place and clearly needed to talk to you. Which was quite the surprise considering the fact you two *broke up*," Val adds.

One thing at a time. Once I get my wardrobe sorted then I can set the debrief with the girls in motion. There's still so much to process. Butterflies flooded my stomach seeing Win sitting side stage, but that might only have been because it's new and unknown. Win is a good friend, he's handsome and charismatic, has very kissable lips, an intoxicating smell, and we clearly have a strong . . . connection. Of *course* I got butterflies. I can feel my cheeks heating up. For John, though, it brings up so many feelings. He betrayed me and hurt me. He broke my trust and that's not something you can build back in a day. But I can't suddenly stop loving him. My heart doesn't work that way; it never will. I truly believed I was going to end up with John—how could I have been so wrong? He said all the right things to me—apologized, admitted he made mistakes—but that doesn't erase the heartache. Or mean that I can trust him again.

"Mmmkay, I agree. I'll wear the blue one." I whip off the gold dress and hand it to Kaitlin. She laughs as she takes the dress back.

"Princess, Cinderella blue. Maya, sexy red. Valerie, giving black widow. My job here is done, you all look stunning." Kaitlin gives each of us an air kiss and turns on her heels to pack up the racks as the rest of us sit in a row, each in a director-style glam chair.

Each of our glam teams moves around us, powdering, glossing, and glittering our eyelids and we finally have a moment to sit and spill.

"Tell me what's new."

"My last trip was insane!" Maya does her best to get the words out as her makeup artist swipes my coconut lip gloss across her pout, which makes me giggle.

"Do tell."

"You'll never guess who was there and made an absolute fool of herself."

It's a long story about another model, who happens to be one of Riley's minions, trying to make a name for herself and maybe gaining attention for the wrong reasons. Maya has us in stitches as she's telling it. She travels the world for work and models for many of the high-end designers and magazines. It's a world she's very comfortable in. Like every forward-facing position in the entertainment business, it is glamorous on the outside, but modeling is no easy gig and yet somehow Maya has such an ease about her when telling stories about work. She puts you right in the action and makes everything sound fun. She's definitely comfortable in the spotlight; she's a magnet for it. Unlike most people, all the attention didn't make her arrogant. Maybe there was a part of her that expected to have whatever she wanted whenever she wanted it, but Maya was also generous and seemed to get genuine pleasure seeing her friends succeed.

Maya's story took a turn right up my and Valerie's alley: she met a guy at an afterparty whom she somehow convinced to change into her pink lacy panties for the rest of their evening together, which had us all nearly in tears laughing at how unbelievable her love life is. Hearing about Maya's party, then hotel, then champagne breakfast with Mr. Pink Panties was a great distraction from my entanglements.

She's never seriously dated anyone, preferring to keep things casual, which is so different from my experience. Sometimes I wish I was more like her. I'm not against dating and I like meeting new people, but I prefer the connection that comes from being in a relationship. Sharing special moments and achieving goals with one person over a long period of time is important to me. I've always been a hopeless romantic, but before John I was laser-focused on my career. Then one thing led to another between us and John was a great support system. He was there for me with the music, and we made a great creative partnership. I felt stronger with him, like I could push myself artistically and feel safe. John was my safety net, ready to put me back on track if I ever slipped, ready to protect my emotions and guide me through. We learned from each other. And then John stopped being honest with me. The betrayal was so deep on many levels—as a boyfriend, as a producer, as a friend. I'm not sure which one hurt the most.

"What about you, Val?" I smooth the blue dress over my hips. They were right; this is the better choice. "How are you feeling now that you're an old married woman?"

Val bursts into a wide smile. It's so great to see her happy. We all worried about Val and how lost she seemed. This girl could party. I love seeing her smile like this. It was torture watching Tripp love Val while she pretended to be aloof for so long, but she finally gave in and admitted to him—and herself—that she was serious about him. It was all new and this is the first chance I've had to check in and get the details.

"Is it official?" Maya asked with a wink.

"Not official-official but yes, it's all good."

"You're looking great, babe." Maya reaches out to hold Val's hand. "Happy."

"I feel like a brand-new woman." Val grins. "Recharging, starting over, whatever. It feels good. I've got my weekly therapy locked in, Tripp's a sweetheart, I'm balancing all the family stuff and spending time with my girls. Life's good."

My phone buzzes and my makeup artist Angel hands it to me from the glam table, completely unfazed and fully in his artist zone. How he does what he does is a mystery but somehow my skin looks airbrushed every time he glams me. I look down at the notification—it's Kimi letting me know there are changes to the dinner guest list. The record label invited a couple of up-and-coming producers they want me to connect with. Her text says, They're so excited to meet you! The label wants to get a new song out soon so we'll have to move fast. My stomach knots but I'm not sure exactly why.

"Everything okay, babe?" Maya asks, seeing me scowling at my phone.

"All good. Kimi's just hitting me about some business stuff," I say. "Every few minutes she's got more thoughts. It's never ending."

A hum in the back of my mind wonders if they're paying me all this attention because they *have* to, not because they *want* to. Then, suddenly, the guilt hits: complaining about Kimi is going too far. Up until now, she and Wayne have always been so supportive. Working to build my momentum, keep me exposed, and amp up my career is their job. I need to push my doubt down. They want to capitalize on the momentum of my performance. I'm trending. I need to remember that I've worked my ass off for years to get here and I have so much further to go. Kimi and Wayne will help me get there.

"They must be so excited about the show and how well your single's doing," Val said. "Everyone wants a piece of you, babe. Is show business everything you hoped?" She chuckles a little sarcastically.

"Speaking of which . . ." Maya twists in her glam chair to face me. "What the fuck—Riley's post? That snake finds a way to make this day work for her."

"Yeah, it was a little weird." I sigh. "It's only a picture of my bracelet, I guess. What harm could come of it?"

Maya rolls her eyes at me like she can't believe I'm letting it slide. "You don't trust her, so why are you letting her make it look like you two are besties all of a sudden?" Maya looks at the makeup artist applying a baby pink blush. "Not a word of this leaves this room, understood?"

The young girl that arrived with Kaitlin nods. Angel tries not to smile and winks at me. They won't spill. They've been with me for years—all through the ups and downs with Riley in the first place. You can't spend hours in a makeup chair and not spill secrets.

"What else was I going to do? I'm not going to fight with her on social media." I push myself up from the glam chair after Angel finishes and head to the makeshift bar to grab a bottle of tequila. To be honest, I'm not okay with Riley making the situation look however she wants, but I am so emotionally drained that I don't have it in me to make a big deal out of it. Dealing with her is exhausting and I guess if it's not a negative interaction I'll just leave it be while I try to get myself back on my feet.

"I'm not going to focus on Riley and try to make sense of what she's doing. Tonight is about us and about celebrating the good things that are happening. For each of us."

Maya fluffs her hair in the mirror when the squad is done with her. "You good?" Kaitlin asks me.

"I'm perfect, thank you so much."

"We'll get out of your hair," she says.

Val says, "I don't trust Riley."

"Me either," Maya says. "Not as far as I could throw her."

Kaitlin announces they're done packing up and does one last check to make sure all our looks are good. After the final 360s, they grab their bags and head out.

"Cheers to that!" Valerie reaches for the tequila bottle to refill her glass.

"Hang on!" Maya clasps her hands together, jumping up from her glam chair. "You let us get distracted, missy. We're talking about Riley and her stupid post but not about the bracelet. Before we start talking about snakes, let's talk about wolves and that sparkly thing you have on your wrist."

"Drum roll, please . . ." I tease and Valerie mimes the action.

I hold out my arm and the girls rush over for a closer look. They both ooh and ahh over it and I can't stop smiling. I am a bit surprised by how glad I am that they're finally paying attention to it.

"Things are good but also maybe confusing." I hand each of them a freshly poured shot. "First, we need to get Jessie on the phone. She needs to be a part of this too."

I can see Maya and Val exchange quick glances while I call Jessie.

They're doing their best to be patient—still, the squirming is a dead giveaway.

Jessie pops up on the screen. She's in her room, clearly studying, her hair in a messy top knot and she's wearing sweatpants, but she looks gorgeous as always. Jessie is much more reserved and shy compared to me, Maya, and Val, but she sure does light up whatever room she's in.

"I'm heartbroken I missed your show, Princess! Summer term is drowning me right now so I couldn't get away and I hate that I missed your big night. Major FOMO."

Jessie's like a sister to me. We've known each other most of our lives. It was hard when I was a kid and spent so much time rehearsing. The other kids didn't understand why I put so much effort into it but not Jessie. She was as ambitious as I was, only in her case, it was about her academics. Because we're on different paths doesn't mean we don't understand each other.

"There'll be a million more shows. You'll make it to the next one if you can." I sat down near Maya and Val and angled the phone so Jessie could see all of us. "But right now, I need you to put the highlighter down because . . . I have news."

I hold up my drink and wait for the girls to do the same. "Here's to a great night and even greater friends."

"Holy shit, you're driving me insane!" Maya downs her shot then grabs my arm. "Stop playing and tell us already."

"Okay, I'm just going to come out and say it." I take a deep breath and bite my bottom lip. Once I say these words to my friends, there will be no taking them back. No more secret bubble with just me and Win. Here goes nothing. "Something happened with Win and me last night."

"Shut the actual fuck up!" Val stands up with excitement then sits back down. "What does 'something happened' mean? What something? The bracelet is from *Win*?"

"I called it! Tell them, Princess." Maya jumps up and down. "Did I or did I not call this when we walked out of our cosmetics marketing meeting? Elevator. Sexual tension. And me. Calling. It!"

"Wait, guys, the phone is shaking too much," Jessie shouts into the phone. She is laughing and trying to get their attention again. "Tell us everything."

"God, where do I even begin?" I take another deep breath. It's a relief that my friends know now. I like that I'm not left to figure all this out on my own anymore. "Basically, the night was great. We talked a lot. He was really sweet. Honestly, he made me feel pretty special."

"Special is good. We like special," Maya coaxes.

"And what did you say to him?" Jessie's voice chimes over FaceTime.

I bite my lip again. I really hope Angel left me a lip gloss because I'm going to need a touch-up.

"I think he knows I wrote the song about him." I'm playing with my hands, clearly anxious.

"That's huge." Val puts a hand on my arm, ready to support and unsure of where the story is going. "What did he say? He must have been happy."

"We didn't exactly talk about it." I start laughing. "Oh. And then we kissed."

"*KISSED*?" all three of them practically shriek at the same time.

"Did I say kissed? It was more like a make out. A hot and heavy one," I say. The expression on my face is cool, hand waving to turn down the heat.

"I love this for you."

"Wow. That's my girl. What now?" Maya asks. "He did some

sweet-talking, basically knows you wrote a hit song about him, he gave you a very shiny and no doubt very expensive bracelet. What happens next?"

"I honestly have no idea. It was perfect. Magical. Surreal. But Win doesn't date and I'm not sure if this means anything more than friends who made out. Did I mention how good of a kisser he is? He is *such* a good kisser."

"But Win knows making out with friends isn't really your style."

Maya stands bracing herself against the bar.

"Maybe it's Win's style?" I'm pacing in front of them now. "We don't know anything about Win's dating style."

"Okay, so we don't know what's going on with Win." Val holds up her glass as a toast and we all drink. "Now what's the deal with John? It seemed like the conversation was . . ."—her voice trails off searching for the right word—"close?"

"Wait! John was there? You talked to *John*?" Jessie leans in closer to her camera. "I really hate that I'm so far away right now."

"Oh yeah, girl, they talked," Maya rebounds.

"John apologized, and he seemed sincere." When Maya and Val try to interrupt, I hold my hand up. "Not saying I believe him. Or that anything is happening. Nothing has changed."

I don't have it in me to say if I believe him or not because I really don't know. Everything is feeling very fresh for me right now. Not to mention the fact that I'd look literally insane to Maya and Valerie admitting I could consider having even a shred of trust in John at this point.

"Well, which is it? Is it Win or John?"

"Who do you want to be with?"

"Who makes you happier?"

I stare at my friends. I try to clear my mind and hope that the answer will be revealed to me.

"Princess?"

"What's your answer?"

I shrug my shoulders and smile, breaking into a hysterical laugh.

"I don't know."

We all fall silent, staring at each other. Maybe waiting for me to say something else. This is an entirely new and strange position to be in. I make critical decisions all the time. Writing songs, what to do in the studio, what I want to focus on next in my career. John was my first love, my first real boyfriend, and we fell into it after being close friends. Win is someone I care deeply about, and he's proven himself to be a great friend and pretty consistent knight in shining armor. He makes me laugh. I feel seen when I'm with him. I know I can count on Win. But he's a very busy and successful man with a whole world that I know nothing about. I'm not sure what kind of future we could have together. Or even if Win's thinking that far in advance. How does a popstar even fit into that picture? The idea that I might have to make a choice between Win and John seems preposterous.

"I only had the capacity to tell you guys. Not to think about it in depth right now." I take a step forward, picking up my phone with Jessie on the call. "We have to get to dinner, Jess. Love you."

"We love you, Jess," Maya and Val say simultaneously as I hang up.

"Okay, fine," Maya sighs, her attention back on me. "But this conversation is far from over."

"I promise, you'll be the first to know once I figure it out."

I have no idea what will happen once we leave the safety of this room but I'm about to find out.

5

Everyone in the restaurant turns to look as we walk through the door of Komodo just after ten. It's like in *Mean Girls* when Regina George is being carried in slow motion across the football field with her long blond hair softly blowing in the wind and everyone goes googley-eyed. Minus the football field, footballers, and bitchiness. Each person stops talking and starts clapping, someone lets out a cheer and a *Yay, Princess!* echoes across the room. I can't lie: my ego is feeling pretty good right now. I love being recognized for all my hard work and feeling like I've earned my spot. Even though I haven't "fully broken," I'm on my way there and people see it—the energy buzzing through me feels new and a little strange in a way. For a second, I wonder if they're going to want me to perform tonight but then I realize this is all part of being a celebrated artist.

My team booked out the entire venue for the late dinner. The tables were set up in a low row and decorated with candles and flowers, which reminded me of my blind date with Win all those months ago, before

John, before all this, and how special it was having that restaurant all to ourselves. I scan the room looking for any sign of him but he's not here yet, which makes my stomach sink a little. Win *will* show up; he always does.

I survey the rest of the room and realize I know maybe half the people present. John is in a group with some musicians who played on the record. He nods to me and it makes my breath catch in my throat. Butterflies? Ugh, stop being so weak, Princess. He's wearing a black hoodie and black jeans, casual but somehow elevated. He looks great.

Riley is on the opposite side of the room with her crew. Seeing those girls makes me want to audibly groan. They're posing for photos and laughing together but as soon as Riley sees me at the door she does a double take. Just like when I was on stage when I spotted her in the VIP section, she looks almost angry at the sight of me—did she somehow think I wouldn't come to a dinner party my label put together after my show? The look on her face disappears a second later. Still, it's enough to make me wonder if there's something else I'm missing. Kimi and Wayne are both talking to people I assume are the producers they want me to meet or more industry executives. It's obvious how many people are interested in me now that I've proven I can make money for them and am "hot."

Val slips her arm through mine. "The place looks damn good."

"Are you ready for a night that is all Princess all the time?" Maya nudges me with her elbow.

"I'm ready." I lean my head into hers and smile at them. Grateful doesn't even begin to describe how I feel having them by my side. "Let's have a night."

We strut into the room and split up. Kimi calls me over to meet with her group, Maya saunters over to some hot musician, and Val does her rounds with familiar faces. As I suspected, executives who wouldn't give me the time of day a few months ago are now over the moon to celebrate my success as though they never dismissed me before. There's a lot of *we always knew you could do it* and *we knew we backed the right horse in the race.* I almost laugh out loud and say *are you calling me a racehorse?* but I keep my game face on. This is part of the game. Network, smile, work hard, prove yourself, work harder. I'm going to make my dreams come true.

It's something I learned from Riley. She could work her way through a room and make everyone feel like the most important person there, even if in reality she'd be whispering jabs about them into my ear only a moment later. When I asked her about it, she'd laugh and say, *This is how Hollywood works, babe. Everyone does it.* It wasn't long before I noticed she was selective in who she talked to and only focused on anyone who could do something for her. I just assumed this was because she was on another level status-wise. Riley and her family don't mingle with those they feel are below them. Which is partly why I always questioned why she'd befriended me. When Riley ignores someone, she can make them feel like a ghost, like they don't exist.

So I talk with the record company reps and industry executives, laughing at their jokes, then spend time mingling with a couple of producers Wayne introduces me to. I don't get a great feeling from any of them. They all want to talk about their achievements and about what record they want to make with me, somehow forgetting to consider any opinion I might have on the matter. They have no interest in my ideas. It's a lot of 'what they can do for me' and almost no mention of true collaboration. Guess I have more to prove and a lot more respect to earn. I look across the room and meet John's eye. I make a quick *save me* face and he laughs. He gets it.

"Princess is going to take over the world." Kimi beams as she looks at me like I'm her most prized possession. A pang of pride hits me; I feel good being something she wants to show off. "This time next year, everyone will know Princess's name."

I give her a quick hug. Many warnings were sent my way when choosing management and Kimi and Wayne have been such a blessing. Despite the ups and downs of today, and occasionally making me feel like a product, they listen to my ideas. I feel like they want me to be an active participant in my career. They support my big plans and never have a problem with the many questions I have or that I want to be aware of, if not outright involved in, all decisions. In the time since we started working together, Kimi and Wayne have backed me and I feel so grateful for all they've done.

They believe in me. Now I just need to convince them that I don't want to work with these producers. Despite our personal issues, John and I have a creative flow few people ever find. This is what we need to stick with. This is what is working.

"We can do it together." One of the producers puts his hand on my shoulder and I consider pushing it off. I know that wouldn't be helpful as far as networking goes but I also didn't give him permission to touch me and we met point-five seconds ago. "We're going to make you a star." I almost throw up in my mouth at the line.

I'm saved from having to respond by the room, once again, turning as the door opens. As always, all eyes are drawn to Win. He's wearing an expensive suit that is tailored to him perfectly, a classic look of his. He moves with the confidence of a man who knows everyone is looking at him but doesn't need their approval. Someone's got to submit him for *GQ* sexiest man of the year, maybe of all time. I'm so damn drawn to his vibe, drawn to him, but it has intensified since last night. I know what it's like to have his full attention, to kiss him, and know how intoxicating he can be. I told the girls it still feels like our little secret and there's something about that I love. A few women try to get his attention but he doesn't even look their way; instead, he heads in my direction and my legs start to go weak.

"Princess." He stops in front of me and for a moment I wonder if he's going to kiss my hand. "You look beautiful as always."

"You never miss a beat." I laugh, trying to maintain my composure as I turn to liquid and feel the drinks start to kick in. "And thank you. Me and the girls had a little too much fun getting ready."

He glances at my bracelet and smiles. "I'm glad you like it. It suits you perfectly."

"You taste great." Oh my god. *WHAT.* "I mean"—I'm stumbling on my words—"you have great taste." Yeah, I recovered that well.

He lets out a low laugh and I swear I could pounce on him right now. I have *got* to get a grip.

"I was referring to the bracelet and your taste in jewelry," I clarify.

"Yes, I'm aware." He smiles and licks his bottom lip. I notice he's got a little twinkle in his eye, which makes me wonder if he's thinking about the same thing I am right now.

"Princess, we need a few more photos before we sit down for dinner." Wayne holds an arm out, indicating I should follow him, and gives Win a quick handshake. "Everyone else can take their seat. There are name cards at each setting."

"Do we have to do this now?" I follow Wayne to the side of the room. "I'm a bit low on my industry battery. Time for mama to celebrate," I singsong.

"Of course, mama's going to celebrate and share the celebrations. This will only take a minute."

DIAMONDS, DECEPTION & DESTINY

I plaster on my best smile and exchange more pleasantries with execs—shaking hands and kissing babies, as they say. The producer who put his hand on my shoulder finesses his way into every photo. I chalk it up as another part of the job, then head over to the table. I slide into my seat between Maya and Val, finally feeling some relaxation wash over me. Maya gets a pic with all three of us and posts it.

"Captioning all fire emojis because we're fucking hot! Duh!"

"Absolutely. Someone get me a drink, stat," I joke.

Maya has a huge following and posts a lot so it's good exposure but it's also an honest post. We're best friends and we're all happy for each other. We love celebrating each other and our friendship. I grab her and Val's hands. They know.

"I love that you are both here tonight."

"Where else would we be?" Val squeezes my hand. "You're our girl and this is the best party in town."

I turn when I hear the chair across from me move and see John sit down, which is when I realize this seating plan must have been made a month ago and wasn't updated to take my relationship status into account. Asking for a quick change would make the situation even more awkward and I'm not going to let hurt feelings ruin the evening. I almost choke on my drink, though, when Win takes the seat beside him. John's jaw hardens at the sight of Win, but he stays silent. The two of them nod a quick acknowledgment to each other, then keep their eyes forward . . . on me. Oh god.

Maya kicks me under the table and coughs. She leans over and whispers in my ear, "Tonight just got a whole lot more interesting."

I give her a look saying *don't cause any trouble* but I know she's enjoying this all a bit too much, which is why she's my favorite drama queen.

53

"John. Win." Maya teases the guys, leaning into her ultra confidence and sex appeal. "So great you could both be here."

"I am always ready to celebrate, Princess." Win looks directly at me. He's doing that thing where he makes you think there isn't anyone else in the room. For a brief second I think about Riley's lessons in networking and wonder if Win does the same thing. "Here's to the great show."

He lifts his glass and everyone around me raises theirs too. But before we can drink to the toast, John interrupts.

"To an even greater artist." He raises his glass even higher.

Maya and Val are giggling beside me. It takes every ounce of willpower not to crumble into laughter too. Win and John are both acting like peacocks strutting around in front of me. It's flattering—they aren't exactly fighting over me, but it's fun to see how all this will play out.

Win flinches slightly at John's toast; his jaw hardens this time, but he recovers quickly. He is still holding his glass up. "To friends and memories that last a lifetime."

John doubles down with, "To great loves—" but Maya cuts him off.

"—and even greater sex."

She holds her glass up then takes a drink, letting everyone know that the competition is over for now. It's my turn to give *her* a quick kick under the table, even though I'm smiling the whole time. Everyone sitting near us who heard the back and forth of toasts laughs and even John and Win seem to relax.

Through chatting and laughing and sipping on our cocktails Riley glances our way and this time there's a glimmer of the friend I used to know. Maybe it's the drinks making me go soft but the look of her pulls on my little heart strings. That Riley was fun and generous. She would have been sitting close by and giggling just as much at the display of male energy. Granted, maybe it wouldn't have been quite as enjoyable for her unless it was her attention they were vying for. Deep down, maybe that person never existed, and she was simply acting like someone I *wanted* her to be. That I *hoped* she was.

The dinner itself is far less dramatic. Everyone makes small talk while Win and John both pretend the other doesn't exist. They take turns talking to me, though, and almost every time one of them speaks, either Maya or Val nudge me under the table. The questions grow more and more obvious the more cocktails we have. I can't look at either of them because I'll burst out laughing. It feels good getting a little loose after the stressful past few days.

Maya takes control of the conversation if it gets tense, distracting everyone with questions like *if this was a horror movie, which of us would die first and which of us would survive into the sequels.* I talk about a tour Kimi and Wayne are setting up. Win asks about my cosmetics line launch. All in all, it's fun and I don't think about the producers or executives hovering on the sidelines. I'm happy in my little bubble.

As soon as the dessert plates are cleared, Riley stands up. Quickly, she makes her way to my side and puts her hand on my shoulder extending her glass to me, Valerie, and Maya. An olive branch? We cheers and down our drinks.

"Come on, girls. Enough sitting and eating. Let's make some jaws drop."

Val shrugs *why not?* and we all get up. Riley backs away and towards the dance floor, waving her arms like she's beckoning me. I laugh because she's right. It is time to get moving.

The DJ puts on a remix of Taylor Swift's "Cruel Summer," and we scream our heads off to it as soon as we hit the dance floor. Alcohol melts away any inhibitions as we work it like there's no tomorrow. The lights change, the music is loud, and I'm feeling fucking great. I close my eyes and let the music take over. Everything that was worrying me—the upcoming tour, Kimi pressuring me to talk to new producers, the record company pushing for the next big single when this one is still out and working—drops away. It's just me, my friends, and the music. Exactly where I want to be.

I open my eyes when I feel someone slide up next to me. John moves in close then spins on his heel.

"Remember these moves?"

He performs a routine that he has perfected over the years and is a running joke between the two of us. Miming his heartbeat through his shirt. He started doing it when we were in the studio and just getting to know each other. It was one of the first times that he made my heart flutter. John is so handsome, those blue eyes locking you in effortlessly. He's got a goofy side to him that only I got to see. This dance routine was a prime example, and it only grew more elaborate once he realized how much it made me laugh. The fact that he is doing it here, in front of others, made my heart flutter again. I miss this.

"How could I forget?" I laughed, charmed.

I move in front of him and we dance together. We don't touch or even get too close but it's a nice flash of friendship. Forgiveness? I'm not sure I want to take it that far. John's moves are slightly sloppy, giving away that he's likely had one too many drinks. Not to mention the liquid in his current glass keeps splashing over the edge and dripping onto his hand. The song switches up and I step back. I'm happy to have him here but it's not time for John.

"Princess, behind you." Maya spins me around and pulls me into a circle with her, Val, and Riley, plus a few more friends. Twenty-four hours ago, if you had told me that the three of us would be in a dance circle with Riley after all the shit she's pulled, I would have never believed it.

We dance to more songs and everything else is quickly forgotten. Kimi snaps photos of us on a little digital camera I had her bring. Val somehow gets into the DJ booth and then my song comes on and the room goes wild. I'm not sure how much time has passed before I feel his eyes on me. I stop dancing and turn to look at him.

Win is standing at the side of the room, leaning against a pillar. He is holding a drink and watching me. The room is alive with energy and dancing, but Win only has eyes for me. Maybe it's the gravitational pull he has on me or the liquid courage burning through my veins, but I smile in return and walk towards him.

"Hey there, handsome. Mind if I get your number?"

Win laughs at my best Jessica Rabbit impression as I lean against the pillar beside him. I don't understand how someone can make a person feel so electric and so zen at the same time. My face flushes; I hope he thinks it's the heat from dancing. Standing this close to him again is definitely *not* the reason. Not flashbacks of last night, or seeing his face side stage, or remembering the feeling of his warm soft lips on mine. Nope. Nothing to do with it. At all.

"You can have my number, my address, my email, my social security number." His smile is warm, and his voice is low and sexy because of course it is. "I'll give you everything."

We both giggle for a second, and secret tears well up in my eyes. I try to furiously but casually blink them back as fast as I can. What is wrong with me? I can't tell if he notices but he brings his hand up to brush my jaw and I lean into it. Safe haven. How can he be real? Win could have anyone but he genuinely likes me as a person. Not for what I can do for him or where my talent can propel him. Win sees *me*.

"How are you feeling after that performance?" Win asks, his voice a whisper in my ear, the sound brushing against me.

It's really nice to flirt, to feel admired, to be sexy in someone else's eyes. My mind races and puts me at ease every time we talk. How can those two things happen at once?

"Honestly"—I shift against the pillar to face him directly—"incredible. The fun of last night, how well the show went this afternoon. It's awesome. I feel awesome."

Things are charged between us. There's no way I am imagining it. But I haven't really given myself a moment to breathe since Coachella. My world was turned upside down, and my insides ripped up.

Win was there for me. Win said such wonderful things. Plus, he's sexy as hell and that's enough to fuck with your head. This doesn't even begin to cover everything that's happening in my career. Kimi is right: I have real momentum right now and I need to capitalize on it. At this point, I'm not sure if I'm flattered by Win's attention, want more, or am riding on the wave of everything happening at once.

Win leans in closer and says, "About last night . . ." just as I say, "Can I ask you something?"

He smiles and doesn't look at all worried by my question. It seems impossible to truly rattle this guy.

"Sure."

"What did you mean about not being able to give me your full attention?" I brace myself for his response.

I wanted to ask him last night, in the moment, but there were other things on my mind. Like practicing my highest level of self control by not ripping off my clothes mid–make out. Win means more than a heat-of-the-moment hook-up.

Win runs a hand through his hair and sips his drink while looking

DIAMONDS, DECEPTION & DESTINY

out at everyone. I know that he's pausing to find the right words. I like that he doesn't take any of this lightly. Even if this is a casual, friends-who-made-out thing, he isn't brushing it off like it's nothing.

His eyes meet mine. "You know I want you. There's no doubt about that." He reaches out to pull me closer to him. "None." He doesn't break eye contact with me and maybe doesn't blink. "But I've got business shit for the next few months that will take me from LA, and—"

"You are away on business all the time." I say. "We've managed to stay . . . friends."

"It can be hard if someone is away all the time," His brow furrows and I want to press my hand against it. Against his cheek. Whatever it takes to offer him comfort. "I don't want to do that to you. Or let you think that you're not a priority. I'm not in a place to be wholly present."

Win and I *both* travel a lot for work. That doesn't scare me. If two people want to make it work, they will. Did I get way too ahead of myself? Maybe he doesn't want me. I don't understand.

"Wholly present?"

He nods and I know that he doesn't want to say anything more. My head spins with so many questions, but somehow I instinctually understand that Win isn't ready to reveal more.

He pulls me tight and wraps me up in his arms, the party swirling around us.

Maybe he never opened up completely. Maybe that's why Win doesn't date—not publicly at least—and doesn't discuss his romantic past. It makes me wonder if he hurt someone in the past or if someone hurt him and I low-key hate that he's shutting down. It's not even about getting more information. The part I hate is that he feels stuck, like he wants to tell me something but can't. Win has been my confidant and such a comfort for me, I want to do the same for him. Why won't he let me? My heart breaks a little; I wish this conversation was going differently.

He pulls back but leaves a hand around my waist. Damn, he's big; his hand can nearly reach all the way across my back. Delicious shivers shoot down my spine.

"If you're going to be mine, it's going to be the right way," he says. "It might take us a little longer but you're worth it."

There's a cheer with a change in music. And it echoes the jumble of thoughts in my head. Win's going to be away, doesn't want anything serious, but the next words out of his mouth are telling me I'm worth it. The music bumps and I can't help but start to sway, leaning into Win, trying to be in the moment, letting myself be happy.

Maya and Val are still dancing away and being the life of the party. Of course. John is at the back table talking to some producers with his back to us. I scan the room for Riley like I need to keep tabs on them and check that they aren't talking. I also don't want Riley paying too much attention to how much time Win and I are spending together. I take a deep breath when I see her with her minions still dancing. I don't like this feeling of being suspicious and I don't want to be this person. I need to snap out of it.

"You've got a lot going on, too, Princess." Win removes his hand from my waist. And maybe I didn't say the right thing, because he caught me staring across the room in John's direction. "With your music. Your cosmetics line. Maybe you don't need the distraction either. And I'd never want to be someone who hurts you."

"You're not a distraction, Win." *And you're not and never will be John*, I want to add.

But what I really want to ask is who hurt you? And how can I help you get over it? He looks far away and maybe he's thinking about someone else entirely.

The crowd bounces again as the DJ mixes transitions into a sexy house vibe. This isn't the time or place to have a heartfelt one-on-one with Win.

"I had a lot of fun this weekend, Princess," Win says. And that sounds like an ending. Not a beginning. The gravitational pull I felt is loosening. The air grows a bit colder between us, like Win's just put up a forcefield around his heart.

"Are you leaving?" I ask.

"My flight out is in a couple of hours; I've got to get back to the hotel to grab my stuff. I didn't want to leave without a proper goodbye but there's an opportunity and I've got to be in New York for an eight a.m. meeting, which means getting a red-eye tonight."

It's time to readjust my thinking about Win. We'll stay friends. He's still in my corner.

And if I continue to let myself think or feel like we could be more, I am only going to get hurt. And I suspect that this hurt, if it happens, will be harder than I can imagine. My body is here but it feels like my mind is somewhere else. I'm already worried that I've lost John as a friend because of a failed relationship, and I don't want to add Win to that list. He already has a relationship: he's married to his job.

Moving my body away from his, I need some space. The moment suddenly feels a bit intense. Echoes of this conversation come through as I think of my breakup with John. It's too raw. And how perfect it's been with Win these last few days, and what happened last night—it's too much for me. I don't want to burst into tears right now, not in front of all these people.

Mixed signals. Win's great for big gestures and the whole knight in shining armor. But is that what he wants me to be? The lady-in-waiting on the corner of his life. Maybe we got carried away this weekend. There's so much more I want to say but now is not the time and the last thing I need is to get ahead of myself like I did with John. Falling head over heels and making him my whole world.

John looks over at us and I'm starting to feel guilty even though I know I shouldn't. There's no reason to feel guilt and there's no reason why I should care about John's feelings. But, of course, I do. I care. Truth is, other than working and touring, I'm not sure what I want. I don't know what anyone wants from me. I'm trying my best to be what I need to be for everyone and feeling like I'm consistently coming up short. Who *do* I want? John is familiar and there's a connection but it's also not so safe. My relationship with Win changing is exciting and new but also uncertain and feels far too risky considering my tender heart. Until a few days ago, I never would've let myself think anything with Win was even possible. He's handsome and the natural center of attention; he's been such a good friend and support for my career. But none of this erases John from my mind. Even making out with Win doesn't mean I am completely over John. To be honest, getting over John seems impossible. I've never loved anyone like that.

I need to step back. Get my head straight. There's too much clouding my judgment. Better to back off before I break anything else.

"I understand. Have a good trip." I step towards the dance floor and feel a little piece of my heart crack. "Maybe we can talk when you get back."

"I'm not falling off the face of the earth."

"You know how to find me," I say. "And call anytime you want to talk. I'm not going anywhere either."

Without second-guessing myself, I kiss Win, deeply, and like I mean it. I like him, I do, I'm attracted to him. I'm single. He's single. Maybe this can be just that: mutual attraction.

DIAMONDS, DECEPTION & DESTINY

Breaking the kiss, I step back and turn, glancing at him over my shoulder one last time before I slip into the crowd to find Maya and Valerie. I take a mental picture of him standing there. The expression on Win's face is unreadable, he tips his drink up at me, and I know when I turn back again, he'll be gone.

I do my best to lose myself dancing, the music taking me over, and enjoy time with my friends.

It's not too late when I convince Val and Maya to leave. They're properly tipsy and laughing as we clamber into our black car. Some random industry exec followed Maya around the whole night trying to convince her to give him her number. She is still laughing at his hangdog expression when we leave.

"Why did Win leave so soon?" Val asks. "I thought he was here for the weekend too."

"Called away on business," I say.

"You okay?" Maya asks.

"Absolutely," I say, hoping she believes me and wishing it were true.

The hotel room has been righted from our earlier chaos. The beds are turned down and they look delicious and inviting. I'm drained and my feet are aching. I pull off my shoes. The show, the dinner, the dancing, it's taken it out of me.

There's a box of chocolate-covered strawberries and a bottle of wine beside the bed. I pick up the note.

So proud of you. Always thinking about you.

There is no name on the card but I recognize the handwriting. The letters are as elegant as the man who wrote it.

6

Sleep consumes me as if it could sense how desperate I was for it, only waking long enough to trek through the airport and get our asses out of Miami and back to LA as fast as possible.

Maya, Val, and I go our separate ways once we land at LAX. I need the comfort of the city and my condo even if it is only for a brief moment before the chaos begins again. I manage to get in a few more hours of sleep before Angel and Ray arrive for hair and makeup and Kaitlin shows up with an armful of outfits to consider for Riley's perfume launch.

She invited me while we were in Miami, and she did it in front of Kimi, knowing that my team wouldn't say no to the opportunity for exposure, especially with the single out now.

Riley flitted over, draped herself on me, and said, "You're coming tomorrow, aren't you?"

The confused look on my face betrayed me for a moment. Kimi interjected, "To your perfume launch? I'm sure we RSVP'd."

DIAMONDS, DECEPTION & DESTINY

"See you there, Princess," and Riley danced away knowing exactly what she'd done. Keeping the rivalry alive. Pulling me back in no matter how many times I try to distance myself.

"Riley's got millions of followers. This will be a big event." Kimi's voice was hoarse from the party. She sounded slightly irritated that this was something she needed to explain. "I understand it might be awkward with Riley but it's just business. We'll have Kaitlin get you an outfit so you can feel your best and get the right press coverage. You don't have to stay the whole night. Make an appearance, smile for the cameras, get those photos out there. You have to play ball."

After two hours in the makeup chair and squeezing myself into a gorgeous gold dress with a pair of sky-high heels, I'm about to step onto the red carpet.

Whenever Riley has a launch, it's always huge and everyone drops what they're doing to attend. The carpet is packed with every A-list celebrity clamoring to be seen and press stacked in bleacher formation capturing every moment. People pose beside cardboard cutouts of Riley holding the fragrance bottle that line the carpet. I step out of the car and wave to the fans gathered outside. Shrieking fills my ears.

This is nice. A little distraction from my own thoughts. I make my way down the steps and repeat, posing for a few different press shots, and head inside as the photographers call my name. I'm used to these events now and enjoy them. Mostly, anyway. Having a little more flexibility with budgets has definitely helped this process become more enjoyable. If I can make it look like I belong here on the outside, it makes it easier to convince myself the same on the inside. Everyone always looks amazing: they're confident and excited, and there's usually a bunch of fans, which makes it that much more thrilling.

I hit my poses on the red carpet and answer some questions thrown at me and tease just the right amount of info on my upcoming album. Considering I don't exactly know what's going on myself, having that conversation is on the top of my to-do list since getting back to LA. Press mostly asks about the record, if I'm excited to be out for the event tonight, but then one PR person asks where John is. They're looking for gossip or to get a reaction from me because everyone saw the posts Riley made of the two of them together a few days ago, but I continue to smile and keep walking. I refuse to take the bait.

There are hundreds of people inside. The see-and-be-seen crowd. Those people who move from one event to the next, one person to the next, hoping to end up in a paparazzi shot or meet that one person who can make the difference in their career. I wish that Maya or Val could have come with me but the invite was last minute and everyone's lives are so busy. Maya had to rush off for work and Valerie had family commitments.

"Princess?" One of the PAs steps up beside me. She looks like a teenager and maybe is. "I can escort you to the VIP section."

It is much calmer once we are behind the velvet rope. There are still a lot of people but also more familiar faces. Riley often has a big team and entourage surrounding her, but only a few ever really get close to her. I know because I used to be in that inner circle and I was the friend who knew her best.

We met when we were sixteen at a coffee shop. I went to see Red, a friend I was making music with at the time, and he introduced me to Riley and we immediately hit it off. She was already famous, a rich kid with an infamous last name. We were around the same age but unlike me she'd never worked a day in her life. She was funny and almost goofy, definitely willing to laugh at herself and this crazy business. We bonded over our mutual love of Ho Hos and rom-coms. We scrolled through Instagram and looked at photos of cute boys. Talked about our favorite designers and musicians. I told her about my music and everything I planned to achieve. She listened and asked questions and seemed genuinely interested. She told me she felt inspired and that she had never thought about what she'd make of her life. I felt kind of bad for Red because we basically forgot he was there. With Riley, it was an instant friendship, and it felt like we'd known each other a lifetime instead of a couple of hours.

She and I became like sisters. One of the things we loved doing was shopping. I didn't have much money then so it was mostly of the window variety on my part but it was always fun. Being creative always came naturally and fashion was one of my favorite ways to express myself. Back then, I wasn't too familiar with the high-end stores or designers; I always made my outfits from thrift stores and my family's closet, tearing clothes up and pinning them in different ways to create my own style. I was so impressed with Riley's knowledge of where to go and what to buy.

One day a sales clerk asked if my shoes were Manolo Blahniks and before I responded with, *No these are from Macy's. What's Manolo Blahnik?* Riley jumped in. "No, they're not Manolos." Riley took my arm and quickly steered me away.

I didn't think twice about admitting the truth about my shoes but Riley knew how I would be judged. *Never provide information that can be used against you.* That was probably a lesson I should have kept in mind as far as Riley was concerned, too, but I really didn't see that one coming. Riley and I felt like a team then and I trusted her almost as much as I did Jessie. It wasn't until later that I realized how little Riley interacted with my other friends. I didn't really question it since she was in a different sphere in more ways than one. But I also didn't really notice when she started to pull away more. There was no altercation; I just chalked it up to both of us being busy. My career really started taking off, which might be why I missed the shift from besties to competition.

"Princess." It was the PA again. "Please come with me."

I follow her to a small staging area with a few photographers. Riley is there posing with attendees and there's a line of people waiting their turn. She spots me and waves me over.

"You came!" Riley looks happy to see me. She nods to one of her assistants who hands me a bottle of perfume. "Come on, let's get a shot."

Riley's assistant holds up her phone up next to the photographers and we stand close together. I hold the bottle up so the label is visible and we both smile for the cameras. She shows me the photo on her phone before posting.

"Everything looks great." I scan the room. There's food on buffet tables and more being served by cocktail waiters. Bars along both sides of the room. More than one selfie station. "You guys really did think of everything."

"Enjoy yourself, babe." She gives me an air kiss.

Riley leaves and I go back to wandering around the space. I take some photos and write a few notes.

I'm collecting ideas for my cosmetics line launch in a few months. My launch won't be nearly as big as Riley's tonight but it's always a good time to gather inspiration. So much of the music business is a hustle and it's necessary to have more than one thing going. I've poured my heart into this makeup line, pondering over colors and palettes and types of brushes. The creative part comes naturally to me but I want to learn more about the technical side of the business.

I wish my girls were here to see all this; I could bounce ideas off people I trust. Plus it's kind of lonely roaming these events without someone; I think I'm one of the few people that braves events solo.

My phone buzzes and I laugh when I see who it is because it's like I summoned them. She's clearly seen the photo Riley just posted.

Maya: 🐍 A light night in Miami was one thing . . . what does she want now?

Princess: Long story. We can brunch about it.

Maya: All right. I gotta get back to set. Check you later xo

Princess: Sounds good babes

I stand in front of a large bouquet of flowers and sneak a quick selfie. I think about what I should say or if I should say anything. Should I send it at all? I decide that maybe it's best if I don't think about it at all. I hit Send and put the phone away. Time to move on and forget that it even happened.

He responds maybe three seconds later.

Win: ♡ Gorgeous.

Princess: I somehow ended up at Riley's perfume launch and it's actually a really beautiful event.

Win: Get in and get out, superstar. 😊

I immediately feel a little less alone. See? We don't have to be in the same place to be there for each other. I slide my phone into my purse and decide to go find a drink. Thankfully I run into a couple of PR girls at the bar and we spend time catching up on life and they give me the lowdown on upcoming events that might be good for me to attend. I make mental notes to have Kimi and Wayne reach out for me.

A couple of drinks later, Riley pulls me aside. "I want to introduce you to someone."

I say my goodbyes to the PR girls and fall into stride with Riley.

We walk towards the velvet couches. There's a tall, beautiful woman sitting on one of them. I've never met her before but I'm very familiar with who she is. She stands up as we approach.

Riley leads the convo. "I heard you're launching your own cosmetics line soon. Is that right? Because I wanted to introduce you to Stephanie Lorne. She helped me with my perfume line, branding, marketing. All that boring stuff."

"And I love all the boring stuff." Stephanie reaches her perfectly manicured hand out to shake my own pearly French tips.

"Yes, that's right! It's lovely to meet you, I've only heard great things." I smile.

Stephanie's reputation precedes her. She's considered a genius brand incubator who's helped launch several celebrity brands. Stephanie has her own very successful companies too. It's known in Hollywood that if you want a successful brand launch, any product, she's the one you go to. Mentally, I make a note to ask Win about her. They must know each other or have worked together at some point.

"I would love to assist in any way," Stephanie says, glancing at Riley. "Riley's one of my favorite clients and I'll make time for anyone she sends my way."

"You mean your *very* favorite client," Riley teases.

Laughing, I say, "Let me give you my info—we can find a time to connect and talk about my cosmetics line."

She passes me her phone and I input my info while she and Riley chat. Stephanie would be an amazing mentor. One day I want to understand and run a business the way she does. She's a shark. She has something I want: respect.

"There you go." I reach the phone back to her.

"Perfect, I'll text you. I have a few more rounds to make so I'll catch up with you later, Rye." She excuses herself and we're left alone.

"That was really sweet, thanks for making that intro, Riley." I can't help my surprised tone.

"No problem, babes. Despite everything, you know I love you." If she notices my surprise she doesn't give any indication. "Dinner soon, text me!" She gives me a quick hug before getting back to her party.

I'm left feeling a little dumbfounded. What am I missing here? What does Riley get out of this? Interactions with Riley are typically all transactional. I figure my mission is accomplished for the night: support Riley, make some new connections, show face. *Get in and get out, superstar.*

It's been two weeks since the Miami whirlwind. I gave myself a much-needed work-break-slash-self-hibernation except for assessing my upcoming music, gathering my notes for where I want to rewrite some lyrics and adjust production. Normally, I'd make final comments with John, either in a studio or here at my place, but I haven't been up for one-on-one time with him for obvious reasons. But it wouldn't be fair to leave him until the last minute to discuss the edits and make the adjustments so here I am curled up on the farthest edge of my couch wrapped in a fuzzy blanket, phone in hand and my thumb hovering over his phone number, working up the courage to dial.

You are a businesswoman.

You and John were friends before anything.

You can do this.

I ignore the twisting and turning in my gut as the ringtone chimes, once, twice . . .

"Hey Princess, how are you?" John's voice comes through smooth.

"Hey, I'm great." Have I been great? My tone comes out much brighter than I want, causing my eyes to roll. Note to self, practice talking out loud before making calls so you don't sound like an elf cosplaying a valley girl.

"So I was just calling to—" I start to say at the same time as John says, "I just want to clear the air about Miami and the photos and Riley."

He rushes out the words and my breath catches in my throat. I do not want to talk about this.

"Oh well, we really don't have to." Because it might kill me if I have to relive the memories. Again.

"You know Riley, you know me—" he starts but I'm quicker.

"John, genuinely I can't have this conversation right now. Let's just pretend none of your guys' make-out photos surfaced and that it never happened.

"Anyway, I was calling so we can catch up about the music before my meeting with Kimi and Wayne at the end of the month." Clearing my throat, I find my calm and confidence. I reach for my notebook on the coffee table and flip to my page of notes.

"All right, let's hear it." John tries to bring a normal energy but we know each other too well—we're both so uncomfortable.

He's quiet on the other end of the line while I walk him through each note per song and I appreciate the space he gives me to get through it all. Thank god the natural bond we have for the music takes over and we fall into an easy conversation and come out with a game plan to get the music ready in time. I miss this and before I have a chance to stop myself, I hear the words come out.

"If you're free I'd love for you to join the meeting. You know, where I play everything for the managers. Having you there might help lock everything in. But of course, no pressure." I cut myself off, unsure if my word vomit was too much.

"I'm there." His confidence bleeds into me.

"Perfect. I'll catch up with Kimi and Wayne for a little bit before you come. It'll be at their office. I think I'm going around noon so maybe plan to come around two but I'll text you the official details on the day of in case we're running late." Excitement bubbles in me, partly because I know Kimi and Wayne are going to be impressed. Partly because I love being like this with John.

"Yup. In the meantime I'll get these edits going and send you the bounces as I get them finished. I'm proud of us, P. They're going to love these songs." His voice gives away his desire to say more but he doesn't.

"I'm proud of us too. Thanks John." I hang up the phone before I get caught up in the slippery slope of remembering how it feels to love John.

7

The last few weeks have been hectic and stressful so I'm a little weighed down as I walk into Kimi and Wayne's office. My nude patent leather Louboutin So Kate pumps clack against the polished concrete flooring. In one hand my Dior tote feels like a thousand pounds and is full to the brim with my computer, charger, Moleskine notebook, lucky Cartier pearl pen my parents got me a few Christmases ago, a scarf just in case I get cold (Maya hates when I wear scarves; she says it's too granny but I think it's cute), and of course a lucky clear quartz crystal. In the other hand, I have my phone, which is chiming with text messages and an iced vanilla matcha latte barely staying in my grip. A few more quick steps and I'll be able to throw all this stuff down and breathe. I got here a little early to get in my zone before the commotion begins.

I exchange pleasantries with the receptionist and assistants on my way to the conference room. One of the girls says, "Obsessed with the last song, Princess. We're all so proud to be a part of your team, even if it's from a bit of a distance."

DIAMONDS, DECEPTION & DESTINY

"You guys are the best, thank you. It takes a village and every team member counts. Couldn't do any of this without you all."

We do team meetings often but today is extra important because there are deadlines approaching and we need to review some items in my cosmetics line. Then John and I will play the updates we have on the new music. Nausea always takes over when I have to present music to the team—you never know how people are going to react, if they're going to support it or if they'll make me fight to release the music.

I also can't tell if the nerves I have in my stomach are from the stress of everything we're about to go over or if it's lingering stress from the drama with John.

I use my back to push open the doors to the empty conference room and breathe a sigh of relief, happy to have a few moments to myself to settle in before Kimi and Wayne join me. I pull out one of the black cushioned office chairs and set my tote down, grab a tiny vinyl record-shaped coaster for my matcha, and get comfortable in my seat. Checking my phone I'm relieved to see none of the texts are urgent and a little happier than normal to see one from the one and only.

Win: Hey, superstar, was thinking of you this morning. What's on the agenda for today?

Holy shit.

Princess: Morning! Just sat down at Kimi and Wayne's office. Bout to talk big business.

I snap a quick selfie, sipping my matcha, conference table in the background and hit Send.

typing bubbles appear

typing bubbles disappear

That's weird. Maybe I was too excited and shouldn't have sent a selfie. I set my phone facedown and pull out my notebook to review

75

my list right as my phone chimes again. It's a selfie of Win, in his glass castle of an office, city view of New York behind him as he too sips on a matcha.

Win: Great minds think alike. I'm about to start my meetings too. Good luck, P, you got this. I should be back on the West Coast in a few more days.

I heart his message in response. Moments later John's name appears on my screen.

John: Morning P, heading to you guys soon, keep me posted on how it's going. Really excited for the team to hear our new music. I made final tweaks last night and they sound incredible. Let's get 'em!

Princess: Can't wait to hear the new bounces, these songs are the perfect followup to keep the momentum going. We're on to something. See you soon.

Relief washes over me—the little confidence boost from Win and the comforting text from John were just what I needed. Perfect timing to give me some clarity as the doors swing open to Kimi and Wayne.

"Morning, Princess." Kimi smiles.

"Feeling good? I see you got your notes ready. Let's rock and roll!" Wayne says with high energy.

"Feeling amazing! So many exciting updates to go over today," I singsong as we all exchange quick hugs and take our seats.

From the beginning I had a vision to expand my career outside music and build an empire. Having an entrepreneurial mind has always come easy to me since I was little but the most challenging part of it all is getting people to believe you and believe *in* you.

Before you can have success, you need someone to co-sign. It's a feat to get gatekeepers to take risks on new artists and songs that

DIAMONDS, DECEPTION & DESTINY

haven't built a consistent track record. I've had to prove myself over and over again and that still hasn't been enough to solidify my spot. My mind is on becoming a strong businessperson, not just in music but in many different lanes. But this is something I have to show, not tell. Something I have to prove.

"We should start with the cosmetics line updates, so we can be completely focused on the music once John gets here," I suggest.

"You're the boss, let's do it," Kimi says. "I got some renderings of the shades and components for the lip glosses for you to review. Jen from the cosmetics PR team says you should have products in hand soon. The formula is the same as what you already approved with her, so all you need to worry about are the shades and if you're approving the actual component."

Kimi clicks her iPad a few times before handing it over to me. From the beginning I knew that developing a cosmetics line would be part of my journey. I distinctly remember how my life changed when I started wearing red lipstick. Not only did I feel something shift inside me but I saw that reflected in the real world. People treated me differently, like *someone*, which in turn made me act like *someone*, which eventually made me somewhat of a *someone* in Hollywood.

Slowly scrolling through the images, I'm inspecting each color and ensuring the shades and fragrances are matched correctly. We've spent a lot of time working out what exactly the packaging will look and feel like. It is really important to me to get it right—I want this line to feel glam but still be accessible.

"Does this shade look right to you?" I hold the iPad up for Kimi to see, even though she isn't involved in any of the creative stuff for this and is just making note of my comments so we can send them back to the team. "It looks a bit off to me."

"I can't tell. That's not really my forte." Kimi leans in to look. "I'm sure it's fine."

"I'd like to check with the team." I scroll some more to look at other renderings. Everything looks slightly off. "I don't want them to get too far in the process if the product isn't right."

"They list the same lot numbers you selected but we can certainly check in with them." She takes the iPad back and looks at the photos again. "It's probably just the difference of seeing the product in real life versus on a device. I imagine it doesn't translate perfectly."

Isn't that something they should take more care to reproduce then? Wouldn't it make sense for a manufacturing company to produce as-real-as-possible photos for clients? How can I approve something that isn't an accurate representation of the product? It irritates me slightly that Kimi doesn't seem too concerned. I'm going to follow up with Jen myself to review this document and go over my notes.

"Okay, let's talk shows!" Wayne claps his hands together. "You're going to be busy!"

Who could not laugh at that level of enthusiasm? "Bring it on. You know live shows are one of my favorite parts of this business, Wayne," I say.

Most of the shows discussed are for the LA area, easy one-offs, but I need to build my hard ticket sales and touring. We discuss starting in Europe and Asia in a few months. But first we have to build my brand, and music, to new heights. This is the gritty part of the business. If you don't build your hard ticket sales, it's unlikely you'll have a long-lasting career as an artist. I've been pushing to build this side of my business for years and was constantly shut down with the whole "you aren't there yet" feedback for the last couple years.

Now with the success of my single, we're able to start having these types of conversations. I just hope I see some follow-through.

Normally an artist starts off doing one-off shows, really small rooms with a two- to three-hundred audience capacity. If they get lucky they are added to special events, award shows, even an early slot on a festival bill. Once you build enough, then you graduate to opening for a more famous artist. Eventually you want to break off and headline your own tour, which is not easy to do. You work your way up to amphitheatres, arenas, getting billed higher on a festival lineup and if you're one of the very lucky ones, stadiums.

"The record label wants to prepare your next single—push it overseas and get a buzz going before we actually send you out there."

"We need to be strategic about what we do next." Kimi flips her laptop open. "Your last song came out of nowhere and really took off. It was perfectly personal and intimate, and the audience ate it up."

That wording definitely doesn't sit right with me. Describing the music as being "eaten up" by the audience feels icky. I get it's called the music "business," but I don't like feeling that Kimi sees my emotions as transactional. Besides, John and I already have a project that's close to being finished and I plan to release it for the album. They'll get it once they hear the music.

"I'm not sure if that's something we can easily replicate," I explain.

Writing, recording, and releasing that song was a natural, almost instinctual process for me.

But so was making this music with John. I haven't been sure about any of it except the fact that the music is special. Just because we fell apart romantically, the music shouldn't have to be thrown away.

"John and I have the songs and album we've been working on together. Trust me. There's one we should release as a follow-up. It's special. He's meeting us to play the songs so let's wrap up any other items before he gets here."

"Sounds good to me." Wayne nods.

"Let's pull up our calendars." Kimi motions to her assistant. "I want to look at the dates and see where we can fit these shows in."

Her assistant starts clicking away. It's always exciting to watch the team get moving.

I shoot a quick text to John: We're on time, see you at 2.

"Oh, we'll make them work, all right," Wayne chimes.

We spend the next half hour going through the dates and deciding what will work. As always, there's a lot of coordinating as we need to work around other singles dropping, the cosmetics line, and being in the studio. With every new date and plan, I get more excited.

I take my phone out and hold it up to film a story.

"Hey, guys. Wanted to give you a quick update on all the exciting things we're working on." I spin around in my chair so Wayne and Kimi are on camera. "Say hi, team!" They both wave at the camera. "We have new music coming, which I can't wait for you to hear. I've been in the studio writing the best songs I ever have. I might not be able to say this yet buuut—we're setting up a tour! We'll stop all over North America and then we head to Europe and Asia. Keep you posted on more details and dates when I know more. I can't wait to see everyone!"

I do a quick check of the video, then upload it. The response is immediate.

There are hundreds of likes in the first minute and tons of excited comments, including a text reply from Riley.

Riley: I can't wait.

Wayne and Kimi are happy with the response. It's proof that people are listening, watching, and interested.

A knock at the door signals John's arrival and I get instant relief that I don't have to fight this battle on my own. Convincing 'suits' to believe in the artist's vision of a rollout of music is always a nightmare. The suits, for whatever strange reason, believe they know the artist, their audience, and what their music should sound like even though they've had zero part in any of it.

If you're a young woman this is an especially difficult argument, if you want to call it that, to win. Having John by my side confidently presenting these records and my management seeing his enthusiasm for them will help solidify my case. These are the songs they should be excited about. This is the album they should support. I am the artist they should back. We need to be unified when we take this to the label. His presence will help them get on the same page so we can lock this in. He's here, we're very strong in a room together, and besides, this music stands on its own even without us.

John steps into the room and I'm happy to see him. Truly.

"Good to see you, Princess."

"You too, John."

I feel calm, like it's old times.

"Thanks for coming in, John. Princess told us about these incredible new songs and we're dying to hear them." Kimi smiles.

"I added in some final touches—let me get the aux and we'll start there."

The assistants hustle to get John's computer plugged in, clearly eager to hear the music themselves.

John presses Play on the track and I feel an instant connection, to the music but also to John. Even without words we've been able to express ourselves to each other in a way that only we know. I can't sit anymore. I need to stand and move around, let the music flow through the air and through me. I close my eyes and start to sing on instinct and just let myself go.

John's smiling, nodding along to the rhythm. We made this song and this project, just us. We've done so much, and this track is proof that what we have is rare. We can't let this go. No matter what happened. We are a good team.

Wayne and Kimi care. Maya, Val, and Jessie love what I do, but none of them can really understand what it's like being in a studio and creating something the way John does, to be willing to be vulnerable and let yourself be open to failure as much as success. We make beautiful music together.

Am I superstitious? Could I do this with someone else? Without him?

When the song ends Kimi and Wayne are grinning—they congratulate John and me and immediately start strategizing how they're going to work this to the label. After some brainstorming between the group of us, Kimi and Wayne excuse themselves for other meetings and calls they need to attend to.

John and I are on a high and part of me doesn't want this moment to end. He starts making his way over to me, sauntering and smiling.

I'm so excited I'm bouncing up and down and he wraps me in a hug. He whispers into my ear, "I love watching you pitch records. You have a way about you that just captivates everyone in the room. It's incredible."

A rush of heat goes through my body as he sets me down and I almost feel shy when I reply, "Thanks, John."

He must be feeling the same way I do. How could he not? We've been entwined for so long, it'd be impossible for him to not think about it. I know John, I can read his face, I know his body movements and his gestures.

"Are you hungry? We could go for lunch." He's trying to act casual, closing his laptop and packing it into his backpack.

And there it is. Reality. This isn't what I'm supposed to be doing. I'm about to cross that line again, putting myself back into the fray and right where I know I don't belong.

"I don't think that's a good idea."

"Now or never?"

"I don't know." I hesitate, heart and head screaming at each other. I can never make up my mind when it comes to him. "Right now, we should stick to work."

"Okay, sure. I get it." John steps closer and puts his hand through his hair, but I wish he was running it through mine. "It's just I have some other music to play for you, and thought you might be feeling inspired."

I have to admit, I don't want this to end either. Lunch it is.

"All right. Let's do it."

8

The view of the city is spectacular. Los Angeles is a lot greener than people think with hills and trees dotting the landscape. Although it can be hard for me to really claim this place as home, I do have love for my adopted city. I love knowing that there are millions of people and stories out there. Even when you feel alone, you know you're not.

John and I try to get lunch at a nearby restaurant, but every place is packed so we decide to grab takeout and head up to the rooftop of Kimi and Wayne's office.

"We made a good choice with the salads." His small talk kills me.

"Yeah, it'll be nice in the heat." I internally scold myself for being awkward and not saying something more interesting. I hate talking about the weather.

The elevator dings for the top floor and honestly, I prefer the privacy. No need to stress about who's who and who might be listening to our conversation. Being in public can be such a distraction. I want to spend time alone with John, just us. I need clarity and the only way

I'm going to get it is if I come up with something more interesting to say.

John chooses the far corner table, the only one with an open umbrella. I slide into the sofa and recline, sipping on my mango green tea as he unboxes the salads we got from Health Nut. We're basically silent except for the occasional *here you go* and *thank you* as we get situated but it doesn't feel awkward.

Our relationship has been complicated lately but there's comfort here too. We don't need to fill in every pause or empty space. Watching him makes me feel happy and I wonder if I'm still riding the high of playing our music earlier or if this is real.

"Get Lucky" by Daft Punk softly plays over the speakers, instantly taking me back to the beginning of us.

It was one of my favorite songs at the time and I remember sitting on top of my bathroom counter, putting my makeup on and trying to psych myself up for a night out. I had been in Hollywood for a while but was still starting out. I'd had my fair share of bumps in the road at this point, got a glimpse of the darkness that blanketed the town so that the real stars could shine. If I was going to stay here I needed to build a stronger network.

Hollywood is cutthroat and I was inching towards the point where I wasn't sure if I should stay in LA any longer. Maybe the music *business* wasn't for me even if I'd never give up on being a musician. You have to be selfish . . . at least that's what I was gathering from what I saw around me. Selling my soul and shamelessly promoting myself was never my style but it was becoming apparent that if I didn't get on the trend soon, I'd be more out of season than those horrible Chelsea boots we all used to wear. Some jobs would spark here and there or I'd release a song that would gain some traction online and then I'd hit a wall. Over and over.

I started to question if hard work and determination would ever be enough. I had some friends, I had a little bit of a network, but I really missed my home, I missed my family. So much had been sacrificed, was it all worth it? I was looking for a sign when I got a DM from John completely out of the blue.

He'd heard one of my songs and wanted to get into the studio together. He told me he loved my style and how unique he thought my image and skills were. We went back and forth on messages a few times and he sent a song he'd been working on. I was instantly blown away. Ideas poured out of me and for the first time in a long time, I was excited. I felt hopeful. John was special, that was clear from the start.

He was in the early stages of his career too—he had had some good cuts with known artists but he hadn't "broken" yet. We were on the map but we were far from established and we were hungry. Inspired by each other. That was the magic. His Instagram didn't have too many posts—just some songs he'd made for artists and some artistic photos of himself. *Damn,* was he hot and he had style. And those blue eyes? Sharp and gorgeous. I pushed that aside though, because this was a creative proposition, not a date. I was dead focused on my career.

A couple of days later we met and as I predicted it was an instant connection. We made two songs that night. Talked for hours. We learned we had more in common with each other than anyone else we'd spent time with in our lives. I'd never felt so deeply understood until John. He could keep up with me when I went on tangents about my favorite music videos or stage performances. His eyes never glazed over like others' had in the past when people had to listen to me ramble on. He was just as enthusiastic and obsessed. He was a musical genius, and he was self-made.

Working together was electric, similar to how I felt when I first got

DIAMONDS, DECEPTION & DESTINY

on stage and realized what music meant to me. We lost all sense of time working all day into the early hours of the next morning. We pushed each other to try new things but it never felt competitive. There was nowhere else I'd rather be than with him in the studio. It was supportive and mutually beneficial. I loved every second of it and didn't even realize how exhausted I was until my head hit my pillow each night.

It never felt like work. We laughed as much as I sang. John created such a safe workspace for me: he was in control, he was a leader, he was a teacher. We spent basically every day together so naturally we got close, revealing more personal details and learning more about each other. We'd linger while finishing up or he'd walk me to my car so we could keep talking. By the time we finished our first few songs, I knew I had made a friend. It wasn't long after that when I started thinking of him as my best friend. We knew everything about each other. He was an integral part of my life.

So I didn't think anything of it when he asked me out to dinner. We'd been sharing meals, sure, mainly takeout on the studio couch. But this was different. A real date. When he picked me up, I teased him about his new shirt, a blue button-down, and how he'd gotten so dressed up for me. He cleaned up nice and I remember thinking how handsome he was. Then he held the car door open for me and took my hand as we walked into the restaurant. He didn't make a big show of it. Just took my hand, rubbing his thumb slowly over mine. That's when it hit me: I was in love with him. The place was humming with patrons, and he led me though the crowd to our table. This felt right. It was easy and exciting and I knew I didn't want John to ever let go.

I've thought about that time in our lives too many times to count since we broke up. I was destroyed. I've barely scraped myself back together. He has no clue how many times I felt like I couldn't breathe.

I took him back. I believed in him, that things would be different. And every single time the rug was pulled out from beneath me. But despite all that, I still missed him. I missed the good parts. Missed talking to John every day, being in the studio with him. Having him by my side. I had built him up, us up, so high in my heart and in my head that when it all came crashing down it smashed me into a million little pieces. Since then I've been trying to put myself back together and I don't know if I'll ever get it right but I do know that I love him and I miss him.

"Aren't you going to eat?" John asks. "The salad's actually pretty good."

I snap back to reality. Right. We are sitting on the roof of Kimi and Wayne's building. We are eating lunch from the big plastic bowls. We have been in love, broken up, reunited, then broken again. I am sitting with the man I thought I would spend my life with and now I'm not sure where we stand with each other.

"The food?"

John laughed. He's wearing his square-framed sunglasses but I know his blue eyes crinkle as he smiles. I know every line on his face.

"Yes, the food," he says. "It's nice, sitting here with you."

He takes my hand and I don't pull away. He rubs his thumb over mine just the way he used to and instant palpitations flutter in my chest. I don't pull away. I missed the warmth and strength of him holding my hand. I never wanted us to fall apart.

"You might not want to hear this again but I'm sorry, Princess. I wish I had a time machine. I'd make it right. I wish I could go back and not just hear what you were saying about Riley but really listen. I'm a better man now. I can do better."

"Can you?" I say, looking down into my bowl, unable to make eye contact with him. I don't know where to begin.

"So much was happening at once." His thumb is still circling mine and I'm not sure if I want him to be holding my hand anymore. "I was selfish, and immature, and I wasn't the leader you deserve. I had so many people in my ear and I was trying to navigate everything the right way but all I did was drag us down. I thought I could balance the momentum but looking back, I see how there was never balance. I didn't prioritize us. You're all that matters to me and I'm lost without you. I got caught up and lost the one thing that matters the most to me in the midst of it. I want to make it right."

You have to ride the wave when it hits. I just never thought he wouldn't keep me safe along the ride. That's what Kimi and Wayne are doing right now with my career. People are looking at me, paying attention to me and my music, and we need to keep their attention. Get more. Get in front of more people. It's not my favorite thing but definitely something we can't ignore or avoid.

"I'm not saying that Riley is innocent in this." I am definitely not saying that. "But you can't blame her entirely for this. You made those choices."

His jaw tightens and nods.

"It's my fault. I fucked up." He squeezes my hand before he lets it go. "I hate being apart from you. I hate not spending nights with you and waking up together. I want to hear everything about your day and tell you what happened in mine too. You're my person. I know you are."

I bite the inside of my cheek to stall for time and to retract the tears burning in my eyes. I take no pleasure in seeing John upset but I'm so scared. Our breakup nearly destroyed me. I wish I could just cut off my feelings but all I know is how much I care about him.

"Can you find your way to forgiving me?" he asks quietly. The warm sun surrounds us, the bright sky betraying my thoughts.

"I don't think it's about forgiveness anymore." What will people think? Val and Maya and Jessie. Kimi and Wayne. The world.

"Do you think it's something we can move past?"

"And go where? John, I'm not sure what you want from me anymore."

"I don't want to lose you. I never wanted to lose us."

My hand is back in his and I should pull away. Set reasonable boundaries. We've slid towards and away from each other so many times now that I'm unclear on where that line is anymore.

"It's so hard, John."

John nods again and I laugh. We're both nodding so much. Speaking our truths and solemnly listening. If only this was how we'd acted a few weeks ago. Maybe we'd be in a far different place right now.

"I do believe you. I believe you regret your actions. That you're sorry. I'm happy you've taken time to reflect on it and can see how you messed up, but it's not that easy for me. I'm still in the middle of it and it's still so fresh."

"This is where the time machine comes in handy."

"I don't want a time machine. I don't want to erase what happened. I mean, I wish I didn't know this heartache or that we even have to have this conversation. But we also need to own up to our actions or we're just going to repeat these mistakes over and over. Being in love with you was the best feeling I've ever experienced. I thought we'd found it. I thought we were invincible, but this has taught me no one is. No couple is perfect. We are young and we made mistakes. I can admit I haven't been perfect either. I can't change that you're always going to be my first love, John. No one can take that away or ever replace you."

DIAMONDS, DECEPTION & DESTINY

I study him for a while. My mom told me once that young love is hard because we both have so much growing up to do. Who we are at twenty isn't the same person we'll be at twenty-four. Or twenty-six. Maturing is a struggle—add Hollywood into that and it's a disaster. We're trying to keep our heads above water. If John and I met now, maybe we could fit together better without having so much to smooth out in the beginning.

"I hate that you speak about us in the past tense." He removes his sunglasses so I can see his eyes. "You aren't in the past for me."

He takes his hand away and I almost sigh. I wasn't ready for it.

"I want you to listen to something." He pulls his phone out, turns the volume up, and hits Play.

The song is mid-tempo and the melody hits me hard. It's a mix of gentle and persistent strings that draws me right in. I don't recognize the singer, but her voice is beautiful. I raise an eyebrow at John, questioning what this is all about, and he responds by holding his phone higher. I twist my head, leaning in to listen. We can't let go of each other's eyes.

The lyrics are sweet, longing. The woman is singing about holding onto things, people, love. The fear and pain of realizing she almost lost it all but she won't give up. She finally understands what's real. She doesn't want to waste another minute. Doesn't want to lose any more time.

"I wrote it for you." He pauses the song then puts the phone back into his pocket. "This song is for you, about you, because of you."

John's hand goes to my cheek and I feel a hitch in my breath. A lump in my throat.

"Can I kiss you, Princess?" He looks from my eyes to my mouth then back to my eyes. "I really want to kiss you."

I nod, again, because that is my default today and all I am capable of at the moment.

The kiss is soft, gentle. His hand cradles the back of my neck and mine intertwines into his hair. Our lips part and come together in the most natural flow, drinking each other in the sweetest way. We've been holding our breath all this time. Maybe we can finally come back to life now. That mix of new and familiar that I've always loved with John. I lean into it, into him.

9

"Time for the dirty." Maya sits back on my couch a week later and tucks her legs under her. "We love you, P, love hanging out, but we are dying for the details. Spill that tea. I want to be speechless. I want to scream, cry, faint, and scream again."

I put my head into my hands and laugh. I brought this on myself by inviting the girls over. I even flew Jessie down from San Francisco. I'm going to tell them everything but, shit, where do I begin?

"All right, buckle up, bitches. Who wants to moderate?" I pull my legs up onto the couch and wrap my arms around my knees. "I won't be holding back, so ask accordingly and hold on to your panties."

"Hold on a minute. We need cocktails!" Valerie chimes. "What are we thinking!"

"Dirty martinis. That's what we need."

In my kitchen, Maya directs us each on what ingredients to grab. Ice, olive juice, vermouth, Grey Goose. She eyeballs the vodka-to-olive-juice ratio into the cocktail shaker. I grab the glasses, Jessie grabs the mini olive skewers, and Valerie provides moral support. In a flash, we all have drinks in hand and are skipping back to my living room.

"Let's get into it." Jessie sits across from me on the floor. She's tucked in beside the marble coffee table holding on to her baby pink martini glass. "Good or bad?"

"Unclear."

"We aren't off to a good start with these answers," Val laughs. "I didn't expect an 'unclear' to show up off the bat."

I sit up straight, taking a nice long sip of my absolutely filthy icy cold martini.

"That's fair. Let's get a little loose. Cheers, girly pops." I raise my glass and we all raise up onto our knees and meet in the middle before I continue. "Everything is good. At least I don't feel bad about any of it so that must be a good sign."

"Mmmkay. Now let's get down to discussing what 'it' is," Maya says.

"Let's start at the management meeting. What happened?" Val asks. "You looked pretty happy on your Insta stories but then you were unreachable for a couple of hours." She raises her eyebrows expectantly.

"John was at the meeting." They let a unified mini-scream out. "He came later to play our music for Kimi and Wayne."

"Oh my fucking lord." Maya half laughs.

"Okay." Jessie perks up. "And how was . . . that?"

"It went well." Reaching for my frosted glass, I take another sip. Count to three before turning back to my friends. "In fact, dare I say it was *really* good."

All their mouths drop at the same time.

"Good how?" Maya.

"What happened?" Jessie.

"Say more things." Val.

I am back to not knowing what to say or how to describe what happened. I have been actively trying not to overanalyze everything because I don't want to get too in my head like I normally would. My plan was to lay it out with the girls so they could help me work through it but now it all seems so convoluted and tricky.

"There are two parts to the John story. First, he came in to play the new music we'd been working on." I pause to look at all of them. "And that was good."

"If you keep leaving the details at 'good' I am going to have a fucking meltdown. We want *more*," Maya drags.

"Do you mean John or the song?" Jessie asks.

"Both?" I laugh. "Okay, okay! I survived in Miami, and maybe I was happy to see him. We work well together, you know?" I smile slightly. "And then, he played the song and I was . . . transported. Not sure how else to describe it."

"Transported by listening to yourself sing?" Valerie raises an eyebrow.

"Sure. Let's say that." I try to skip over the comment. "The song we want to release is great and that I can say is a fact."

"Okay, babe! Let's go!" Maya says.

"I was transported back to the feeling of us in the studio and making the song and being inside it. That moment. Singing along like a crazy person without realizing it. John's final mix is like an ear orgasm. The song is so lush. I felt like I was swimming in it. It was really an incredible feeling."

"That's beautiful." Jessie sighs.

"I love that for you," Val says.

"When I opened my eyes, John was staring at me. You know the look."

"Uh-oh." Val narrows her eyes. "I'm not sure I like where this is going."

"If this is going where I think it is, I need a refill." Maya grabs the cocktail shaker and refills her and Val's glasses. "Okay, ready."

"We got lunch. Nothing fancy. We sat on the roof and talked. He apologized again."

"Wow, John? Good at apologizing? I never thought I'd see the day," Maya singsongs.

"I believe he's sorry." I know why they're skeptical. "It was actually a good talk. We both got to say our piece."

"How are you feeling now?" Jessie moves the convo along. "Have you forgiven him?"

"I'm not sure if I've *forgiven* him but I'm not angry anymore. He made mistakes, but I've been duped more than once by Riley. He should've known better but I do understand how that could happen."

"As your boyfriend, he should protect you. He should guide you and move in your best interest. Without you giving him tips," Maya says, matter-of-factly.

"Speaking of snakes, what do you think is up with Riley?" Jessie leans forward. "She's trying to be buddy-buddy with you guys again, right? So should we be assuming she's up to something?"

"It's very suspicious." Val rolls her eyes. "But I'm not surprised. Riley always pops in and out whenever she needs something from you. Your music is doing well, you're playing shows, producers want to work with you, you're becoming harder and harder for her to silence. If Riley can't control it, she's going to be there to take advantage of it."

I hesitate a moment before speaking again. "I swear, if you knew the Riley I used to know, you'd know there is a sweet person underneath all that." I pause before my next thought because I know the reaction I'll get. "If it was that Riley around now, she'd fit in perfectly with us. Part of me thinks we should give her a chance."

"Hold on now. You can't be serious." It's Maya's turn to roll her eyes. "Why should we give her another chance?"

"Because she does have a sweet side to her." I finish the last of my martini. "Or she did."

"Or maybe that was all an act too. Not everyone deserves a second chance," Jessie suggests, noticing my empty glass and reaching to refill it.

"Thanks, babe. I'm just saying there's more to her than what you see. You and Val especially should understand the pressure she's under. You all come from really successful families and it can't be easy. There are a lot of expectations. You guys know how it is."

"It's not that hard either," Maya almost mumbles as she takes another sip.

We're all silent for a few seconds and it doesn't feel like the same comfortable silence that John and I enjoyed. It's unusual for the girls and me to not be on the same page and for a second or two it has me worried.

"You said there were two things about John." I look over at Jessie, grateful that she's broken the spell. "What was the other thing?"

"He wrote a song for me." I try to hide my smile but it's impossible. "It's not like anything else he's written before. It's personal and very sweet. Honestly, I didn't know what to do with myself when he was playing it. And then . . ."

I pause for dramatic effect because I know it will drive them all mad. I don't start talking again until Maya threatens to throw a pillow at me.

"Okay, okay! And then we kissed." My hands shoot up to cover my mouth.

The girls all respond exactly as expected with gasps and *get the fuck out* and throwing their bodies to the ground in disbelief.

"He fucking kissed me!" The words come out in a rush and an octave higher than intended. "He *asked* to kiss me."

I feel the warmth of the kiss again. Familiar. Exciting yet comforting. It didn't have the same intensity as when Win and I kissed but that was brand new and unexpected. It really isn't fair to compare the two. And my stomach dips at the idea that I have two men—a past and a present—and don't know what to do about either.

"It was such a sweet moment. We talked and let some confessions out and we fell right back into it. It was like a conversation we were having that got interrupted. Like we both had more to say. Do you know what I mean?"

"It pains me to say this because you know how I feel about John." Jessie almost sighs as she speaks. "But if you really think that there's something there, you shouldn't ignore it."

"No way, fuck that!" Maya holds up her glass like she's making a toast. "Past is past, girl. It's better to move on."

"Don't listen to her. Maya's never even been on a second date." Val laughs as Maya pitches the pillow at her head.

"Suddenly you're an expert on relationships because you've been in one for what? Three weeks?" Maya counters.

"It's true. I *Tripped* and fell into love . . . no pun intended." Val bats her eyelids and shrugs like, *what's a girl to do?* "But my point is, love never makes sense; all we can do is follow our heart."

"Try telling that to my head too. My head and my heart are not on speaking terms these days."

"Okay, so your head is telling you to be cautious." Jessie rests her elbows on the table and leans forward. "What does your heart tell you?"

This is a very, very good question. I straighten up again. Stretch my back and neck and take a deep breath.

"My heart tells me that I've never had anyone write a song for me before. Not like that."

"I guess now you know how Win felt." Maya laughs and I know she didn't mean anything by it, but I feel a small twinge all the same.

"Except John and I have a history, a base for it all, and Win and I decided to stay friends." Saying it out loud twists that mini-knife in my side.

"Are you sure about that? It looked like you were having a pretty intense and intimate conversation at the afterparty."

"I'm not sure exactly . . ." Why wasn't anything straightforward these days? It was so much easier when John held my hand and it all made sense. "We did talk. He said he was going away for business and that he didn't want to commit if he couldn't give me his all. He was cagey about people getting hurt when he goes away for long stretches of time or can't fully commit. He didn't give me any details but I'm guessing he's been the culprit for some heartbreaks along the way."

"All those mysterious girlfriends that no one ever sees," Val says.

"I got some intel on that; I guess someone's heart was broken. And it was big enough that Win shut down the idea of anything more than casual happening with me." Am I disappointed? He said so many sweet things to me, he's definitely a flirt, he has natural charm, and I swore I felt a connection. But clearly I was wrong. Our conversation would've ended a lot differently if Win had any long-term romantic feelings for me. "I've already accepted that truth."

That's right, I think. *Keep telling yourself that.*

"Maybe it was Win's heart that was broken." Maya looks at me and shrugs. "It's possible."

"Possible but not probable. It still doesn't change the outcome. Nothing is happening with Win and me."

"Have you spoken to each other since Miami?" Jessie asks.

"We text." I don't add *every day, several times a day*. "It's all been friendly . . . *how was your day* type of stuff. Some harmless selfies. Little updates here and there. Nothing big. He's still in New York."

That part is true. It's a lot of checking in and saying *hey* but nothing more than that. No real emotions. But I'm always happy when I see a text from Win and a bit disappointed if he doesn't respond right away. There's nothing I can do but chalk it up to having a friend and liking the interaction.

"Fine, I accept defeat." Maya raises both her hands. "I will drop the Win subject. We can officially move on."

We ease into a regular hang. We switch to wine and hot tea. Val fills us in on her time with Tripp. Everyone piles onto the couch with me as Val shows us videos of them out on the town. They're adorable together. Tripp still looks like he's in disbelief that Val is dating him, like he'll never stop smiling. Of course, this leads us down a TikTok path as we show each other funny videos we've saved. It's my turn to scroll through my feed, holding my phone up for everyone when a text pops up.

John: Madeo tonight? You and me.

Everyone squeals and I almost throw my phone across the room at the surprise.

"This is exactly what keeps happening. Is God testing me and if he is . . . am I passing?!"

"Oh girl, it's not looking good for you." Maya jokingly winces. "Are you going to go?"

"Yesss? Nooo?" Val is jabbing my shoulder trying to prompt a response. They are all staring at me. Waiting for me to make a move.

"Come on! Someone say something! I genuinely need your help here."

"I vote don't go." Maya looks serious. Mama Bear speaks out.

"I say do what you need to do but be aware. Think about what you're getting yourself into if you go," Val says.

"Do it! If someone is trying to right their wrong, let them!" Jessie cheers.

My mind screams *don't go*. Don't be an idiot. You've been down this road *too* many times. But my heart argues that John is sincere when he wants something. Maybe he was neglectful when he had me, but he said he regrets that. My heart. Despite the very recent heartache, it isn't quite ready to give up. In music and in life—I lead with my heart. It hasn't always worked out for me—recent heartache being an excellent example—but things don't feel resolved with John. Reopening that door is the only way I'm going to be able to close it for good. Besides, maybe this time it will work.

"She's going," Jessie says to the girls. "Your face says you're going." She looks matter-of-fact to me. She's known me a long time and reads me like a damn book.

"We better get to glamming then," Maya says with a sigh of resignation.

I text John back: I'd love to.

"Let's get moving, ladies. Chop chop." Maya claps. "I'm making another round of cocktails."

"I'll raid the closet." Val gives my hand a squeeze before heading into my room.

"Guess that means I'm going to jump in the shower."

If I'm going to do this, then I'm going for it. There's nothing happening with Win, my career is on the move—this isn't the time to sit around and mope.

10

John stands in front of the restaurant waiting for me. Dark denim, crisp white T-shirt, all-white Common Projects, and his Rolex. Hot. His hair is messy and looks a little longer than he normally keeps it. Suddenly I wish I had a photographic memory. He looks me up and down as I walk towards him. He looks happy to see me and I find myself smiling right back. As hard as I try to stay present, I rewind to the last time we were here.

"Hi, P," he says sweetly, opening his arms so he can fold me into a hug.

"Hey, you." My face heats up and I want nothing more than to cuddle up into him.

Madeo is my favorite Italian restaurant in LA. The off-menu lemon pasta and a crispy glass of Sancerre are just what I need to start a night off right. This was our special occasion restaurant, the place we'd go when we had an achievement to commemorate, or we wanted to cele-brate each other just because. I held on to those moments with white knuckles, desperate for them to burn into my mind so that if one day we weren't happy or we weren't together anymore I could recall what a love like this felt like. The first time we were here was when I signed my record contract. A ribbon of bittersweet wraps around my heart and pulses; a lot can happen in two years.

Back then, paparazzi swarmed as we approached the front doors. But I was in my safe John bubble. Normally I'd be overwhelmed by the cameras and people shouting my name, saying anything to get a reaction for the perfect clickbait photo. More of a reaction, more of a payday. I'm all for posing and letting paps get their shots when I'm at an event or a red carpet—that's part of the job. But it takes on a different energy if I'm at the gym or out to dinner with friends. The Princess that shows up in artist mode is different. Always on, always aware, always perfect.

"Are you okay?" John asked me back then, intuitively checking on me.

"Yes, babe, I'm good." We smiled at each other and kept moving.

The flashing lights can be intrusive and triggering. That night though, it didn't bother me. John had his arm cradling me, hand secured at my waist, and pulled me in close. He was my shield. I felt so cared for and it was the greatest feeling in the world.

On that night, the doors swung open as the hostess greeted us warmly. John hugged me from behind and walked in step with me as she led us to a corner table. Perfect. People-watching with privacy. He gave me the booth seat as he always does and slid into his chair.

"Can we get you started with still or sparkling?"

"Still is good," John replied for both of us.

When she left, John got up from his side of the table to squeeze into the booth next to me and I scooted my body as close as I possibly could. We couldn't get enough of each other. I didn't care if anyone was watching. We were an island of two. In the studio, in life. Every day brought us closer and stronger. I realize now that some of this might have been the euphoria of new love, but I had no perspective then. It was all new to me, exciting. I thought I was the luckiest girl alive, and I knew beyond a doubt that I only wanted more.

"We're so lucky we found each other." I wrapped my arm around his and pressed my forehead into his neck. His hand gripped my inner thigh and I almost crawled into his lap because I wanted to be closer to him, consume him, but I kept to the booth. "People search for a love like ours their whole lives and I'm just so grateful that I found you."

"There's no one else like you and me, P. Nothing compares to this."

He leaned in and kissed my cheek. He was acting polite and gentlemanly but that look in his eyes. He wanted me as much as I wanted him.

"If I were them, I'd be jealous of us," I said, looking at the other patrons. "I wonder if any of them will ever find this too."

"Highly unlikely, but even if they get to experience a fraction of what we have, they'll be lucky." He rubbed my back and I felt like I could melt.

This wasn't anything I'd planned for. Yes, I'd had crushes on guys and gone on dates here and there. I was a hopeless romantic who loved rom-coms and weddings and was always happy for friends when they found someone special. But I never knew if or when it'd happen for me. I spent my fair share of time fantasizing about being in love and having a relationship, about finding my soulmate. But I'd always been so focused on my music, creating a foundation for my career. I wasn't actively trying to reach goals in the love category of my life. So falling in love with John was a surprise. One I wish had happened to me sooner.

John picked up my hand and kissed it.

"When should we start having babies?" He winked and I giggled.

"Whenever you're ready," I joked. I wasn't against having kids but that seemed like a future Princess question. Not a just-getting-her-career-rolling Princess question. "But we should probably get a rock and the white picket fence first."

I always knew I'd lead a bit of an unconventional life but somehow I'd find a way to fit in the house with the yard and babies and maybe a golden retriever. I wanted a family but I also didn't want to give up my dreams and my career. John felt the same and I loved him even more for that. No one gets this. No one finds a person they don't have to sacrifice for, but I did. We were made for each other.

"Whatever happens, Princess"—he leaned in close and kissed me softly—"it's you and me forever, whenever and always. I love you."

I knew we loved each other before we ever said it out loud but hearing the words roll off John's lips for the first time sent delicious tingles throughout my entire body like I'd never felt before. I. Love. You. Fuck. How could anything feel this good?

"I love you too."

John opens the door to the restaurant for me and my mind swims. We are not in that moment. This is not when John tells me he loves me for the first time. There has been so much heartache and pain since then. But once again, that's my head talking. My heart skips a beat when he puts a hand on my back to guide me inside and I'm hit with the sudden image of John and me sweaty, hungry for each other, in bed, how he put his hand on my back to ease me down there too. I try to push the memory away but, damn, it's hard to shake.

Once inside the hostess shows us to our table. The place is busy enough for us to blend in but not too loud. No one looks up as we walk past, everyone's deep into their own conversations and cocktails. John holds my chair out so I can sit down and I realize I'm a bit disappointed we aren't sitting closer together.

"You look so beautiful tonight."

I hold my hands out like a show model and my outfit is the product on display.

"I'm Maya and Val's work of art."

"I'll have to remember to thank them later," John says. "I'm glad you agreed to come out tonight. I was worried you'd say no."

"To be honest, I'm a bit surprised too." Neither of us has picked up a menu. "I'm happy I did, though."

"It's good for us to be able to spend time together. Just us, no distractions."

"Like Riley?" I regret the words the second they leave my lips. *He's trying to make amends, don't be a bitch.*

"I don't want to talk about Riley tonight. Can we do that?" John asks. "We've given her enough of our time."

"Fair." I lean forward on the table. "In fact, that's probably something we should have done a long time ago."

The waiter comes back to the table to tell us the specials and asks if we've had a chance to look at the menu. John looks at me knowingly.

"All the usuals?"

"Absolutely."

I feel a bit giddy as John lists off all our favorites. Calamari, caprese, Spaghetti à Limone, Bolognese, a Sancerre for me and tequila on the rocks for him. I'm not sure if it's good or bad that we can fall so easily into old patterns, but I choose to ignore that thought. This feels good and I'm going with it.

Our conversation switches and we start talking about going into the studio soon. Wayne and Kimi are talking to the label about the new songs and said they have "big plans." John and I spend time wondering what that might mean.

We talk about my tour—Kimi texted me the tentative UK plans today. It'll be my first time playing shows in Europe. The dates haven't officially been confirmed yet but I'm still excited. I'm opening for a bigger artist, which is a good look for me, and the venues will be filled with twenty thousand people. I'm buzzing with excitement just thinking about it. We don't discuss the possibility of John joining me on tour but we hint at it—I've already set the plan in my head. We talk about how great it would be to travel together and to be able to work on new material. Who knows what kind of inspiration could hit when we're overseas. This is what I've always wanted. To experience new adventures, new music, success, and travel together. All this is great, but if you don't have someone to share it with . . . what's the point?

I've made music for most of my life but the truth is, it often feels like my musical life is tied to John. I found my voice and created my sound when John and I started working together. I don't know where to draw the line between music and love. They're both completely intertwined with John.

"Remember when we came here and sat in that corner booth?" John sips his drink and I'm instantly locked in on his lips.

"Of course I do." I take a sip of my drink and slowly slide an olive off the pick with my teeth. His eyes lock on my lips before meeting my eyes to catch me watching him.

I look away and take in my surroundings. The décor, the people passing by outside the large windows, the jackets the servers wear. I recognize a lot of the staff and some of the customers. Being here reminds me of happy times with John and that brings me safety, security in knowing how all these pieces fit together. And yet, something is nagging at me. A low hum, an almost prickly feeling in the back of my head—something is off. I dismiss it as my usual overthinking.

John takes my hand, laces our fingers. "We were really good together."

We *were* good together. Past tense. Like we were but not now. Maya and Val's voices creep into my mind—this isn't a good idea.

"Give me another chance. I won't mess up again."

I feel so relieved. This is all I want to hear. I'm tired of being in a constant battle with myself. Maybe I'm being naïve, but I want John, I love John, we should try this again. It's okay. People make mistakes and grow and try again. Maybe he's not the same person who first said *I love you* in this restaurant. But I am also not the same person who said *I love you* back. So much has happened since then. We've stumbled and learned. We're both better people. We can't go back to who we were. This time, if anything happens with John and me, my eyes are wide open.

"Please don't break my heart again." I can feel tears welling but I'm not sad. There are just so many emotions rising up at once. I'm scared but this is what I want. "There will really be nothing left this time around."

He rubs a thumb across my cheek to wipe away a tear.

"I will not hurt you. I promise. You are my priority. You come before everything else. Everything will be different this time."

I nod and kiss his palm. This is good.

DIAMONDS, DECEPTION & DESTINY

Our food arrives and I dig in. It's as delicious as I remember. We reminisce about trips we took, other dates we had at Madeo and other restaurants. The time I tried to make him eggs and almost set my kitchen on fire. When we fooled around in the back of an Uber on our way home and John got a one-star rating from the driver. We are laughing so hard that I feel drunk, even though we have barely touched our drinks.

Our hands keep coming together. He traces fingers along the inside of my wrist. He draws on my forearm a map of the studio he wants to build. He has a plan. He's going to be more than a producer. He's shooting for mogul. And he can do it. I know he can.

I love seeing this John. He is ambitious and focused and it's such a goddamn turn-on. With every bite of food, as we drain our drinks, I wish for time to speed up because I want this dinner to be over. I want to go home with John.

We finally finish up and John calls us a car to go home. We don't talk much on the drive but we hold hands. I rest my head against the seat and watch the city out the car window. Lights and people passing by. It's beautiful and I am so at peace and content.

John holds my hand as he helps me get out of the car and slings an arm over my shoulder, holding me close as we walk inside. We say hi to security and head towards the elevators. As soon as we step inside and the doors close John pushes me against the wall. Hands in my hair and mine in his. Pulling hard as he teases a kiss, brushing his lips over mine. Kissing the corner of my mouth on the right, then on the left, giving me a little taste but not his full mouth. I moan his name in protest. I need more. I push my hips forward to meet his, feeling him hard. It's easy, so easy to do this. My body is a bundle of nerves and electricity. I know all the moves, all the places to turn him on, and he knows exactly what to do to make me crumble. I'm pinned between him and the wall of the elevator, and I have no desire to escape. His mouth meets mine straight on and his tongue slips into my mouth. Warm and soft. I wrap my lips around it as he moans, sliding his hand down to cup the top of the back of my legs, his fingers barely grazing that warm spot aching for him. My body is begging me to just let my guard down completely and go for it. But then the elevator doors open again and I'm in my apartment. My senses return. John follows me, hands on my hips, looking for the cue, but I place a hand on his chest and push him back.

"I had a really great night. Thank you for taking me to my favorite place." I look up at him, a little nervous to see his reaction.

John bites the inside of his cheek to dampen his smile. He is disappointed but he gets it. He puts both hands on my cheeks and kisses my forehead.

"To many other nights like this one, babe."

He backs away, still smiling, and gets into the elevator. And I'm left there standing, staring at the doors long after he's gone. Instant nerves are going through me. Did I just make a huge mistake? Just because it feels good doesn't mean it's right. Maybe we crossed the line. How am I going to know if I'm making the right choice? I'm rewarding bad behavior. Maybe he'll think that if he messes up again it'll just be a matter of time before I break and forgive him. Am I teaching him a pattern? What about the signs? What about what Win said in Miami? What does it all mean? There's nothing I can do right now—we aren't official. We had dinner, it's fine.

I'm frozen, staring at the elevator doors and trying to process everything that just happened. Keep it cool; just because you had a good dinner doesn't mean anything. I can't push the thought out

DIAMONDS, DECEPTION & DESTINY

of my mind fast enough and I do a silent full-body victory shimmy, unable to control myself and skip my way into my kitchen. My nighttime ritual and a cup of lavender chamomile tea is exactly what I need right now. With a steaming puppy-patterned mug in hand, I make my way to my bathroom, slip into my fuzzy Four Seasons bathrobe, and start my skincare ritual. Calming music, on. Candles, lit. Very mature.

My luxury skincare is laid out in order, customized especially for me by my esthetician. Double cleansing with my Barbara Sterm foaming face wash, I'm lathering the suds into my eyelashes, erasing any trace of mascara when my phone chimes.

I bet it's John, I singsong to myself. Or maybe Win. When he texted earlier, I'd told him I was going out with John, and he didn't seem mad. That thought makes me slightly more excited. Far too eager to know, I almost drop my iPhone into the running water, not bothering to finish washing my face or dry my hands.

John: Made it home, thinking of you.

Happy it was John but slightly disappointed it wasn't Win. Boy, do I need a therapy appointment with the girls ASAP.

Princess: Happy you made it back safe. I'm finishing my skincare and about to get in bed. Thank you for dinner; I really enjoyed myself.

John: I wish we could've spent the night together but I know I have a lot of making up to do.

Princess: Well, dinner and the elevator kiss was a step in the right direction.

John: Thinking about your lips is going to keep me up all night.

Hot.

John's typing . . . delete . . . typing.

John: I have a feeling we have plenty more dinner dates and time for just us in our future. I want to make you feel like the most special girl in the world.

Princess: I hope you're right. I'm looking forward to it. Goodnight, John.

John: Sweet dreams, P.

Going backward, going forward.

11

Good news rarely comes on a Monday, but Kimi calls to tell me that the London show is a go, which means they are trying to line up some other dates in the UK to make it worthwhile flying all that way. The summer's flying by and my fall is shaping up to be just as busy.

"I'll send over the rehearsal schedule—it'll be a bit of a stripped-down show as this is a one-off for you to open for Avery Heart, so the budget is going to be tighter than we'd like, but there's a chance if this show goes well, they'll ask you to do the latter half of their European leg. If that happens, we'll be able to get a bigger chunk of money from the label's tour support budget."

I put my phone on speaker to check the texts that have been coming in since she called. First I notice the time—11:11 a.m.—then I notice the names, John and Win, right there at the top of my list.

John: Been thinking of you, P, hope you've had a good last couple of days.

Half listening to Kimi and not feeling like typing back a response to John, I double tap the message and react with a heart. Why does he have to remind me that he hasn't thought to reach out to me since the night of our dinner? Maybe just send a nice text and we can pretend that you didn't forget about my existence for the last couple of weeks. That might be petty, but I'm right.

"Thanks, Kimi," I say, directing my focus back to work. "I'll loop back if I have any questions after reviewing everything."

I end the call and swipe back to my text messages to see what Win has to say.

Win: Morning, Princess. Are you already out and conquering the day?

I smile down at my phone. Sweet, consistent, and open-ended. I look forward to these morning texts from Win. It doesn't feel like my day has officially started until I've heard from him. There was a brief pause, or a slowing down, after my dinner with John but we quickly picked up again. Only a few texts a day that first week but now we're up to dozens. A lot of my messages with Win are silly, carefully designed to make him laugh or distract him from the stress of his day. Photos of my morning matcha or a wig I found (but didn't touch) outside a club, or me wearing headphones and PJs with the caption *hard at work*, a video of a dog going down a water slide. It amuses me thinking of new things and I find myself snapping and recording content throughout the day to send to him. It's like I have a side art project called "Will this make Win laugh?" I feel so completely myself when we talk.

I take a selfie of me on the treadmill and smiling for the camera. I'm sweaty and don't look particularly glam working out but Win and I are past that now. I don't worry too much about impressing him anymore. Even if we're not in a relationship, I still love talking to him. Win hasn't been back to LA since he got the last-minute news he was

DIAMONDS, DECEPTION & DESTINY

leaving for business the night of my show in Miami. And that was almost two *months* ago. Since I got back to LA, I've been consumed with doing everything in my power to get this music released, keep my team invested and my label happy, and maintain some shred of sanity.

Princess: And what are you doing? Clearly not too busy to text.

He sends through his own selfie. I can't see his face but he's pulling his hair with one hand in a gesture of frustration and he's surrounded by mountains of perfectly organized papers. It's Win telling me that his work is endless and he needs a break.

Princess: Oh please! Aren't you the same man who brags about how many meetings you can do in a day?

Win: I was not bragging! That was my cry for help.

Princess: Poor baby! So dramatic.

Win: I am speaking my truth, Princess.

I double tap his message and hit the 'haha' then put my phone down to finish my 12-3-30. I know so much about Win's patterns now. There's always a burst of texts in my morning (his lunch hour) to check in, then a break while he's working or in meetings. The whole day follows that schedule. Bursts then break. Bursts then break. But even when he can't send an actual text, he always acknowledges mine. Either a tapback, an emoji, or 'Ha!' He never leaves me on Read or waiting for a response. In fact, he is so reliable that when I didn't hear back from him for a few hours the other day I started to worry. I didn't double text or try to call with concerned messages but it was so unlike him. Turns out, he left his phone in a car, and it took him a minute to get it back. Now I jokingly remind him to sing *phone, keys, wallet* before doing anything. He usually replies with the eyeroll emoji or a *Yes, ma'am*.

I finish my run and jump in the shower. I'm slightly behind

schedule so I need to get moving. I want to go over some music I've been working on before meeting up with the girls. I am on my phone, deciding whether or not I should break the silence and text John. Reading our last messages still makes me mad.

John: Hey, P. You hear anything from the label yet?

He'd been out of town for a song camp with an up-and-coming artist for a few days. Busy in the studio and not responding to texts or calls. Which is why I was irritated that his first contact with me was about business.

Princess: Wayne says they're waiting on the numbers.

John: Damn. We need to get going. Get this song out.

Princess: We will. Gotta stick to the plan and keep pushing.

Maybe I threw the vibe off when I cut the night short. It's not ideal if we're trying again—but work always comes first, for both of us.

He's either been in the studio late or I was booked. Last week he flew to Atlanta to work with another artist. Now I have a quick trip to New York for a corporate event, and my show coming up at the top of the year in London has me busy with rehearsals.

John's communication is so inconsistent. Being excited over the bare minimum is so embarrassing it's slowly becoming easier and easier for me to detach. Him sending a *thinking of you* message followed by a work text just isn't going to do it for me. I know what it means when the texts start getting spaced out. I just wish he'd man up and say he's not interested in the situation. If he wanted to spend real time with me, he'd make a plan to do just that and he hasn't, so the writing is on the wall.

John: Are you doing anything tonight? I get back to LA around 5 p.m. Want to do dinner?

Maybe I spoke too soon.

Princess: That'd be nice.

DIAMONDS, DECEPTION & DESTINY

John: Great, I'll make us a reservation and plan to pick you up at 8. I'll text you right back to confirm everything. How does sushi sound?

Princess: Sushi sounds great, see you then.

This should be interesting, I mutter to myself. I bring my laptop to my kitchen island countertop and prop myself up on a stool to bang out some work over the next couple of hours. I have a quick shopping trip later with the girls to find pieces for my upcoming shows in New York and London and Val's upcoming date. Then I'll need to tear my closet apart to find the perfect outfit and eyelashes for the evening. I decide not to tell the girls about my dinner tonight; best to err on the side of caution for the near future with John. Especially when it comes to our romantic relationship. Call me crazy but I'm excited and looking forward to tonight. My phone bings again.

Win: Finished up my last meeting. Light day. Done with your workout?

Princess: About to go shopping with the girls. I'm on the lookout prepping for the New York show. I leave in a couple weeks, and then London in the New Year.

Win: Anything in particular you're going to buy?

Princess: Probably nothing today. I just love looking at pretty things.

Win: That's a great way to describe window shopping ☺

I realize that it's time for me to leave, and I need my five final touches: a spritz of perfume; one last blast of hairspray; lipliner touch-up; final outfit adjustments and grabbing my stilettos, which will elevate and complete my casual day of shopping outfit comprised of gray sweatpants, a crown-bedazzled white tank top, and a string of pearls hanging down low from my neck.

Princess: This is mostly for Val. She and Tripp have a big date so we're trying to find her something special.

Win: How special?

Princess: Drop-dead gorgeous, have him weak in the knees and wrapped around her pinky finger special, of course.

The house phone rings, startling me, and I drop one of the stilettos I'm debating over. Red or cream . . . I can't decide. I can hear Maya and Val calling my name as they exit the elevator into my unit.

Princess: Girls here. Need shoes. Gotta go. Red or cream?

Win: Cream. Have fun shopping.

I greet them at the entryway with the shoes in hand and everyone laughs. I hop on one foot, sliding the cream pump onto the other.

"Don't kill me, I'm ready! It's been a busy morning."

Jessie holds my arm so I can put on the other one. She's visiting before her classes start again in a couple of weeks now that her intensive summer credit is done.

"I really think we should hit Dior first," Maya says. "Or, wait, maybe we should do matchas first. We're going to need our fuel."

"Yesss! I'm dying to try the Croft Alley matcha," Jessie half-moans, which makes me laugh.

"There are only a few things I'll never say no to in life: binge-watching anything starring Jason Bateman, a vodka cocktail, my girl time with you three, and a pre–shop till we drop matcha-fueled cup."

"Amen, sister!" Valerie cheers.

It's been hard for all of us to get together lately too. We're all so busy with our schedules, which is a blessing but makes me sad that we haven't had as much girl time lately. Finding a night when everyone was available was nearly impossible—we were each exhausted from the day and had an even busier next day. I couldn't complain because I was just as busy as everyone else. Everything was changing. I wanted to make the most of the day with the least amount of stress so I booked my security and driver, Mark, to be with us.

DIAMONDS, DECEPTION & DESTINY

We grab our matchas at Croft and decide to walk to the newly renovated Chanel store right around the corner. It's three stories and none of us has been in it yet. We're in heaven going through the racks, pulling items out. We're supposed to be shopping for Val but I spot Maya and Jessie in another corner of the store racking up items the former wants to buy.

"Val, I'm going to have a few things I want to try on put into your fitting room, okay, babe?" Maya says more like a statement than a question across the store.

"Whatever you want, darling."

Maya cracks me up sometimes. This girl has taste and let me tell you it is ex-pen-sive. She loves shopping and doesn't understand the concept of money. Whatever she likes, she gets. But she would never brag. I love tagging along on her shopping spree days; it's so motivating to me. I do well but I always think twice when I'm making an expensive purchase. Maya has never had to and honestly neither has Val. I don't think humble is the right word to describe them but opulent yet kind-hearted might do the trick.

Maya does her rounds trying on potential pieces and decides on black trousers and a silky black tank to match. She gives the sales assistant her credit card to charge while Val takes over the dressing room.

"What do you think of this one?" Val holds up a baby-blue mini dress with the classic CC logo right in the dip of the sweetheart neckline. She presses it against her body and hits a pose.

"Not sure." I put my hands on my hips as I examine Val and the dress. "It's a good color but I'm not sure about the cut. It might be giving too much babydoll. We need a more striking, *I'm the woman of the hour* kind of statement."

"You're right. You're always GD right." Val assesses herself in the mirror.

"Wait, I saw a different option that might be perfect." Jessie walks off to find the piece.

"What do you think of these?" I look over at Maya dangling a pair of ballet flats but she's distracted by her phone. I nudge her arm. "Are you with us?"

"Sorry?" She stops texting long enough to look up. "Right. Yeah, of course!"

"What's going on? Who are you talking to?" I ask.

"No one." Maya winks and I get the feeling she's up to something. She's not usually one for secrets, at least not from any of us, so I'm not sure what's going on. She puts her phone away and smiles. "All yours."

"Val wants our opinion." I nod toward Val and the baby-blue baby-doll dress.

Maya looks over and waves both her hands. "Hell motherfuckin' no. I love me some Coco Chanel, I really do. But mama isn't giving us what we need right now. On to the next."

After Val changes, we thank the SAs and make our way out of the store. I don't mind where we go; I'm here for the company and to support Val. That said, Dior is way more my style. Lots of clothes I'd like to own someday but I really can't justify the price tag right now. I'm making good money, and the cosmetic line is promising in terms of brand building, but I still have to be mindful. When you didn't grow up rich, you have to be smart. I have no expectation that the money will always be there.

Maya holds a dress up to me and leans back to get a good look.

"This is so good on you. You need it in your closet."

I raise an eyebrow and laugh. "It's gorgeous. Are you going to explain why you are being so very, very weird?"

"Who, me?" She hands the dress to the shop assistant who's been following her around and nods. "I'm never weird. How dare you."

Maya has a twinkle in her eye that looks extremely suspicious.

I pull out my phone and turn the ringer on to make sure I don't miss any calls or texts. It's been hours and I still haven't got any confirmation from John for tonight, which is making my fight-or-flight instinct start to kick in. He's not going to play me, I know that but it's still not a good feeling. I can feel my energy drop; I hope the girls don't notice. I decide to shoot him a text to ease my anxiety.

Princess: Hey, checking in. Were you able to get a res? Let me know the plan.

Val steps out of the dressing room and we gather to review the latest option. It's a little different than her usual style but she looks hot as hell and we all give it our approval. It's a bit edgy for a Dior piece which I like, very Lara Croft–esque.

Valerie checks out and we move on to the next store. Still no word from John. Val and Maya buy bags full of clothes. Despite Maya repeatedly holding up countless items of clothing and shoes and purses and sunglasses, confirming my size for each, I stick to my rule of only looking today. I'm smiling through it all and truthfully I am having a great time with the girls but dealing with John tends to put a damper on things. So yes, I am happy but also slightly worried sick that he's going to let me down again. I haven't told the girls, anything but they know something is up. That's why no one believes me when I say I'm fine, but Maya is persistent.

"You can say you're fine but I know there's something going on up there. I won't pry, you tell me when you're ready." Maya pushes a strand of hair back from my face. "Just remember, a little retail therapy always does the trick." She winks at me. She's always encouraging me not to think twice and just buy what I like. *The money will always come, that's what she believes.* I love her for it.

"I will. Love you." I wink back at her and change the subject.

"What's the plan for tonight? How's it going with you two?" I wrap my arm through Val's as we walk back to the car.

"We're getting sushi! I've been craving some yellowtail jalapeño and Tripp says he wants to satisfy me so . . ." Val squeezes my arm and raises her eyebrows. "I'm obsessed with him. He's the sweetest thing, he's driven. Funny. Kind. And he's crazy about me too!"

My heart pinches—John and I are supposed to be getting sushi and I haven't got a damn text confirming or canceling. I literally want to sob from this anxiety-inducing man but I don't because I'm a strong independent woman. Who sometimes jumps the gun when it comes to being emotional over John. Chin up, carry on.

"Of course he is!" I laugh. "Tripp has been crazy about you for a long time. I still don't know why you took forever to figure it out."

"Maybe I was afraid. He's gorgeous and has the best personality but I was afraid of getting sucked in. I can't stand when you start dating a guy and they do the whole love bomb 24/7 thing. I want to spend time with Tripp—like a lot of time—but I also need my space. I don't want to feel suffocated. I'll legit panic."

Pang, pang, pang in my stomach. Love bombing, my old friend, I'm too familiar with. I glance at my phone; still no word from John.

"And this is why I avoid all romantic relationships." Maya places her bags in the trunk of the car. "Fuck. Leave. Repeat."

"Maya, always the picture of romance." I shake my head and laugh.

"As long as we all know the score, we're good. No one gets hurt."

DIAMONDS, DECEPTION & DESTINY

With John, I want to know what we're doing one way or another. Brutal honesty doesn't upset me; breadcrumbing does.

"That's one way to look at it." Jessie shrugs.

"There's a time and place for casual dating. I've done it and had a great time. But this feels different with Tripp." Val stands by the open trunk waiting for Jessie to put her bag in then hits the automatic button for it to close. "You just have to find the balance for it. I'm not saying Tripp and I have it all figured out, but we're navigating it day by day and we're happy."

Hearing Val is really making me consider my situation. She's right: I really don't need to be making myself sick over a bullshit situation. I'd never stand for someone treating my friends like this, so why am I putting up with it for myself? If I haven't heard by now I'll just assume it's not happening. There, now I don't have to think about it anymore.

"Tripp's always been like that. Interested but respectful. Never wanting to force anything." We pile into the car and Mark closes the door behind us. "He's a great guy and someone you can really depend on. I'm happy you're happy, Val."

"Me too." She laughs. "And I'm surprised as anyone else that it's all worked out this way. But enough about me, what's going on with John?" She joke-winces. "You haven't talked about him in a minute."

Boom. Back to thinking about how John hasn't reached out to me since this morning asking about the record label and slipping in a comment about dinner tonight. I bet mentioning the dinner was just to soften the fact that he only really cared to know about the business stuff. His curiosity ended then and there. The reality sinks in more and more. *He's standing me up.*

"There isn't anything to add. You know everything."

He asked me to dinner, got my hopes up, and he's not going to show. I should've known better.

"No encounters? No meet-ups?" Jessie asks.

Meet-ups? Haha, I can't get the guy to text me back on whether or not I should be preparing for a fake date. That's how much I matter to him.

"More importantly, no sex?" Maya quizzes.

My emotions are going to get the best of me.

"No!" I raise my hands up in frustration. "Guys. He barely. Even. Texts." They all murmur their disapproval. "I honestly don't know what's going on. We're both busy but, fuck, this is insanity. His consistent inconsistency is killing me."

There's a moment of silence—the girls know there's more to it than I'm revealing.

"You deserve the world. I'd hate to see you settle," Maya gently says.

"Trust me, I'm doing my best not to," I reply.

Thinking of my inner child, as lame as that sounds, makes reality click into perspective. I don't deserve this. This is not the type of relationship I'm meant to have. I close my eyes tight. *Show me a sign, show me there's a better love out there for me.*

Maybe John is only interested in the chase and the fantasy of claiming me as his girlfriend. It's the exact opposite of how my relationship has been progressing with Win. There's no chase. No end game. We're just two people talking and getting to know each other on a deeper level. No pressure. No rules on how we should act or what we should do. We're choosing to invest time in each other. Maybe it's the distance, but with Win it feels like there are fewer walls between us.

Win mostly listens, responding with words of encouragement, but he tells me things too. He only mentions his father in passing but I know it's a difficult relationship. One he wishes could be better. He talks about his mom in almost gentle terms, like he's trying to protect her. I still don't know much about his past relationships, and I don't pry. He'll tell me if and when he wants to.

"To be clear, you did want to have sex." Maya shoots me a knowing look.

"I did." I half cover my face and let out a little laugh of confusion. "But I thought it was too soon. I didn't want to jump right back into it. I am willing—or I *was* willing—to give John a chance. I think I'm still willing to, but something held me back that night. Maybe it's still holding me back." Was it possible that I was pushing him away? Was I making it difficult to get together? "I'm really afraid of being hurt again. We should both be clear-headed before we make any decisions. It wouldn't be fair for me to commit myself to someone I can't trust and isn't showing me he can protect me."

"You hold back as much as you want, baby girl." Maya is on her phone again. "I still don't like him."

Maya only giving us half her attention is starting to piss me off. We're all busy. We all had to shift schedules around to hang out. Why is Maya's time more important than anyone else's?

"Well, you're still not official, right?" Val said. "So you should just feel it out and see where it goes."

"Pffftt, official! Girl, he is barely hitting me back. We couldn't be further from official." I think for a moment. "But yes, I'm just going to let things unfold naturally and hope I don't get destroyed in the process. John has to know he's lucky I'm even speaking to him. He's getting an exception because of our unique history and dynamic. If this was anyone else, I'd be long gone because I know for damn sure I deserve more than this."

"Maybe you just need a certain someone to come back into town." Maya finally looked up from her phone and I feel a hint of guilt for my quiet judgments.

"Right! What's happening with Win?" Jessie lights up.

"We've been in contact." I didn't say exactly how much contact. Suddenly it feels like maybe it's been a lot. I don't want to hear their reaction about how much, especially from Maya.

"Say more things," Valerie coaxes. "Gimme the good stuff."

"If you must know"—I pause for their attention—"sending selfies, texts, FaceTime." I brace for the reaction and they all squeal. "But I don't know! He's being super sweet. He said a lot in Miami but it's not like that now. We talk. We're friends. Maybe that's it. He's got boundaries, remember? The whole *I'm-too-busy-to-commit* sitch."

"Fuck off!" Val slaps my shoulder.

"If Win professed his love to you—"

"Puh-lease!" I say.

"No listen. What if he confesses his love and told you he couldn't live without you?"

"Please don't feed my delusions," I joke while picking up my phone to read the notification that popped up on my screen. "You guys…" I flip my phone around so they can see the message.

Win: Thinking of you.

My jaw is on the floor and everyone in the car lets out a slow *Aaahhhh*. *I'll take that as a sign.*

After a moment of silence and staring at each other, Jessie breaks the silence. "Um, is this a sign?" Jessie looks at all of us. "That's some kind of sign, right?"

I'll take Jessie calling out the sign as confirmation of said sign.

"You're a scientist. You don't believe in signs," Maya replies.

DIAMONDS, DECEPTION & DESTINY

That makes us all burst out screaming, which turns into hysterical laughter.

"Of course I believe in signs!" Jessie tries to form her sentence through the belly-aching giggles. "Believing in science doesn't negate believing in love."

Mic drop. We gasp and go silent.

"Marriage material." Jessie sighs almost to herself.

"Preach," Valerie finally says.

Just like that John and our phantom date are gone from my mind.

Mark pulls the car up in front of my building. I know Val is heading out to her date and Jessie is flying back home so I ask Maya if she wants to come in.

"Sorry, babe. I'm expected elsewhere. Here's my car now." A black SUV pulls into the driveway and Maya jumps in faster than we can say our goodbyes.

Okay, weird. She still had that look like she's up to something. I don't want to jump to conclusions, but this is giving me Riley PTSD.

I get back into my condo, dinner ordered and ready to settle in when I'm stopped dead in my tracks. A mountain of packages from all the stores we visited this afternoon crowd my entryway.

"What the—" I whisper to myself as I gather all the bags to bring them into my living room. I open them to find the outfits Maya had been asking me about and they are all in my size. I'm searching for a receipt or a note, desperately trying to figure out how they arrived here when my phone starts ringing. Win pops up on FaceTime.

"Surprise, superstar."

"Stop it!" I blush. "You did not! How did you do this? Why?" I'm so confused and excited. *Maya*—that's what she was doing on her phone. "This is too much. I can't accept all this."

127

"Of course you can. And don't worry your pretty little face. My bank account is bottomless." He laughs. "You've kept me sane this entire trip. It's the least I could do."

Hot.

"Do you even know what you bought?" I pan the phone across the room to show off the opened packages. "Are you busy right now?"

"No. Meetings are done. Room service is on its way. I'm resting up at the hotel."

"Grab yourself a cocktail and make yourself comfortable. Because I'm going to give you a private fashion show."

Win's eyes go wide and he mouths *wow*. I laugh again and prop the phone on the table so the camera points towards the bags. I pull out the first dress and he mimes his enthusiasm. I step off the camera to change. I strip, then redress, and step back into the camera's view. Win is blushing—actually blushing—and looking to the side.

"What's going on?"

Win coughs and points behind me. "Did you see there's a mirror there? I could see everything."

I look back and see the full-length mirror and this time my eyes go wide in mortification. I let out a slow *oh shit* as I step back and almost trip on one of the bags. I cover my face with my hands.

"Oh my god, I'm so embarrassed."

"Don't be. You're beautiful." He's not laughing anymore. "I liked what I saw."

"Did you, now?" Now it's my turn to blush.

"In fact, maybe you should do it again."

He followed it up with a wink so I knew he was kidding. At least I think he was kidding. I have to admit my ego is sparkling knowing Win enjoyed his accidental preview.

"The fashion show is still on but I'm afraid the peep show is over."

Win snapped his fingers and shook his head. "That is a damn shame."

We both laugh and I'm reminded how Win can make any moment, even a ridiculously embarrassing one, easy.

"When are you back?" I really want to see him in person. I'm tired of this long distance thing. I miss him.

"Next week. Dinner?"

"I'll be there." I smile and pick up the phone. "Maybe I'll wear one of my new looks. But for the next quick change, the phone is going down."

I place the phone camera-side down as Win protests the injustice of it all. I grab the next outfit to try on, smiling the whole time, vowing to thank Maya for her part in this surprise.

An hour later, finally a text from John arrives, begging for my forgiveness. He's on an insane deadline for a project with Kraze and the session went way longer than he anticipated. Promised he'd make it up to me. Reinforced that he understands this isn't ideal—we're both so busy. Right now I don't know when I'll see him next. And for once, that thought makes me more relieved than angry.

12

"No one wanted to go out for drinks?"

Win puts his glass of scotch down just out of the camera frame and leans back in his chair. He's still wearing his dress shirt with the top few buttons undone but no jacket. He looks relaxed despite having another long day of meetings and work. There's something so sexy about a man that's driven, a killer when it comes to business, who doesn't complain and still makes the time for a woman to know she's a priority. He really amazes me. "Thought Maya at least would want some adventure."

"Oh, I have no doubt she's out adventuring right now." I move the pillows behind me to sit up straighter. The hotel bed is wide and luxurious and overflowing with personalized embroidered P's just for me. "Val and I said we were in for the night. Maya made no such promises."

Late June

Summer in New York is beautiful. We're here for a couple of nights because I have a corporate event. Win and I crossed planes. He's back

DIAMONDS, DECEPTION & DESTINY

in LA, and now I'm here, where he's been the last few months. We can't catch a break. John's been in the studio so much that I haven't heard much from him except apologies that we can't see each other. We're talking. I'm not closing down any communications but I'm not truly opening my heart either.

This kind of gig isn't my favorite but they pay good money and it's all expenses covered. It'll turn into a fun couple of days. Plus, the girls came with me and I'll always take the opportunity to travel with my besties. It's usually not fans in the audience so I miss that fun give-and-take you get when the whole venue is vibing with you, screaming the lyrics back. There are always a few audience members who are really into it so that's fun, but it's not quite the same thing. There's definitely no sea of pink glitter and tiaras in that audience. I'll have to convert my non-believers into tiara-wearing scream queens.

"Do you have plans for tomorrow?" he asks.

"It's a prep day. I need to rehearse with the band because they're all local musicians. Then soundcheck. Wayne also hired a local stylist so I'm a bit worried about working with someone new. I don't know why he did that since Kaitlin is my go-to."

"You're going to look gorgeous no matter what."

"I appreciate the vote of confidence. But Kaitlin and I have built such a strong work relationship that it's become second nature. She knows me and my preferences so well that she arrives ready. Working with someone new means reviewing the basics all over again."

"Send them to me." Win taps his chest. "I can fill them in on whatever details they need."

"Good to know." I laugh. "I should really have you on speed dial."

"You don't already?" He flashes an expression of mock horror and I laugh again.

"Tell me about your day. Did you crush the competition? Did you disrupt? Make your rivals cry?"

"You still have no idea what I do, do you?" An inside joke we created since Win does business in so many different fields. He's so successful he can tap in to whatever he wants.

"Enlighten me. I'm all ears." I make a show of snuggling into the pillows like I'm getting ready for a long story.

"If I described my day in detail, you would definitely fall asleep. One of my main goals is to not bore you, so that might be counterproductive."

"You listen to me talk about my day. I spent twenty minutes yesterday describing the difference between a major and minor chord."

"It was a difficult concept to grasp. We can't all be musical angels." He shrugs and smiles in a way that melts my heart and I am actively fighting against sighing. "Besides, I love the sound of your voice. You could read the telephone book and I'd be enthralled."

"What's a telephone book, old man?"

"Ouch." His hand goes to his heart and he winces.

"My point is that I always talk and you always listen and we should switch it up." I can see his jaw tighten slightly. He doesn't look angry but his defenses are activated. "You said once that I could ask you anything."

"I did say that, didn't I?" His jaw relaxes and he looks like my comfortable Win again.

My Win? Did I just think of him as *mine*? That was unexpected and definitely something that I need to keep in check.

"We can start with an easy one. Win, tell me about your day."

"My day." He sips his scotch then leans forward with elbows on the table. "It started way too early. I was supposed to go to the gym but my client wanted to do a meeting before the meeting. Then the actual meeting was delayed because half the people were online and the tech didn't work. By the time the meeting was done, my inbox was full of demands that apparently couldn't wait another minute and that led to two other meetings that were supposed to be five minutes and lasted thirty. I had planned a lunch with an old friend and business colleague that I was looking forward to and then I was supposed to go on a site visit but both were canceled because another client had an issue I needed to deal with so we could finally close that deal. The rest of my day was more of the same: A meeting that could have been an email. Repeat."

By the time Win's rant ends, I'm laughing. I try to look serious but it's not possible. Ranting Win is just too funny.

"This is my life, Princess."

"I'm sorry. I shouldn't laugh."

"I like it when you laugh." His stare is so intense. Focused. "I like it even more when I can make you laugh."

"Start prepping more jokes because the second I get back I'll be ready for giggles, cocktails, and dinner."

"Believe me, the prep work for you has been long underway, Princess," he says smoothly.

There's a sudden heat in my chest, radiating over my body, through my limbs. I like it when Win stares at me like this and I wish we weren't separated by so much distance. I've dreamt about him more than once and woke up wet, hot, and bothered. Told myself that this is what happens when Win is often the last person I talk to before sleep so, technically, this was a mess of my own making. And when I get this way I'm not sure what I would do if we were in the same room. If that's something I could even handle. I'd want him to touch me, to stand close. I'm still in the will-we-won't-we phase with John but I don't know what's happening with either man. What the fuck am I doing? I really need to get a grip.

"Do you hate your job? All the meetings and clients in distress?"

Win takes a moment before he responds. He doesn't want to give me the standard line about working hard to play hard or some brag about being busy because the job is important. He gives me a small half-smile before he speaks.

"I don't always react well to not having full control. It pisses me off when things go off the rails and they don't have to. I get irritated when people are manipulating a situation or being deceitful to get what they want. Being up front and direct is always the better option."

I think about Win in Miami telling me I can trust him, that he's with me. And then Win at the dinner party saying he can't commit to anything when he has so many other priorities. They were both honest statements. He's never been anything but honest with me.

"But I actually really love my job. Love that I can do so much of it myself. Love being hands-on. Love working with most of my clients and all my staff even if I complain about some of the day-to-day. And I love knowing that I am really good at my job. Being in charge. Taking chances. Because it feels really good when it hits."

I can feel his confidence even over FaceTime. He never has to shout it because it oozes out of him. Everyone standing near him knows and it is intensely attractive.

"Speaking of always being hands-on." Win lifts up his phone and I can see the screen lighting up with a call. "Sorry, Princess. I have to get this."

"Of course. I'll talk to you tomorrow." I give him a small wave then hang up.

I need to get up and finish my nighttime routine—I was in the middle of it when Win called—but I'm not feeling so exhausted anymore. Not energetic enough to see if Maya wants a drink but also not ready to go to sleep quite yet. I jump when FaceTime announces another call. I think it's Win calling back already but it's John. I pause with the cursor over the Accept button, not sure if I want to answer. It feels strange to talk to John right after Win. We didn't talk about anything personal, but it also felt intimate. Wide open.

"Hey, babe." John is sitting on a couch, holding his phone up in front of him. He's in the studio still. "Sorry I couldn't call earlier. You know how it goes. What have you been up to?"

"I get it. It's been pretty hectic here too. We only got to the hotel about an hour ago."

I almost tell him that I've been talking to Win but I don't. I've never hid it in the past. John wasn't crazy about it, but he trusted me. Or he didn't suspect I would have interest in anyone but him. Technically it's none of his business anyway; we aren't in a relationship.

"You talk to Wayne?"

"At all?" I laugh. "Of course. We had an entire plane ride to talk, ride from the airport, checking into the hotel."

"But did you talk about anything? Big. New. Whatever."

"What's up with you? You're acting cagey."

"Just catching up."

"And that sounds completely like something a non-cagey person would say." I raise an eyebrow at him. "Do you know something I don't?"

"Like what?"

I know him. He's beating around something.

"We didn't talk about anything big. Tour. The usual."

John nods a few times then leans back on the couch, trying for casual.

"Are you set for tomorrow?"

"Yeah, but also nervous."

We walk through the details of the show, what I'm worried about, and how to fix it. John understands all the technical details and he's both encouraging and practical. He knows what I should say to the soundman, what kind of microphone they should have for me, what should be included in my rider. He understands where my preshow anxieties stem from and knows how to calm me down. John plays our songs that he's working on and we spend some time going back and forth about what else they need. We typically don't argue about these things but we both have opinions and can be stubborn. It's all good, though.

"Riley was at the studio today."

He sounds normal, completely casual, but my breath catches in my throat. Fuck. Just hearing John say her name, knowing they are in the same place, and I don't know what's happening. I'm right back at Coachella and John hasn't come back from Riley's party.

"Did you talk to her?" My voice is strained. I am definitely not calm about this.

"Yeah. We caught up for a bit. Nothing crazy." He shrugs and I can tell that he's not hiding anything. My instincts are pretty honed to detecting lying John.

"Cool."

He's not bothered about seeing Riley and doesn't seem too concerned about me worrying about him talking to her. I guess I don't even have a reason to be upset at this point. We haven't had any sort of conversation about what's going on with us, no dates since Madeo. Maybe the distance between us isn't about our location anymore.

John and I were already together when I introduced him to Riley. I was so excited for my boyfriend and best friend to meet. She came to the studio with me. John was so adorable, lost in his work. Headphones on and hunched over his computer. He was so absorbed in the music that he jumped when I snuck up and kissed him on the cheek. John yanked off his headphones and grabbed me. I squealed when he pulled me in close and went for my neck.

"Hang on!" I laughed. "We're not alone."

John looked past me and at Riley. He let me go but still held my hand.

"I wanted to finally introduce you guys. I've told Riley so much about you so it seems kooky that you've never actually met."

"It's true." Riley smiled at John. "She never shuts up about you. It's so annoying."

"I'm not that annoying. He's just the sweetest thing in the world and I'm lovestruck!" I laughed but then became self-conscious. "Am I?"

"No, of course not!" Riley waved her hand like she was brushing away my concerns. She sat down on a chair near John. "You guys do your thing. I'm just going to sit over here."

"Let's play Riley the song we were working on last night?" I leaned into John with my arm over his shoulder and kissed the top of his head. "Can you pull it up?"

"Got it right here." He kissed the palm of my hand, then turned back to his computer.

I glanced back at Riley to see if she was okay and she mouthed *so cute*. I smiled and turned back to John. I had no doubts about John but earning Riley's approval checked a box for me. *I'm one lucky girl.*

The song filled the room, and it sounded incredible. I could hear that he'd already done so much work since last night. I moved my hips in time and John nodded his head. We both get lost in the music so easily, especially when we're together. After our second full listen I looked over at Riley again to see if she was enjoying herself. I was about to ask what she thought of the song but stopped short when I saw the look on her face.

I had hoped she would love the song. At worst, I thought maybe she'd be staring into her phone because she did that a fair bit too. Instead, she didn't look happy. Her brow was furrowed, legs crossed, arms over her chest. I couldn't identify the look at the time because I'd never seen it before with Riley. She was always so funny and in the moment. I didn't know then, but I know what that look was now. Jealousy. My best friend hated that John and I had this connection, and that we were creating incredible music together. That we were creative and romantic partners. She hated that I had a direction for my life and up until that point she had only spent time hanging around, shopping, and chasing boys. Riley Vega, from Hollywood's A-list top of the top family, world at her fingertips, who could do anything in the world she wanted, was jealous of *me*. A nobody from a tiny island, in Hollywood with a dream and no connections, little money. I can see now that I was the perfect prospect to sink her fangs into. I'm kicking myself now that I didn't recognize the signs or understand what she was truly capable of. Riley wanted what I had, literally, and would do anything to get it.

DIAMONDS, DECEPTION & DESTINY

Riley could've told me that coming to the studio piqued her interest in music. I would have loved to be there for her journey, to be in sessions with her, picking tracks and writing songs that fit her. Instead, she kept me in the dark. Her family pulled strings to get her a label deal, and she was in sessions with all the top writers and producers. She was working with top music video directors and singles scheduled for release with unlimited budgets. Riley kept me out of all those conversations; she hid it all, only bringing me around when she needed someone to coax her through a heartache or a real friend to sit around to talk about life and watch movies and bake cookies.

I wasn't smart then. I was a pawn. I was a walking mood board. I had unknowingly become Riley's enemy and, boy, was she keeping me close. Always curious to hear the songs I was making, taking notes of every move I made. From workouts, to clothing, to makeup, you name it. I was going through life finding inspiration, working hard, doing what I could to make my dreams come true and turn nothing into something. Riley was studying me. Picked all the parts she liked. It was like one step forward, two steps back. We were building a friendship and becoming enemies right before my eyes. By the time I realized what was happening, it was too late. She had ripped off my sound and my style, but she was my friend, right? Isn't it natural for friends to end up having similar tastes? I was in way over my head. I know better now.

My exhaustion hits me again and it hits hard. Riley, John, Riley, John. I feel so tired of this shit. Going around in circles and not knowing who to trust.

"It's getting late. Rehearsals start early tomorrow. I'm gonna call it a night."

"Right." He looks at me with narrowed eyes. "Feels like you're doing that thing where you're being short with me, but okay. Get some rest. I'll talk to you later."

I don't have the energy to protest. I say a quick goodbye and end the call.

Never thought I'd be in the middle of a love triangle. There's no one to blame but myself—I can't go deep with Win and I won't let myself get hurt by John. But all that means is that I'm alone, and even if I'm living my best life, sometimes that hurts.

13

It is still early but the club is already packed. Wayne leads us towards the VIP section, which makes me smile. You'd never know Wayne had never been to this venue before today. Whenever I have an appearance, party, whatever, he'll come to the venue, do a walkthrough, and bring security with him so my team is prepared and can handle me smoothly when I arrive. Another reason to be grateful that he and Kimi are on my team.

The show goes well; not the easiest crowd but I'm happy with my performance. The event is so random, very corporate, some retreat for insurance salespeople or something. The audience starts off a bit stiff and cautious, but by the end of my set they are into my show. Most of the crowd is new to my music but they quickly get into the groove. I even get them to sing along with me for a couple of the bigger songs with choruses that do well with call and response. Smaller crowds are harder to perform for but it doesn't matter; if I'm playing in front of twenty or twenty thousand people, they get my all. I love being on stage and no one who sees a Princess show will ever think that I phoned it in.

We step into the roped area and Wayne speaks to the woman checking names. The place is starting to pick up but it's not too loud. It's been a long day with rehearsing then the show and I'm ready to people-watch and decompress. First a drink, maybe two, then dancing.

"We have the table over there." Wayne holds an arm out, indicating we should lead the way. "I made sure they'll have a bottle ready and waiting for you."

"Oh, Wayne." Val touches his arm as she walks past. "You always take good care of us."

Maya's scanning the room, looking for new prospects. Maya is a woman on a mission and I love that she always knows what she wants. She was in Utah for a shoot right after our shopping spree. And Val had been busy with her family business and Tripp. This was the first time we'd seen each other in a couple of weeks.

We all slide into the booth with Val and me on the inside. Wayne pulls his phone out and is immediately back at work. Or who knows, maybe playing Candy Crush. It's hard to tell when he gets like this. No expression, concentrating, rarely looks up. Maya sits for maybe two minutes before standing up again.

"I'm gonna check that one out." She points to another table and a very tall, very good-looking man. "I'll see you later."

"Not even going to stop for one drink?" I joke.

"This is what happens when one best friend is an old married woman and the other is already tangled up with two too many men." She holds out both arms while backing away from our table. "A girl has to fend for herself."

Maya laughs then spins and walks away. She swings her hips like she's on the catwalk. Her auburn hair is effortlessly thrown up in a French twist with soft curled tendrils naturally framing her face and falling around the nape of her neck. The man's eyes go wide as he watches her approach.

"We should've put an airtag on her." Val pours us both a drink. "We have an early flight tomorrow."

A couple arrives at the table and Wayne gets up to greet them. He introduces them to Val and me—concert promoters from Europe. Apparently, they were guests at the show tonight and had a great time. They want to talk about doing the festival circuit next summer if my London show goes well. They're nice and complimentary. I do my best to be professional, kind, and approachable. I stick with their conversation for a few more minutes then leave it to Wayne. The promoters know what I can do and they are impressed. Now Wayne can work his magic.

It's not a huge surprise when the man pulls out some coke and does a quick bump, though I am concerned about Val. There was a time, not so long ago, when Val would've been right there with him. There have been plenty of nights when we had to pull Val from not-great situations and pick her up off the floor. We could all be having the best time, Val happy and laughing one minute, then a complete mess a minute later. It's hard to watch someone you love struggle and I worry that Val might have difficulty navigating this situation. The man with the coke nods to us, asking if we want any. Val holds up her hand and shakes her head easily.

I look over at her. "Are you okay with—"

"Of course." Val shrugs and brushes it off. "But thanks for checking on me."

"I worry. Only want the best for you, always."

Val gives me a quick hug. "Babe, you always have my back."

Years ago, I met Val at a club when she was always the life of the party. The most fun. The most adventurous. I liked her immediately. For a long while, we were club friends, running into each other at events and parties. Then one night we spent hours talking. She told me about her family who were kind of fucked up. It made sense that Val often self-medicated and found drugs and booze to distract herself. But once we started spending time with each other outside the circuit, there was a whole other side to Val. When she's sweet and funny and completely loyal. When the partying started going a little too far, we made sure to have that open conversation with her.

"Maybe being an old married woman is good for you."

Val rolls her eyes and laughs. "Excuse me! Old?! I don't have one forehead line!"

"You can thank the tox for that!"

"Touché. To be fair, Maya thinks anyone who goes on a second date is old and married. I refuse to be classified by her ridiculous standards."

We both look over to the table Maya joined. She's sitting very close to the man, practically on his lap, and laughing as he whispers in her ear. She's been gone maybe ten minutes and already has her whole evening locked down.

"Maya lives by her own rules, that's for sure."

"Listen." Val nudges my arm so I turn back to her. "I really am doing okay. Coke is the last thing I want to do tonight but even if I did, it wouldn't be a problem. I don't feel the need to fill the void."

"The void?"

"I'm realizing more and more that I used drugs to cover up a lot of other problems. Family shit."

"That's really hard, babe. I understand."

My heart aches for Val. I have such a good relationship with my family that I can't imagine growing up with one like hers. Her dad is a tycoon who always pushes Valerie to be the best and her mom is distant and distracted by her own life.

"I'm really proud of you. It takes a lot to turn things around and take control the way you have. You should be proud of yourself too."

"I used to think if I'm going to be a disappointment, I might as well be a *big* disappointment." She shakes her head. "Talk about unhinged. L. O. L."

I squeeze her hand. "I love hearing that you're feeling stronger."

"I don't want to give Tripp all the credit." Val laughs. Her eyes get brighter whenever she mentions him. "But he's definitely helped. Being with someone who trusts me and gives me space has been a game changer. You and I haven't talked about this much but Tripp and I had a bit of a struggle when we first got together. Well, when we stopped having sex twenty-four-seven and had to have some conversations." She laughs again. "It was hard for me to regulate my emotions at first. I was so used to drama, to causing a lot of the drama, and it was confusing when Tripp refused to participate. He wouldn't take the bait. His attitude was 'I'm crazy about you and I'm not going anywhere so you might as well get it out of your system now.'"

"Okay, *Tripp*! This boy has been one of my dearest friends but I didn't know he was capable of all that. I am very impressed and so fucking happy for you."

Val laughs. "There's a lot more to learn of course, but he's a steady guy and we make a good team. He's supportive. Isn't frightened off by my sharp edges or emotions. It was like a switch was flipped realizing I could have healthy communication instead of setting everything on fire. I talk, he listens and isn't scared away."

"You deserve all of it."

"So do you, Princess." She raises a shot glass and hands one to me. "Enough of this heavy talk. Cheers to us and always moving on to bigger and better."

"Cheers, babe!"

I look around the table. Wayne is still talking to the promoter and more people have joined the table. I'm not sure when it happened but we are now surrounded by strangers. Suddenly, I'm exposed, like the situation, the evening, is getting away from me. Wayne's doing his job, but it also doesn't feel like it's about me anymore. I've been struggling with feeling like a product to Wayne and Kimi. Maya and I talk about this a lot—with her modeling, she's also her own product and has to get used to people talking about her like she has no feelings. We have a keep-it-down saying—a hard shell we put up to get through the awkward, tough moments like this when we feel like we're on display, ready to be bought by the highest bidder.

There are more things happening, more wheels turning, that have little to do with me and my career. I look over at Val and she's on her phone, probably talking to Tripp.

I don't recognize this feeling. It's new. I feel floaty, but not in the good way. It's not transcendent but unmoored. This doesn't feel like my space, my night, my world. John could probably help ground me if he wasn't so busy. If he would even reach out to me after the bad end to our call last night. I still don't know what's going on with him. He was hiding something that may or may not be Riley-related and definitely has something to do with Wayne. I snap a quick selfie and play it up for the camera. Win responds almost immediately.

Win: 😍 I wish I was there.

Princess: You're stuck in endless meetings, don't you remember?

Win: Who, me? Never. All my time is yours.

This quick exchange is exactly what I need. I immediately feel more like myself.

Princess: What are you wearing?

Win: Gray sweatpants

He adds a wink emoji for good measure and I respond with a melting one.

"Princess?" Wayne holds up the bottle asking if I want a top-up. I nod, then lean forward across the table as he pours.

"Hey, have you spoken to John?" I ask. For a brief second Wayne looks startled but quickly recovers.

"Why?"

"I'm curious. He was asking about you yesterday, wondering if we'd talked."

"We always talk."

Well, that clears the air. This conversation was in the same loop as the one with John.

A friend of the promoter arrives at the table and I've lost Wayne's attention. An hour or so later, I decide to head out.

Princess: We're about to leave, you staying or coming with?

Maya: Coming with. Mama needs her rest.

I have the excuse of it being a long day and flight tomorrow. Maya meets us back at the table and it's an easy exit. Wayne navigates us with security through the crowd and out front to our car. There is a group of fans and some paparazzi calling our names as we exit the club. I stop to sign a few photos, remembering to keep my face in the perfect soft smile while photographers blind me with their flashes, but keep it quick before blowing kisses to my fans and jumping into the black SUV.

Back at the hotel, my phone buzzes and once again my first thought is Win. Why is he always my first thought? I stare at my phone. Riley. It's almost 1:30 a.m. my time. I'm exhausted. Why the hell is Riley texting me?

Riley: Hey girl! You won't believe the day I had.

Riley: I was up in Malibu and saw Leo. He was asking about you.

This is surreal. Insane. Riley is sending me casual, friendly texts like it happens all the time. Like we're still friends.

Princess: Oh, yeah?

Riley: He's as cute as ever.

Riley and I used to take rides up the highway at sunset, usually ending up in Malibu. It was a fun ritual. Gorgeous scenery, the ocean, songs blasting. We talked about music and boys and whatever else came up. It was a lot of fun and something I always looked forward to. I was down to do anything with Riley but hanging out just the two of us was tons of fun. She wasn't putting on a show. It wasn't about being a celebrity or star or anything more than just two good friends hanging out and listening to good music.

In Malibu we often ended up at the Country Mart, one of Riley's favorite places. There were shops and spas, restaurants and coffee shops, lots of places to hang out or wander around. One night we ran into Jaxon Ray, a famous DJ, whom I'd had a little crush on, and was a fan of his music. He's way cuter in person. We hit it off immediately and jumped right into talking about music. It was early in my career, and he hadn't heard my songs so I pulled one up on my phone and played it for him. He was into it, started getting into the beat, when Riley slid in between us. Purposely moving so Jaxon faced away from me, and that was the end of that. She knew of my little crush but that didn't stop her. When we got back in the car,

DIAMONDS, DECEPTION & DESTINY

Riley acted all excited, saying she had such a crush on him, and it was so amazing she got to talk to him. I didn't point out that in all the time we talked about boys and her crushes, she'd never mentioned Jaxon Ray even once.

Our friendship changed after that night. Riley distanced herself bit by bit. We still hung out if she needed someone for an event and I was always available when she needed to talk—a heartbreak or she didn't get the publicity she was so desperately seeking. I always checked in and she gave me the time if it suited her.

Maya pointed out that Riley was dressing like me. She wore the same designers right after I did, layering pieces almost identically. She got her hair done in the same style, twenty-two-inch extensions, long layers, big bouncy blowout waves. We were easily mistaken for a duo, and when Maya pushed me, I insisted it was a coincidence.

Then, one day I was working out with my trainer at a private gym and this woman came up to me. She said she was trying to place where she knew me from only to tell me she was a stylist assistant and had seen a picture of me on Riley's mood board for styling pegs. It was my mistake, a supreme error in judgment that it took me so long to realize that Riley was so competitive. Keeping me around was a way of keeping me down or at least trying to. And that wasn't my way at all—my friends were like family. We were tight. We didn't lie to each other. Competition wasn't a thing; we didn't cut each other down to make ourselves feel better. I wanted to work hard for me. Riley worked hard to be better than me.

When we both had songs out and mine would catch more virality, or when a brand reached out to me first, she didn't even try to hide her jealousy. When we were on a red carpet, posing together, and the photographers called out for photos of only me, she stormed off and didn't answer my calls when I called her later.

Riley's connections. Her family's money. They both meant her fame and connections grew quickly. And I couldn't compete on those levels, which put me in her shadow, fighting every inch for my own opportunities. That's why it hurt so much when she and John collaborated. When they did more.

Prime example: her stealing my dress and leaving me with no other option and no time to problem-solve. And then she and John slept together, and that was it for me. The dress fiasco was one thing. Losing opportunities, sure, sabotaging my career, not great, but I was strong. I could bounce back. But then I saw John's ambition matching Riley's, and how much that cost me.

What am I doing? Why am I talking to *either* of them? Val's words echo in my mind, how maybe this life drama is my own addiction. No, I've got to take back control like Val did. If she can do it, so can I.

Princess: What's up?

I don't want to straight-up say *why the fuck are you texting me?* because I know that would only cause problems later. And also, I wasn't sure where we stood after our half amends that had been made.

Between the call with John, the promoter and hangers-on doing coke at the table, and now Riley and her potential fake friendliness, I'm worn out. Worn down. I'm tired of Hollywood politics being thrown at me. I need to act. Things with John aren't perfect but talking and facing the situation straight on took away the sting. Maybe it was time to face her too. I didn't need to give Riley the power by letting her call the shots. I'm not afraid of her so why not face it—her—head on?

I take a deep breath and call Riley. I know she already has her phone in her hand but I'm still surprised when she picks up.

"Hey, Riley. I'm back in LA tomorrow. Do you want to meet up for brunch on Friday?"

There's a pause, then I'm positive I can almost hear her smile.

"Sounds good, Princess. Text me the address and I'll see you there."

14

We're at Republique, a famous brunch restaurant on La Brea Avenue. I'm finally over the bit of jet lag and haze from the New York performance and totally looking forward to hanging out with my girls. The restaurant is one of the trendiest spots in LA. Famous for its brioche French toast, this place is always packed. Tall ceilings, brick walls, huge windows to let in the morning light, checkered flooring and long tables with benches to sit community-style. My mouth waters at the sweet scent of pastries in the air.

"Explain it to me again." Maya leans back in her chair with arms crossed over her chest. She doesn't look angry as much as deeply confused. "Because this makes no sense."

Maya's reaction is exactly what I expected when I told them I'd invited Riley to join us for brunch. She is not pleased.

"It might be insane but it's something I need to do. We all should. I tried ignoring her but that's impossible. She is literally everywhere. Let's test the waters and see if we can at least be on friendly terms. My history with Riley isn't all bad. She was a really good friend for a while there. And I know who she is now. So, she's not dangerous. She can't hurt me like she did before."

"Past tense. She *was* a good friend. History."

I know they're trying to be supportive, maybe even provide a shield if things get tense, but in this moment they are adding to my stress. I gave them the chance to bail, and they decided to come.

"I get it. I might be playing the fool here, but I've decided to open the door a crack and see what happens." Our server puts my coffee on the table. "I'm asking you to keep an open mind. If this is a crash and burn, you can tell me 'I told you so.'"

"We don't want this to crash and burn." Val is the peacemaker between me and Maya. I know she's sensitive to people fighting around her, since her family is such a nightmare. "We absolutely don't want you to be used and abused again."

I put a hand on Val's shoulder to say thanks. Even though I am playing tough guy, I'm nervous about all this. I don't think there'll be blood or anyone will lose an eye but it might be an added annoyance that none of us needs.

"Showtime." Maya nods towards the entrance as Riley walks into the restaurant.

A few heads turn as she passes, recognizing a famous face, but she doesn't acknowledge anyone.

"Ladies! You're all looking good."

Riley sits down, acting like we are all the best of friends. I can't tell if it's all a bluff or if she truly thinks that everyone loves her and desperately wants to be in her presence. This is what happens when you've been famous most of your life, when everyone knows your entire family: you come to expect a baseline of adoration. There is something disarming about her despite the past having some horrible moments. How can all that investment in someone be for nothing? I'll give it my best shot.

"You too."

I do a quick visual check with Maya and Val and they both offer small, not terribly believable smiles.

"Are we doing mimosas?" Riley looks around the room and waves to a server. "How many do I need to catch up?"

"We've only just started," I say. I nod at my cup. "And this round is coffee."

"That's ridiculous. We need to put an end to that."

Riley orders a round of drinks for the table and no one objects. There are a few awkward pauses at first, but Riley pushes through like nothing is off. Again, I can't tell if she even notices that Maya and Val are slow to respond. It's almost like old times, but I keep my distance—I can play the game. Riley's holding court and telling stories and eventually everyone is sucked in, even Maya. We're laughing and chatting and I feel a twinge of sadness because this is how it should've always been. We all should be hanging out together and having fun. We should all be friends. None of the bullshit needed to have happened.

"I need some help. I have to make a serious decision and need your advice." Riley holds up her phone to show us a photo of a guy. She swipes the phone to show a different photo of a different guy. "I need to choose."

"Between the guys?" Val leans in for a closer look and Riley hands over her phone.

"Two guys? That's got to be tough." Maya doesn't look at me as she says it but I know she's laughing.

"We need info—tell us about them." I take the phone from Val and swipe back and forth between them. "We need a pro and con list to go along with the photos."

"You're so right. What have I been doing without you all this time?" Riley laughs. "Okay, so boy A . . ."—she points to the photo of the heavily tattooed guy in a black T-shirt—"I met him up in Malibu. He's an actor, just moved from New York, and he's obsessed with me. Hangs all over me, desperate for my attention, so that's hot."

My phone rings. "Sorry, I need to get this, it's Kimi. We've been playing phone tag since New York."

"You don't have to work all the time, you know." Riley sounds less jokey with that comment, like maybe she's offended that I'm taking the call.

"It's Kimi. If she's working then so am I."

I answer the call while walking to the restaurant foyer, hoping I don't disturb too many people.

"Finally! I was starting to wonder if we'd ever connect."

"I know, I know." Kimi laughs but she sounds stressed. "It's been more hectic than usual and I wanted to make sure we had time for a real conversation. More than a check-in."

"Okay." I like talking to Kimi, look forward to our conversations but her comment puts me on edge. "What's up?"

"Don't panic. It's the label. They aren't crazy about the new song?"

"What?" I'm in the foyer now and do a quick scan to see if anyone is too close. Privacy seems key right now. "I thought they were on board."

"They were. But they've decided they want you to go in a different direction."

"Why did they change their minds?" I'm trying to remain calm but panic courses through my body, desperate to find a way to fix this.

"Listen, we all know the song is brilliant. No one is doubting how good the song is. But the label knows what sells and knows what they can sell and they want 'Supernova' to hit the market next."

Hit the market. Hit the market. That sounds like the least creative response anyone could have to music.

"'Supernova' is good, I agree, it's my song. But I don't think it's going to hit as hard as 'Never Mine' right now. You're always talking about momentum and we should build on the last song. I have a really good feeling about 'Never Mine.' It's the perfect follow-up."

"I know, I know." That is the second time Kimi responds this way, which now starts to feel more like a nervous tic. "But we don't have a lot of wiggle room. You're doing well and people are paying attention, but we don't have the power to make these demands. We don't want to piss off the label. We have to keep playing the game."

"It's not a demand. I'd like to have a conversation about it. Would they meet with me and John?"

"We don't want to be difficult. You've put in work and are on the right track but in reality we need a delicate balance. We're at the next level right now with this song. A big label is involved. It's not like your YouTube channel. You're not at a place to call a meeting like this yet. One day you will be, but for now play along and we can make bigger asks later."

Difficult? How is asking questions being difficult?

"If they don't want 'Never Mine,' John and I are finishing up another song that can compete. It would be a rush to get it ready but we can do it."

"They've already prepped the packages and PR for 'Supernova.'"

"Kimi, how did this happen without any input from me? We have no other options? We could release 'Supernova' on its own like we did the last one."

I want to add that the last song was all me. I wrote and recorded it on my own. Posted it on my own account and it was my fans who spread the word. It was a hit before the record label started to push it and take the credit. But I know that this business isn't a one-person game. This success is built on previous success and future success isn't guaranteed. I don't want to take away anything that Kimi and Wayne, and even the record label, do but this feels like torture, like I'm not being heard.

"You have a contract and you can't release songs from the album whenever you want. We need to let this one go." Kimi's tone reminds me of a teacher trying to keep her class in order. It's not something I've heard from her before and I'm not sure I like it. "We need to give them one, then we'll take one. That's how this goes."

Her tone rattles me. It always felt like a partnership and now Kimi is playing the tough authority figure. Acting like I need to be put in my place.

I'm silent on my end of the phone. Kimi has always been on my side; how can she not be fighting for me?

"This part is hard, Princess. But we're playing the long game here. There's compromise and we have to trust the process. The label wants this to be a success as much as we do. We all win together."

"Sure." I'm trying to stay calm. Keep my voice at a reasonable and level-headed volume. I don't think it's a good idea if Kimi knows exactly how upset this makes me. "I'll try to keep that in mind."

There's no way Kimi doesn't hear the defeat in my voice but she chooses to ignore it.

"Now, let's talk cosmetics." I can hear Kimi typing. "We've decided to switch the promo up. Instead of the big PR launch we talked about, we're sending out boxes to a select group of influencers for review."

"What? Why?" That sounded angrier than intended but it was a surprise. We had a whole plan for the launch. "We wanted it to get into more hands, didn't we? Reach more people and get the buzz going?"

"We'll get more bang for our buck this way. We could never reach the amount of people these influencers can. They'll get the word out."

"Can you please send me a list of who will receive the boxes? I want to review and approve the list. We need to make sure Maya receives one too."

"Maya is at the top of our list." Kimi covers the mic on her phone and says something to her assistant that I can't make out. "We'll reach a lot more channels this way. They're called influencers for a reason."

"I'm a bit disappointed that we won't have the full launch. I told you that Stephanie wanted to help."

"Princess, we can't afford Stephanie. The profit margin will be cut so short if we're paying someone at her level. This way is better, trust me."

Trust. How do I trust them when I'm cut out of all the conversations? There isn't much of a goodbye as we sign off. I can tell Kimi's head is already with her next call. I'm feeling stunned, then angry. It's irritating to be pushed aside so easily, to have my opinion so definitively ignored. Wait, the producer has a say. John can pull rank, as negotiated in his contract for final say, and demand we stay on track with the song release.

He answers my call and I start venting. Recap my conversation with Kimi and tell him about my plan. Get them to release "Never Mine" as planned.

"You know, P, the label can see the big picture. Kimi's right. We should trust them."

"People went crazy for the teaser we posted."

"Because it's a great song. But we've got to let the label have this one."

"You sound so calm about this. Last time we talked about the song you were all fired up."

"It's how it goes, Princess. It's business."

"You already knew. That's why you asked if Wayne and I talked. They checked with you first because you have veto rights."

"Look, Wayne said they should talk to you about it to emphasize it's business, not personal."

"What did they give you in return?"

"What's that supposed to mean?"

"I assume they softened the blow with something. I want to know what it was."

"They set up the Atlanta sessions." Guilt coats his words.

"I have to go." It was a sudden and determined feeling to flee. To get off this call and get the hell out.

"Babe, you can't be mad at me. You're a businesswoman. This stuff happens all the time."

"We're supposed to be a team. Have each other's backs."

"This is good for both of us. Gives both of us a boost."

"You didn't say anything, and you had plenty of opportunities. You blindsided me, *again*." I bite my cheek to push my emotions down. "Why do you keep doing this to me?"

"I'm sorry you had to find out this way. I wanted to tell you, but Wayne said they had to take the lead. I couldn't overstep your team. I'm honestly pissed that it took them so long. Should've told you days ago. They put me in a shitty position."

Not too surprisingly, I find it difficult to have much sympathy for him. But I did understand why Wayne and Kimi wanted to talk to me.

It wasn't John's fault that they were delayed. And honestly, there was no reason why Wayne didn't tell me when we were on the road. I guess that's a fight for another day, though.

I get back to the table and everyone can see that something is wrong. I don't even take a moment to consider that I shouldn't say everything in front of Riley.

"My label has completely fucked up my release and my management isn't even fighting for me." A single tear falls down my cheek and I quickly wipe it away. "I'm sorry for ruining brunch. I don't know what to do right now. My hands are tied."

I let out all my frustration though I have enough sense to not talk about John. My friends are all sympathetic and angered for me. And as it turns out, Riley is a good person to talk to about my career problems because she understands the business.

"Labels can be the worst. I've had so much trouble with them. This is going to sound gross, but considering my dad could buy the label if he wanted and fire them all, it says something that they think they can push me around." Maya and Val side-eye each other at the comment. Riley goes on unknowingly. "Most labels are bullies and they think they can push you around because you're a young woman." As much as her comments can rub me the wrong way, this one brings me a little sense of comfort.

I'm not sure if it's true that Riley's dad could buy then fire everyone, and I know that statement says a lot about her viewpoint of the world, but it feels good to hear that she's frustrated at times too. Throughout the end of our mimosas and pancakes, I'm still frazzled by the phone calls and changed plans. I'm not sure where I stand with the label, management, or John. But at least this brunch turned out well and it was nice seeing Riley. Maybe we've turned a corner.

15

Time is flying. August is here already. It's been a few weeks since "Supernova" dropped, and I'm underwhelmed to say the least. I pace back and forth on my balcony, trying to keep my cool. Training for my London show has me under so much stress, and I feel like my career is spiraling out of control. The single isn't the one I want. Rehearsals keep getting scheduled then canceled. I'm in a holding pattern. Kimi's assistant called, after another long round of phone tag, and she promptly put me on hold. I understand they are busy and I'm not their only client, but this is starting to feel like the runaround.

I saw the first influencer review of the cosmetics line posted online yesterday morning; I've been trying to get answers ever since. Maya came by with the box she was sent, and I was mortified. It was nothing like what we discussed or even the samples shared earlier. I'm no scientist but I can tell these products all have different formulas. The eyeshadows aren't blending how they should, the pigments are not as smooth and vibrant as they should be. My lip gloss is supposed to be a crystal-clear smooth shine and it's the complete opposite of that. How the fuck do things keep changing without my input or approval?

"Princess!" Kimi jumps on the call sounding like she ran to the phone. "Too many fires to put out today. What can I do for you?"

"You can tell me what happened with the line. The reviews are shitting all over it and I don't blame them. I'm looking at the product right now. The lipstick and eyeshadow aren't pigmented enough. The lip gloss isn't clear, it's cloudy and grainy. These aren't my formulas. This isn't what I approved. What the hell?"

I had put so much care into these products. Spent hours thinking about shades and texture. Tried dozens of samples with the cosmetic chemists. We went back and forth about all the products until we got it right. Or that's what I thought. Because the products the influencers reviewed are not the products that I approved. Or the samples I have in front of me. These are not products I would use, let alone put my name on.

"We're looking for ways to salvage the reviews. Get the products in more hands. These things happen."

"How do these things *happen*? That's the part I'm trying to understand. Why don't my products have the correct formulas? Can the manufacturers confirm whether these formulas have been changed?"

"That was only our first round of sending out the boxes. The team is researching who might provide friendlier comments."

"The *product* is the problem, not the reviewers."

"Try to look on the bright side. If we'd gone with the full launch like you wanted then the line would be out in the public and there would be nothing we could do."

"Kimi, I know a lot of the people who reviewed the line. It's embarrassing that they think I approved any of it. This is destroying our brand credibility."

I'm more than embarrassed. I'm humiliated. This line wasn't a lark. I really cared about it. Countless hours of sampling and researching. Also, I had hoped this would be another source of steady income and not a project we try to sweep under the rug. Having a cosmetics company was meant to be a pillar in my business. It's a long-term investment but not if we can't even get it off to the right start.

"Princess, I can tell you're upset. Let me take it offline and see if there's anything we can recover."

"No, it's okay." My voice was sharp, half of me didn't care and the other half felt guilty. "I'll call my contact at the cosmetics company. I want to hear it for myself. I'll call you back when I know more."

"If that's how you want to handle it. I need you for a few more minutes, we need to discuss something else. That's why I called."

Except I called her and it took a day to get a reply.

"Please no more bad news."

"I have updates from the label." Kimi sighs, an actual, long, audible sigh. That is not a good sign. "Your single isn't doing as well as they'd like. They were hoping for a bigger splash right out of the gate. There's some interest but not even close to the traction they were hoping for. The acoustic song's numbers were so good so quickly and they wanted to see something closer to that if not better."

"How bad is it?"

"They aren't pleased."

"Are they taking responsibility for not releasing the song John and I wanted? It was their choice to go with 'Supernova.'"

"There's no point in laying blame. We need to move forward."

And let them make more bad decisions? I was a number on a spreadsheet to them. If my song didn't sell, they would move on to the next artist on the list. But this is my life. My art. My music.

"What are our options?"

"We need to strategize. Get you back out there and recapture some of the glory."

How is it that only two months ago I was their best new thing? We were going to go places together. Do shows. Be on everyone's list. I've proven I make money for them, I bring eyes, so why has everything shifted with one stumble? A stumble that they *caused*?

"Get me in front of an audience. My fans are there. I can get more people on board." I sit on a deck chair and lean back. My body feels tight and stressed. "We can still push 'Electric Love.' We could do it like I launched the acoustic one. Let's get it remixed. I'll post it on my own and get the fans involved right away."

"The label has other ideas," Kimi says with that teacher voice again. "And Wayne and I agree that it's the way to go."

Why am I so out of control of my own business? I can tell right away that I'm not going to like this idea. Kimi sounds stern, like she already knows this is going to be a problem so she needs to be firm.

"They want to try something different. Go in a different direction."

"What does that mean exactly?"

"They think—and again, Wayne and I agree—that we should try you out in a different market. Connect you with someone with a proven track record."

"As in producer? It's not ideal but I'm sure I can get John to let someone else work on our records. I'm open to bringing someone in, of course, but we have a whole album of songs that John produced. We still have a lot to work with there."

"The label wants us to focus our energy elsewhere. They aren't convinced that the John album has the necessary momentum anymore. They think it's better if you build more of a foundation first."

"Kimi what does that mean? John and I have made all our music together and the music has been successful. What do you mean *you and Wayne agree*?" It wasn't a question because Kimi had already said it more than once.

"Princess, we don't have a lot of bargaining power right now. The last song wasn't a hit. In all honesty, we should be grateful they are giving you another chance."

I want to point out the discrepancy that a hit song is *our* success but a bomb is somehow my fault. My nerves are raw at this point.

"The label picked the last song. Doesn't make sense that we don't we go back to what works and leave it to John and me? But fine. What's the big idea?"

"They want you to do a song with rapper Lil D. He's on their label, knows your music, and is willing to collaborate."

Willing to collaborate. How generous.

"And John can produce."

"No. No John. The label thinks you need to branch out."

"That's a mistake but okay."

I've worked with other producers before and have no issue working with anyone new. But it feels strange how regimented Kimi is being. Whether or not Kimi wants to impress or please the label, it wasn't long ago that Kimi and Wayne listened to our music and were blown away by it. What's changed since then? It really feels like they are fighting for the record label's concerns, not mine.

"Good. It's already set up. We'll send you the date and studio details shortly." Kimi sounds relieved that she's finally made it through this call. "This is going to be great! Thanks for being so understanding and being a team player. This is going to work, Princess."

"Yeah." It's not like I really had a choice, though. This whole phone call really didn't feel like a discussion. I was basically given marching orders and expected to follow.

Kimi ends the call with a few other compliments, telling me that this next song will be the one to push me to the next level. I try to take on some of her enthusiasm but I'm feeling a bit (completely) crushed. None of this feels like good news to me.

I need to do something. Solve these problems. I don't have access to the label, and doubt they would listen to me anyway, so cosmetics company it is. I spent so much time working with the company and planning everything that I got friendly with one of the chemists, Kara. She even came to my record launch and one of my shows. I get myself a large glass of water because all this stress is making my mouth dry and call her.

"Princess!" Kara answers her phone and I can actually hear her smile. We had a lot of fun working together. "It's been way too long. You must be really busy these days."

"I am. It's crazy around here with all the music dropping and the line." I hope I'm covering my anger, disappointment, and frustration well enough that Kara doesn't notice. She's always been direct with me about what will or won't work. "Hey, listen, I'm calling because I'm concerned about something and not sure what went wrong. The reviews are coming out and they're not good. Actually, they're pretty bad and I'm shocked about them. The items don't look like the product we talked about. The color and pigment are off. The gloss is grainy. I don't understand what happened."

"We had to make cuts to the formula."

"Cuts? What cuts?"

"Your note." Kara is getting flustered. She sounds just as confused as I am. "You sent a note saying the line needed to be more affordable. We had to change the formula to meet that goal."

"Note? I didn't ask for changes. Yes, I want to the line to be affordable, but I would never sacrifice the quality." Was I going crazy? How was this happening? "Who approved this?"

"I-I'm sorry." Kara's voice is low. She is apologetic but I'm starting to realize that this isn't her fault. "The request was passed down to me. I can ask my manager to see who sent it."

"Please." I paused to steady my voice. "I'd really appreciate it."

"Princess, I'm sorry about this confusion. They told me the request came directly from you. We'll get to the bottom of it."

"It didn't. Thanks for helping me figure out who did this."

There's a mix of emotions working through me. Disappointment, anger, sadness, confusion. I asked so many questions along the way and tried to stay up-to-date on all the details but, somehow, something this big happened without my knowing.

I sit back down on the patio, my instincts cue me to text Win but I overrule them and text John instead.

Princess: Call me. Label isn't happy. They're pulling our next few songs.

I give it a few seconds, hoping that bubble will pop up, but nothing. Why can't John make me feel supported the way Win does?

Princess: I'm really stressing. They want me to make the next record with Lil D. Fine. No big deal. But what about our songs!

Still nothing. I know it's not entirely fair of me to expect an immediate response. He's probably working and in the zone so might not even see my texts. It's also that it's more of the same with John these days. It's become harder and harder to connect. We went out for dinner the other night and it didn't go well. Our phone calls have been tense. It feels so forced with John. I turned him down when he wanted to come upstairs, and knew that made him mad, which made me feel resentful and want to pull away even more. Our kiss wasn't deep or even all that special.

There's also the not-so-small detail that spending time with John didn't bring up the soul connection I usually feel when we're together. I'd be making a mistake to keep pushing forward with John, deep down I can feel that. The passion and anticipation we both felt after our dinner at Madeo had dissipated. The writing was on the wall.

But my fantasies are alive and well and they're all Win-related. I think more and more about our time in Miami. His soft lips and hard body. We might be having a perfectly normal and innocent talk on FaceTime, and I picture him beside me, naked, in bed, my legs wrapped around him. I want to hear him whisper in my ear, tell me anything and everything. As soon as I let myself start down that road, it is getting harder and harder to rein it in.

I need to refocus. Trust my instincts.

Princess: Just had the worst conversation with Kimi.

Win: Why?

The fact that he almost always replies instantly doesn't help. Yes, I'm aware that texting and calling is not a good way to get Win out of my head but he also, somehow, helps me recenter. It's confusing, I know.

Princess: Record label drama. Cosmetics line is a disaster. I'm spinning out.

Win: I'm sorry. What can I do?

Princess: Can I call you now? I need to talk this out.

Win: I want to hear everything. But I'm in a meeting right now. Can't talk.

DIAMONDS, DECEPTION & DESTINY

Princess: Why are you texting? Go back to your meeting.

Win: I'll be done in a couple of hours. Will call then.

Princess: Don't worry about me. Honest. Sorry to bother you.

Win: Don't ever say that. You are not a bother. I'll speed this up. Take a bath. Have a drink. I have a free night on Wednesday. I'm booking dinner for us.

Why would he text when he's in a meeting? He should be focused on work, not my crazy drama. After giving dinner a thumbs-up, I still don't want to be alone with my thoughts, so I text the girls.

Princess: Shit is going down. 😥 Label is pissed about the song not doing well and won't release any of the songs we recorded.

Val: None of them? What the hell?!!

Princess: They want a new one. Have to record with Lil D instead.

Val: He's got some good songs. Could be good?

Princess: Yeah, could be. But pissed they don't have faith in the record. Bc it's fucking good!

I'm about to go on my rant about "Supernova" being their choice and they won't take responsibility for it when Maya jumps in.

Maya: That's so messed up! What did they have to say about the cosmetics?

Val: What's wrong w cosmetics? What am I missing?

I let Maya take the lead on explaining this one. I am heartbroken about everything that's gone wrong. It's comforting to read their reactions because they are so offended that it was even a thing we had to talk about.

Maya: What do you need from me? I won't review or make any sort of statement obvs. Are we still doing the shoot?

Princess: No clue. Will let you know.

Maya: Gotta go! They're calling for me.

169

Val: Love you, P. Call later if you need to talk.

It's good to have friends who listen and are by your side. Makes me feel a little less crazy. They understand the business side of things but they're not as hands-on with the creative. They don't know what it's like to put your heart and soul into something and have it fall apart through no fault of your own. In fact, if the label or management team had listened to me about the song or the cosmetics, we might not be in this position.

I stare at my phone. I can't believe I'm considering this . . .

I call Riley. Surprisingly, she picks up right away.

"Princess! How's everything?"

"Not great. You got a minute? I need to vent."

"Got all the time in the world. Lay it on me."

So, I do. The cosmetics line and bad reviews, finding out that someone ordered changes without my knowledge, and I have no idea who. The label's bad decisions about the songs and me feeling ignored. Having to record a song with Lil D when I want to focus on the album I have right now. It's a relief to let it all out in a stream.

"The cosmetics stuff sucks. This is where Stephanie can help. She knows her stuff. And doing a song with Lil D is a great idea. He's a good guy. The fact that he's massively famous, respected within the industry and with the public, he's got a real team behind him—they've stuck with him through some tough things—and puts out hit after hit. It can't hurt to be in his spotlight. Take advantage of it."

"I don't have a problem with that part. It's not my first choice since I already had my album put together but I can go along with it. I can compromise with the label, I can be flexible. I want to be a team player. Win says the same thing. There's no harm in taking advantage of opportunities if they feel right."

"Win? You still talk to Win? You never mention him."

I didn't mean to mention him now either. I hope this isn't a misstep.

"Yeah, sometimes. He's great to talk to for business and career advice. He's really helped over the years."

"Right." There's a brief pause and I wonder if I can hear the gears working in Riley's head. "Let's meet up and drink. You vent, I buy."

I laugh. Getting out of the condo is a great idea. Change of scenery, more people, more distractions. Maybe I can turn this day around after all.

"I'm down. Where do you want to go?" Weirdly, meeting up with Riley in person is bringing me a sense of relief. Like maybe I'll be able to brainstorm a realistic way of saving this shit show.

"I'll pick you up. I'm a member at Black Bird now. Let's go there."

Black Bird is the hottest members-only club that just opened in Los Angeles. It's a two-story venue with velvet dinner booths downstairs and upstairs is a half-indoor, half-outdoor bar area. Normally there's a DJ spinning, sometimes a live pianist, and a bunch of tables where you can play games like backgammon. I've been dying to go.

"All right. Let me stick on some eyelashes and I'll be ready." I make my way to the master bathroom and dig through my makeup bag for some clear eyelash glue.

"Good idea, me too. See you in twenty."

Riley hangs up the call and a small wave of hope flashes in my chest. An hour later we're sliding into the velvet booths at Black Bird, sipping on spicy margaritas.

"I genuinely don't know why things had to get so messy with us." Riley shrugs.

"Well, I guess that's because somewhere along the line you decided to become my frenemy and steal my boyfriend," I say, trying to half-joke the whole truth.

"Ouch. But fair enough." She nudges my shoulder. "I can be such a bitch. Honestly, I don't know why I act the way I do but I swear I'm trying to be better."

"People make mistakes, and what you did was beyond messed-up, but I believe in people changing for the better. So, you made some petty choices . . . people make mistakes, and I have to believe our friendship was real."

"Let me just be blunt. Insecurity bubbled out of me when it came to you; I couldn't control it. You're so driven. You're so talented. You were able to build something from the ground up, no one handed you anything. I had this constant nagging voice telling me I'd never be able to do what you did if it wasn't for the family I came from . . ." Her voice trails off and I snap my hanging jaw shut.

"Rye, it's okay, you don't have to tell me all the reasons why. What matters is how we move forward. Friendships have ups and downs."

"You're a sister to me. I want you to know I'm aware of the horrible things I've done but I'm hoping us having an open conversation can be the first step to rebuilding your trust."

"Done. I forgive you." I squeeze her hand tight. "You're like a sister to me too, Rye. Let's move forward and vow to be honest with each other, no matter what."

"Done." It almost looks like her waterline is welling with tears but she blinks them back and lifts her glass. "Cheers to us."

"Cheers to us." Relief washes over me. I'm so happy to have my friend back.

16

Instead of booking the entire restaurant for our dinner, this time Win only reserved one of the private rooms at Mr. Chow. It seemed like a good compromise between privacy but not completely hiding away. The room was intimate with low lighting and felt distinctly romantic. I expected Win to put on a bit of show because he liked to do things up right, but this one felt more personal. There was no bouquet or jewelry or sparkly things waiting for me. Just Win looking perfect and that was more than enough sparkle for me.

"It's easy to pretend the rest of the world doesn't exist when you're in here." I rotate the wine glass slowly by the stem. "I know it won't last but it's nice right now."

"It's healthy to have an escape sometimes. A chance to recharge. We all need it now and then."

"Honestly, this is exactly what I need right now. I'm starting to think you might have a sixth sense for this kind of thing."

"No." Win laughs. "I'm not a psychic and have no special powers.

I've got a Princess sense but that comes with close observation and a dedicated attention to detail."

"Some might call that stalking." I regret the joke as soon as it leaves my lips.

"I'm trying to put a good spin on stalkers. We're not all bad. Plus, I wanted to see you in three dimensions instead of through our phones."

"As long as you promise not to break into my home and give me a heart attack."

"Dammit, Princess." He reaches out and grabs my hand. It is quick and instinctual. "I didn't mean to make fun. I wasn't thinking."

I squeeze his hand then pull mine back. That feels altogether too good. "Honestly, it's not something I think about often. If I did, I might never leave the house."

"No one should have to live like that. You never have to worry about things like that when you're with me. If I could, I'd keep you on my person at all times." He tries to make light.

My god, wouldn't that be a dream come true. Warmth swarms in my lower belly. *Relax.* I want to tell Win that I already know that. I have always felt safe when I'm with him. That I can let my guard down when it's just the two of us. I feel like me.

"There's so much about this job that I love. Fashion and glam and big stages. Hollywood and all its glamour. Guess there wasn't much time spent considering the not-so-pretty parts." I felt a quick rush as Win laughs. I will never have my fill of that sound. "But I really love all of it. It's not just the final outcome but the whole process. Experiencing the journey is one of the most special parts. Working with everyone. Deciding on dresses and colors and themes. I love meeting new designers and not using the obvious, well-known ones. I think that's something that comes with being an outsider. We stick together. We recognize each other. If I can pull someone into the spotlight with me then it's that much better."

Win is watching me, listening. I still can't tell if or how much he likes me, wants me, but I definitely like how he looks at me. There were different versions. There's the engaged and amused one when his eyes sparkle. Intense and maybe concerned, which is the one I'm getting right now. Then there were times, though maybe not as often as I'm now willing to admit I like, when he looked like he wanted to eat me alive.

"But it's been a challenge to get people to take me seriously. Especially the execs. They don't want to see past the pretty or my age. They want the songs and me on the red carpet but they don't want to hear what I have to say. It's not even that they don't trust my opinion; they just don't care to listen to it. The label wouldn't listen to me about what song to put out and they don't want to use any of the songs we have. Somehow Kimi and Wayne made the call to cut the cost on the cosmetics without consulting me and now everything looks and feels cheap." I let out a huff and take a beat to compose myself. "I'm just really frustrated and it feels like my life is getting away from me."

"It's difficult to feel like you don't have any control over things."

"And that's what you like. Having control."

"At work, in business, sure. But I'm not interested in controlling other people."

"Maybe that would make things easier. Stop all those idiotic, so obvious mistakes from happening."

"Some mistakes need to play out to get through and over them."

His hand went to mine again as he absentmindedly ran his thumb along the back of my hand. When he realized what he was doing he pulled his hand back and cleared his throat. "What's the record label's next big plan?"

"Heading back into the studio. A collaboration with the rapper Lil D."

"Never heard of him."

"That's impossible." I snort, a very unexpected sound, and Win's eyes go wide. "He's global. Everyone knows him."

"Sorry. Not me."

I'm still laughing when the waiter arrives with our dinners. We order a mix of things. Chicken satay, lettuce wraps, steamed baby bok choy, shrimp fried rice, noodles. There's plenty more than the two of us can consume.

Our hands touch repeatedly while we reach for food, so often that it can't be an accident. He's sitting in the chair next to me, instead of across the table, and he puts food on my plate urging me to try things. I do the same for him and challenge him to up his hot sauce game. When he tries too much and sputter-coughs, I laugh so hard I start crying. I am happy. Content. Excited. Turned on in a way that feels more than sexual but also intensely primal. I feel fully charged and lit up.

I'm not a prude but I also haven't had the same level of experience as many of my friends. Maya and Val, or even Riley. I associate sex with emotion. I've had a total of *one* one-night stands and that was when I was twenty and I wasn't a fan. Nothing against the guy but not something I wanted to repeat. I had a few boyfriends before John but nothing serious. John wasn't my first, but he was my first as far as love and commitment goes. Believing we were building something. Stronger together than apart. When we broke up the first time, and the second, I couldn't picture myself with anyone else. One of the reasons that second breakup was so terrible was not being able to comprehend how quickly he was with Riley.

"Are you ever going to tell me about your past girlfriends?"

DIAMONDS, DECEPTION & DESTINY

Win doesn't flinch this time. His defenses don't go up.

"I might sound evasive but I'm not hiding anything. There really isn't much to tell. I've had girlfriends but nothing monumental. Nothing that lasted for long."

"You've never been in love?"

"I've loved a few, cared about them, but never been *in* love. My work has always come first. I'm ambitious, and I won't apologize for that. A relationship deserves more than I can give. I want to make *Forbes* before I'm thirty-five."

"And if you can't commit to someone completely, you don't want to string them along."

There it is. My answer. I could never be a priority at this point in his life. Never be enough to hold his attention for long.

"How did these non-relationships end? Have you left a trail of broken hearts?" I ask.

"Not broken. The occasional bruised one but I've always been honest. I never make a promise I can't keep."

I believe him. He might work at keeping up the mysterious aura but it's there as protection, not subterfuge. He isn't hiding. He's making sure that no one gets hurt.

"Did you learn these noble qualities from your father? You said once you took after him." I'm hungry to know more about this side of Win but am also trying to be gentle and not push him to share more than he wants to.

"Not necessarily the good parts." He laughs but I don't believe that he thinks it was funny. "I'm not following his example, but I've learned from it. He gave me a head start. I'm not complaining. But I've built my firm on my own. Took a while for the other venture caps to take me seriously. I was lucky, early. Hit a few big wins that allowed me to diversify. I'm close. The deal in New York will get me there—if it goes through. But if it doesn't . . ."

"That sounds ominous." I put my hand on his forearm. "I don't want to pry but I'm here to listen if you want. I'd like to return the favor and let you vent for once."

"It's more obvious than ominous." He took a drink of wine, then rested his hand on top of mine. "My father is very good at what he does. Successful, rich, powerful. We lived in a big house, had the best of everything. He worked constantly, traveled most of the time, complete devotion to business and the dollar, and when I was a kid he was my hero. I idolized him. Felt like the most important person in the world whenever he came home and paid attention to me. As I got older, I realized that didn't happen very often and that there was likely something shinier to steal his attention. Usually a woman. Both before and after the divorce. He wasn't terribly subtle about it. I did the usual high school stuff, acted out, made an ass of myself. Then I decided I was going to make a name for myself and prove to him that I could be just as good as him. Better."

"So he inspired you in business."

"He did." Win nods. "But the part that gets me, that I'm so ashamed to admit, is that it took me years to realize what all that did to my mom. She was always the steadiest person I knew. Loved me unconditionally. Was my biggest supporter. But he broke her heart. Made promises that he never intended to keep. He broke her. She lives a good life now and has lots of friends, travels. Always pushing me to get married and have kids, but she never remarried. She lost something by trusting Dad. I promised myself a long time ago that I would never do that to anyone else."

"I'm sure you won't. I don't think you have it in you to hurt anyone."

DIAMONDS, DECEPTION & DESTINY

He pulls my hand closer, claps it in both of his.

"This will sound strange, but it's never really bothered me. That I never found that person to fall in love with. Who makes me want to leave meetings early or skip them entirely. Answer phone calls at all hours of the day or night. Everything made sense because it was easy and straightforward and exactly to plan."

"And something changed?" My voice is low, almost trembling. "Does your life not make sense now?"

"It does. In fact, it's crystal clear. I just had to open my eyes and it was all right there in front of me."

I don't know if he leans towards me, or me him, but we meet. Our lips touch, gently, carefully. I close my eyes and gingerly touch his jaw with my free hand. The kiss is almost innocent. Slow and longing. When I open my eyes again he's staring at me. Watching my every move, our joining.

"I'll wait for you, Princess. You need time to figure out what you want and what you need. I'm not pressuring you about anything, but I want you to know that I'm here until you tell me not to be. And I'm not John."

After a fitful night of sleep, I finally get a chance to catch up with my girls. Maya's back from her shoot somewhere in the desert, and Val's board meeting was canceled. We have a rare weeknight together. I mean, Thursdays aren't bangers—but that's not what any of us needs. We're at South Beverly Grill having comfort food.

I am still reeling a bit from my dinner with Win and trying to understand everything that happened. We're pulling it all apart, talking about what he meant by "I'll wait for you" and "you need to figure things out first." I fessed up to how much I liked hearing those things and how delicious the kiss was but I still didn't have a complete picture of what was going on.

"It's obvious. He doesn't want to fully commit or put himself out there until you're done with John."

"Is it obvious? He could say that if that was the case. He's a pretty direct guy."

"In business. Seems like he's a lot more careful with girls."

"He told me that he's honest when he starts relationships or whatever. Tells them how much he can do and that it's casual."

"So maybe he's more careful when it's not casual. Maybe he's figuring out what to do when it's not casual because it's all new."

Maya is making good points but I'm feeling defensive. She's making a lot of assumptions about Win and it's my heart on the line. I'm not quite ready to make that same leap of logic.

"It does make sense that he wants to know what's going on with John." Val looks between the two of us, sensing the rising tension. I know it's especially hard for her these days because her nightmare family have amped up their crazy. She feels caught in the middle of all of it. "They don't exactly have the best relationship so Win is probably wary."

"I do need to deal with the John thing. Or do I? What is there to say? Nothing's been happening outside of work. There's still love there. And I'm not sure how to end something that never really got started again. The plan was to try things out, experiment in this new space. But that never happened. The apology happened, we kissed, and then things kind of stalled. But stalled doesn't mean over. Right? Every relationship hits that rough patch. It can't all be the excitement of a new romance."

I don't doubt that John loves me. I'm just not sure what kind of love it is. Are we friends or lovers? Can I rely on him for either? Is it like what Win said about wanting to find someone he wants to leave work for? It was never an issue for me and John when we were working together. There was no question of which we prioritized—career or relationship—because they were essentially the same thing. Now that there's more separation, it feels like the relationship is losing out. I can't blame John entirely for that part because I'm also very focused on the business side of things. But I would give up work to spend time with him. Or at least I would have. I'm not sure what I would choose now and I haven't really had much opportunity to test it out since John is rarely available.

"Princess. You're not holding on to John because you want him or don't want to lose him." Maya sounds more frustrated than supportive. Maybe she's getting tired of these conversations too. "You're holding on because you need John as an excuse. If you finally and definitively end it, you won't have the maybe boyfriend. Then you'll have to deal with your feelings for Win."

"But I've never denied that I have feelings for Win. My point is that he hasn't said he wants to officially be with me. It's always if he can't commit, then he won't do it."

"Why should it always be Win who says it? Why can't you admit your feelings and see how he reacts?"

"That's a huge risk!"

"Of course it is. And it's one you should both make if you want this to happen. Besides, it wouldn't be fair for you to be doing this if John really did have feelings for you. Make your decision." Her words are harsh but true, putting me on the defense.

"You've got a lot of nerve offering up relationship advice. You're more commitment-phobic than Win." The words come out with a bite I instantly regret.

"Just because I don't want a relationship doesn't mean I don't understand how they work. And I know you, Princess. You've been hurt and you're scared."

"I have every right to be. These past few months have taken a lot out of me." My emotions are a twisted mess of denial, hurt, and embarrassment.

"Of course you have the right to be hurt! Val and I have been with you through everything. But you can't keep asking us to sit by and say nothing while we watch you floundering around and making the same mistakes over and over again."

"Great. *So* nice to know. Thanks, pal." My gut knows they're right, which pisses me off.

I want to talk to Jessie. She's known me the longest and will be on my side. But I also know I can't bother her too much because she's in the middle of exams. I'm starting to feel more and more isolated here and it's only making me lash out more. I should just fucking quit. All this is falling apart. I can't get a hold of my team, I can't figure out my relationships. I'm fighting with my best friends. This is not how things were supposed to go. Maybe it's all a sign.

"You need to face some facts, Princess. You can't expect Win to hang around indefinitely while you work up the nerve to officially dump John, who doesn't deserve you by the way, and figure it out with Win."

Except that Win literally said that he would wait for me to figure it out. So now I'm sitting on the studio couch desperately wanting to text him, even just to say hi, but I'm paralyzed with indecision. My body is in the room but my mind couldn't be further away. I should be present here. Finding a way to win them over so I can get involved. Instead I'm sitting here thinking about guys. Everything about Win feels like the right choice and everything about Win tells me that it not working out will absolutely crush me.

17

It's been a long few days and neither my head nor my heart is in it. Not just from arguing with Maya, but I still don't have a good answer about what happened with the cosmetics line. We pulled the rest of the planned release to the influencers and sent out a press release about a bad batch—trying to salvage the situation. So, everything is fine. Not great, not terrible. *Fine*. And I'm starting preparations for my London show in a week so I don't have a ton of time to figure it out.

I'm used to the energy of being in the studio, the excitement that comes with collaboration and creativity, but there's a lot more sitting around this time. Lil D and his producer are busy, bouncing ideas off each other, listening to takes, and talking next moves but they aren't asking a lot of me beyond singing then waiting. I try to interject to give my opinion but it feels fucking awkward. This is the first time I've had a recording session that felt more like a job than a partnership. There's a bottle of tequila sitting next to me so I decide to help myself to a glass while I wait. Yes, I'm lucky: so many artists end up doing sessions

DIAMONDS, DECEPTION & DESTINY

and one-offs to make money and I've been able to work on projects I connect with so this is a bit of an adjustment. I can play the game once in a while. There's nothing to complain about but also nothing too memorable. It is what it is.

Riley was right about Lil D: he's nice. Welcomed me to the studio with a hug, checked if I needed anything, and told his assistant to get me anything else. Everyone is friendly and positive but they ask me to do a rough pass then tell me to sit down while they work on a comp. Lil D and the producer—and occasionally even an A&R guy from the record label—huddle together and discuss how things are going. I keep trying to join in, offering my opinion, but they aren't interested. I get a *for sure*, then they go back to doing what they're doing. Sometimes they give me additional direction like, *Let's just get a few more takes. Want to make sure we have enough options* but don't specify what exactly they're looking for. They seem happy with it all, though, so that's a good thing. I'm smart. I'm valuable. Why don't they see that? This isn't my show to run, clearly.

I've been keeping myself amused by scrolling, sipping, answering emails, and texting. Talked to John for a bit, looking for advice on how to navigate this situation but he admitted there wasn't much I could do if they were icing me out. Best to play along, do a good job, then move on.

John: They can't all be great experiences. You will be great. You're a strong artist, that's why they want you there.

Part of my problem is that I'm in a bad mood, period. All these problems are coming to a head at the same time and I don't feel like I'm on solid ground. I'd hoped that this session would prove me wrong, get things back on track. New beginnings and all that. But it's only reminding me how stalled my career feels, my lack of respect and control, and that I don't have the support I need to get it moving again.

"Hey." Lil D pops his head around the corner. "Wondered where you went." He sits down beside me, a bit too close for my liking, but I don't say anything. Maybe it's a good thing that he's being so familiar? "They're setting up for a playback, then we'll see if there's anything else to do before calling it."

"Sure. Sounds great."

"It was a good day, right? Been cool working with you. You have the prettiest voice. It's like angels are singing."

"Yeah, I had a great time. Thank you, that's very kind."

"I have some shows coming up, we should talk about maybe you coming out and surprising the crowd."

Lil D lists off the shows and festivals he has booked. I feel jealous; I could be on these shows too, even if I did have more of an opener's slot. I will work and earn my place. I should be out there too. We talk about finding a date when I can jump on stage with him. I tell him I'm all for it, which is true. The song might not be my favorite but the entire point of doing this song was to get me into new markets and in front of new audiences. I'm here for it all. And now that I'm pretty sure my time with John is up and I'm not sure what's happening with Win, leaving town more frequently sounds like a great option.

"There's a party at my place on Saturday. It's gonna be pretty low-key but lots of people you should meet. Come by."

"Yeah, that sounds great." I already know that I don't want to go but this is the kind of thing where you nod and smile and deal with it later.

"Put your number in and I'll send you the info." He gives me his phone and stands up. I never give out my info but I can't say no. "They should be good to go now. Ready?"

"Yup." I stand up as my phone buzzes. "I'll be there in a sec."

Riley: Babe! I hear the song is great.

How the hell does Riley know what's happening with the song? I haven't even heard the whole thing yet.

Riley: Having fun?

Princess: Yeah. All good.

Riley: See you later, babe. Gotta run.

That was an odd exchange. It was like a drive-by text, like Riley didn't even need me to be there.

I put my phone away and head in to listen to the song. I really hope it blows me away because I really need one thing around me to make fucking sense.

I've been to some fancy over-the-top places since moving to Hollywood, but Lil D's place is unreal. Could the whole house actually be made of glass? It looks like a Barbie dream house (minus the pink) with all the rooms visible from the side. It was cut into the hill and the view over Los Angeles was incredible. It literally looked like something right out of the movies.

I recognize a lot of famous faces but no one I personally know. It's a different crowd than I usually encounter. I can even feel the difference in the air. There's a mix of industry people here, some music publishers, agents and musicians and singers, a few actors. Mostly men, which seems a bit weird, and I don't recognize any of the women. Everyone is friendly, though. A couple of the women recognize me and come over to talk, which brings me momentary comfort while I try to get my bearings. We do some selfies and compare our posts. It's a fun, quick exchange that makes the place feel a bit less intimidating. I've become somewhat used to attending events or parties alone but it still hasn't become a natural feeling for me even though I've done it more times than I'd like. The usual antics are going down—lots of drinking and people doing coke and other drugs in their little huddles—but nothing seems out of hand.

I can sense my displacement loud in my body. I love a good party, but this is not my scene. I tried to get Kimi to come with me. Told her that if she wants me to do this for my career then she should keep me company. There should be plenty of people for her to connect with too. But Kimi had another client with an industry event and Wayne was out of town so it was a no-go. I could've asked Maya to come but things still feel strained between us. We've texted but I think we're both holding back. Maybe we both need some space.

Most of the time I don't have a problem walking into a new space and putting on the charm. I genuinely like meeting people and having new experiences; I remind myself this will all be fun to look back on later in life. But something isn't right here. The guys' eyes are lingering longer than normal. There's lots of ogling of all the women. Since I tend to overthink, I try to read the women's body language to see if they're picking up the same vibe but it doesn't seem like it. From one person to the next it's just smiling, cheers, laughing, light physical touching— from what I can tell they look comfortable. Maybe I should too.

I continue through the house, keeping an eye out for anyone I know. There're a few rooms, more couches and people talking. In the back of the house, there's a room that is a bit more secluded with large windows that look out onto a wall of trees. I do my usual scan then stop. Shit. There's Riley and John in the group of people talking. Everything looks casual and relaxed, but I immediately go into internal panic mode. My brain doesn't care that I've already been thinking that John and I were drifting apart, or that he and Riley are tentatively attempting a friendship again, because I'm right back in that moment where John didn't come back from the party when he said he would and Jessie told me she saw Riley and John together. I take a deep breath and swallow hard. My first thought is to text the friend chat but I don't know if my hands will shake too much when holding my phone. And that is not a vulnerability I'm prepared to show right now.

Mind racing. Did Riley and John come together? Did they know I would be here? Have they been talking this whole time while John and I have been discussing getting back together? Riley didn't mention John once during this time. John said they ran into each other at the studio but that was it. How much were they hiding from me?

I feel completely stuck so I do the only thing I can: walk up to them and pretend none of this shit bothers me.

The group dynamic shifts as soon as I approach them, which doesn't feel like a great sign. The other people they've been standing with drift off and then it's just the three of us standing together.

"How did the song go? Lil D seems hyped. He's so great, isn't he?" Riley is being extra enthusiastic, which only makes me more suspicious. "This is going to be the boost you need. Get you out of the slump from your last release."

Wow. That was a painful way to word it but okay. I look to John to see if he makes any effort to soften that blow. He doesn't.

"Yeah, the song sounds great." I didn't feel like going through the details of being in the studio or my issues with Lil D and the producer. This wasn't the environment to talk those things out. And any sort of weakness is the last thing I'm going to show right now. "Kimi and Wayne also thought this party would be a bonding moment. Networking and all that."

"Totally! That's why I wanted John to come tonight. He needs to widen his network too. Can't work with the same people all the time." Hiding the bewilderment on my face is becoming more and more difficult as each moment passes. Riley continues. "I don't mean you, Princess. It's good for both of you. We need to get John a session with Lil D. I'll see what I can do."

Riley is being helpful but it bugs me. She is saying what everyone is saying. John and I need to record and work with other people. But she makes it sound as if she is going to be responsible for any or all of our success. I try to push that nagging feeling aside.

"I didn't realize this is where we were going when you invited me." He waves his hand around and my curiosity piques . . . so he *didn't* know this was a work thing that she was trying to set up. "Not really vibing with all this."

"Relax, you guys." Riley rolls her eyes. "It's a party full of people who matter and can help both your careers. Here's a crazy idea; try to enjoy yourselves. Talk to Lil D. There's a lot more he can do, especially for you, Princess. You've already got your foot in the door so get in the game instead of fucking it up. Stop being so precious about it all."

She walks away like she's done dealing with us and has much more important things to do.

She does have a point: I *am* being a bit precious about things. Sure, the guest list seems a bit lopsided with powerful men and girls desperate to make an impression, who may or may not have been paid to be so attentive, but I could still make the most of it. In this business, it never hurts to know more people.

"Hey stranger." He pokes my side trying to be funny but I wasn't seeing the joke.

"*You're* the stranger." I wasn't feeling very generous. "You haven't responded to a text or call since I was in the studio with Lil D. And then I walk in and you're with Riley. As her . . . I don't know, date? Guest? So I guess that means you're talking to each other more than you let on."

"That's a bit hypocritical. You're hanging out with Riley again too. What's the big deal if we talk?"

"You know that we're hanging out because I told you. I haven't kept anything from you. But you, clearly, aren't giving me the same courtesy. Somehow you've forgot to mention you and Riley talking."

"Nothing's going on." He holds his hands up in defense. "I swear. I told you I ran into her and we caught up."

"That was weeks ago."

"She told me about the party then."

"And you failed to mention it to me."

"I didn't think about it. Didn't know if I'd come. Didn't know if I'd be busy. You're making it sound like some big conspiracy but it's a thing she told me about then reminded me today and here I am."

"Reminded you today when you couldn't be bothered to reply to me. I thought you said you didn't know this is where you were coming tonight." I'm so sick of fighting with him at parties but this is complete bullshit and I'm going to speak up.

"For fuck's sake, Princess. How many times can I say it's just business?"

"Just business with me or Riley?"

"You're blowing this out of proportion. You know my schedule has been insane with work. And I'm not in a place to say no. Riley is right; I do need to get in with new artists and that's what I'm trying to do. I'm not finding an excuse to spend time with Riley but she knows her shit. I'm doing what's best for my career and I'd hope if anyone would understand it would be you."

"Well, it's always been about you and your career, John." Am I complaining about John working too much or Win? If John suddenly said *I'll give everything up to be with you,* would I even want that?

He's about to respond when I cut him off. "I really don't think this is the time or place for this conversation. Go mingle and make your connections."

He shakes his head and walks away. Doesn't even bother to say a proper goodbye, which I suppose is what I wanted. Maybe there isn't a point in dragging this out any longer. Rip off that Band-Aid. Close that door.

I step out into the hall to watch him. He's in the front room at the bar. Downs a glass of whisky, then heads to the exit.

I look around the room. There's no one that I know or feel like approaching. Guess it's time I got moving and figured out how to make this night count.

18

I work my way through the party, mingle with people, dance with some of the girls, but my mind is elsewhere. The fight with John came from out of nowhere. I already felt on edge even before I saw the two of them together. At this point, I believe him. It was a mistake to press him the way I did. It's not my place to question him. I don't think he's lying about how much he and Riley talk or how he ended up at the party but I'm still angry. Or maybe disappointed, and I'm not sure if it's at me or John.

What the hell have I been doing these past few weeks? It's suddenly hitting me that having John, or at least the possibility of having John, has been an anchor point. Something steady when the rest of this shit felt like it was spinning, sometimes out of control. But loving him is ruining me. Win feels unattainable. Desirable—deeply, *deeply* desirable—but also maybe out of reach beyond being a friend. Maya and I are fighting. Val and Jessie are busy with their own lives. It all adds up to me feeling very unmoored.

I need air. The party still isn't very crowded but I'm feeling a bit claustrophobic. The chilled breeze and a moment to soak in the view of Los Angeles at night should do the trick. I step out onto the balcony and, as hoped, it's just right. Quiet and beautiful.

I resist looking at my phone. I don't expect John to have texted but I also don't want to confirm that he hasn't. I know Win is at an event. He already told me it would be difficult to get messages out. He joked that it was like being off grid but with multimillionaires and seafood towers.

"Princesssss," he drags my name out.

I turn around to see Lil D step on to the balcony. He closes the door behind him before walking towards me.

"Hey. Watch your step," I warn since he's wearing black-lensed sunglasses.

"Having a good time?" He stands beside me. Leans forward, resting his elbows on the railing.

"Yes, thanks for inviting me." I nod a few times. "Just taking a breather."

"You know who you remind me of?"

"Who?"

"Sophia Loren."

"Oh." I chuckle. "That's not what I was expecting but thank you."

"No one's ever told you that?" He keeps his eye contact with me and I do the same. If this is a powerplay, I want him to know I am equal. He looks away first.

"Thinking we might put the song on. Give everyone a taste of what's to come."

"Is it ready? I haven't got an updated bounce yet." It charges me up knowing that he's excited about it.

"It sounds great. Not final but there's plenty to show off."

"I'd prefer if they heard the final version. Plus I'd like to hear it and make any changes before it's played for other people."

"Got everyone here. Could be a big moment to impress."

"Maybe. But songs only get one first impression. We should play this smart, not fast." I hope I don't offend him in disagreeing, but he seems unaffected. A little hard to tell since he has sunglasses on.

"I like the way you think. That's some businesswoman-type shit." The compliment lands perfectly and I'm disarmed. "Shots to celebrate?" He turns to reach for two mini crystal glasses, brought out on a tray by a staff member.

"You are so stealth! Thank you," I joke to the woman as I take the glass from Lil D. She presses her lips into a thin line and returns inside.

"We're going to do big things." He winks and it doesn't feel as warm and flirtatious as Win's. "I've got plans. I've always got plans."

He lifts his glass to mine and we down the clear liquid.

"I'll see you back inside." I hand my glass back to him and watch as he returns to the party.

About fifteen minutes later, I push myself away from the railing and suddenly feel light-headed and my body feels loose. I steady myself before heading inside but it gets worse. For a couple of seconds, my vision goes blurry and I wonder if it's because of the lighting change from outdoor to inside. The music starts to sound a bit warped. I reach out to a waiter but must have misjudged the distance as I miss him entirely. He doesn't seem to notice me at all.

This has to be obvious, though. I'm feeling too fucked up for no one to notice. The group of girls that I was talking to earlier looks over and laughs. They think I'm drunk. I take a step towards them but I stagger and almost trip. Everything is moving in slow motion and fast at the same time. It's difficult to process what's happening around me but I know that they turn away and ignore me rather than help. This is not good.

I can barely make out the apps on my phone screen. Somehow I manage to type a text to John: I don't feel good.

I spot Lil D on the other side of the room. He's sitting on a couch, surrounded by a group of people hanging on his every word. He's still wearing his sunglasses and laughing. I carefully make my way over there without falling or running into anyone. Lil D smiles when he sees me and leans back against the couch. He takes my hand and pulls me closer.

"Hey, I'm not feeling so well. Can you help me?" I'm scared to death and my voice is shaking but I don't want the group to know so I'm trying to be discreet.

"This is Princess." He motions to the group. "Did you miss me?"

Miss him? What is he talking about? Something is wrong and I need help.

He pulls more and tries to maneuver me onto his lap. I don't have the ability to drag myself away or even fully refuse him, but I manage to land beside him rather than on top. The group sitting around Lil D stands up and leaves. Even through my haze, I understand that we are being left alone.

"'Cause I missed you, pretty girl."

My stomach feels sick. Lil D lifts his sunglasses and rests them on the top of his head. It's hard for me to see his pupils but his eyelids are heavy and half open. I try to sit myself up but I'm starting to slouch over and lose control of my body.

This is dangerous. I was drugged and I'm alone. I need to get the hell out of here before anything else happens. Fight-or-flight kicks in and I launch myself off the couch.

"No, no, no. Sweetheart, get back here. Who upset you?" He reaches out, tries to grab me again, but he's even less steady than me and misses.

The room spins and the panic has set in. If I don't find a way out of here, I am going to die. Getting to the door and ordering a car, or getting myself down the hill in any fashion, seems unlikely. Impossible. I need to find a safe space. Alone. Away from everyone here. I try the first few doors I find but they're all locked. Lil D doesn't want anyone getting into his private space without his permission. I scan the room again. It's hard to see anything at a distance or get past the shadows and the blur. A shape is moving towards me and eventually Riley comes into focus.

"Riley." I have to say her name a few times to be heard over the music. Or because my voice is so quiet and fucked up. "You have to help me."

Riley turns to look at me. I don't think she heard me. She gives me the once-over, full top to bottom, then laughs. She says something to the group of girls standing there, the same ones who ignored me earlier.

"You're fine, babe, go find some water."

Her words sound hazy. I can barely make them out. Everyone laughs and Riley turns her back to me. I cease to exist. Riley thinks I'm drunk. I was supposed to make connections, network, and gain new access, but in Riley's mind I've wasted my opportunity.

"Where are you going?" A couple of other girls call to me. I stop and turn to look at them. One of them has a drink in her hand half spilling onto the floor. They don't move and neither do I.

"Imjustgoing." My words come out as one and I leave them.

I walk down the hall trying to hold on to the wall as I go. Finally find a door that opens. It's a bathroom. I get inside and lock the door. I'm bracing myself on the countertop over the sink as I try to turn it on. Eventually manage to splash water on my face before collapsing on the floor.

The girls. I could text the girls and they can send help. The problem is texting doesn't seem possible. My fingers aren't working properly and I can't focus on the screen to even see what I'm typing. I need to call. My eyes are so heavy they're daring to close but I'm too afraid that if they do, they won't ever open again.

The floor is cold and hard but the chill might help keep me awake and it's better than trying to stand. I try everyone—Maya, Val, Jessie—but no one picks up.

My mouth is dry. I need water. I push myself off the ground and grab onto the ledge of the sink to pull myself up to stand. Another splash on my face, then I cup water in my palm to drink. It's not enough, feels like there will never be enough, but it's good. I step back, unsteady, and hit the wall behind me, slowly sliding to the ground.

"Hi, honey. Are you already back from the party? How was it?"

"At party." My voice is slow and slurred. I'm dragging my words together. "I'm so sorry, Mom. Somethingwronnngg. Mommm. Think I've been drugged."

"What?! Where are you now?"

"Bathroom."

"Lock the door, Princess. Right now." I can hear the panic in her voice. She's trying to be calm to keep me calm, but she's terrified.

"Locked. Already." I rest my head against the wall and try to make out her face on the screen. "Already locked."

"Good. That's my girl. Now listen to me. You need to stay awake. Do you hear me? Don't fall asleep, Princess."

"Awake. Stay awake. I need to go home." There's a loud banging and I turn to the door. "Someone's here."

"Princess. You in there?" Lil D's words come out messy as he shouts through the door. The door handle shakes furiously, moving up and down. I can hear him talking to someone else near him before he calls to me again. "You okay? Let me see you, Princess."

"Do not open that door!" Mom can obviously hear everything and she's much faster at responding than me. "I'm calling Wayne."

"Yes. M'here." I'm fully slurring my words now.

Lil D calls out a few more times. I can also hear him swearing, there's another voice talking with him outside the door. I can picture him right there. Lil D. Maybe even Riley. The rest of the party is alive—they don't know or care what's happening to me. No one cares.

"Voicemail." The panic in her voice is getting higher. "It went to voicemail. I'll try Kimi."

"Away."

"Yes, love. Stay awake. Stay with me."

"Here. Mom." It seems important to say her name. Like she needed to remember who she was talking to. I needed to remember.

"I'll call John."

He won't answer. He's mad at me. We fought and I basically told him to fuck off and he's not going to pick up a call from my mother.

"He's not picking up."

No shit. John is gone. He stormed out and there's no way he's coming back for me.

"What are you saying? I can't understand."

Did I say that part out loud? I need to lie down. I can lie here on the floor just for a little.

"Are you still awake? Say something, sweetheart. You need to stay awake. Tell me what happened."

I try to take a deep breath. Swallow. Push my voice and the air out as forcefully as I can.

"Win."

"Win? You want me to call Win? Sweetheart, I don't have his number."

I lift my head off the tile so I can look at my phone. Blink my eyes until it comes into focus. It takes all my strength to lift my arms and concentrate, my body feels like it's swaying back and forth, to add Win into a three-way call.

He picks up right away.

"Hello?"

"Win? Hello, can you hear me? It's Princess's mom. I need your help. Something happened to her. She's at Lil D's house and she's been drugged."

"What?"

I can picture Win. He's on immediate alert. Standing up and ready to run. Do. Save.

"I tried calling Wayne, John. Everyone—"

"Give me her location."

"Lil D's. Bathroom." I have the address, somewhere but not sure I'll retrieve it from my phone. I close my eyes, trying to remember the street. It's a long road and it's dark but maybe . . .

"I've got it. I'll get her out of there."

I hear my mom saying my name, trying to keep me awake. Hear Win saying something to me, or maybe my mom, but I don't recognize any of the words. Things are getting dark and I am done. I've got nothing left. I need that cool floor. It's the only thing I can do right now. The only thing I want. To lie down. Close my eyes and let the cool tile take over.

19

When I open my eyes, I don't recognize where I am. It's not my bedroom. Or John's. No, it wouldn't be John's. I haven't been there in a long time and I'm starting to remember the fight. I shut my eyes again. I let the memories flood back, trying to recount what happened exactly.

We fought and he stormed out. We were at a party. Lil D's party. I was drugged. Locked myself in the bathroom because I had nowhere else to go. No way to get out on my own. Riley thought I was drunk and turned her back on me. No one answered my calls. John ignored a call from my mother. Why would my mom call if it wasn't an emergency? He left me at the party and didn't pick up his phone. He didn't care.

There was more but my memory is so hazy. I take some deep breaths to calm myself, afraid my desire to remember will scare the events away. The phone call with my mom then Win. After that, there were voices, distant then close. A crash that must have been the door. My eyes opened as I was lifted up and I recognized one of Win's bodyguards.

DIAMONDS, DECEPTION & DESTINY

"Got you, Miss."

I tried to say thank you but all I could do was nod. I rested my head against his shoulder and closed my eyes again.

And now I am here, in this strange room. Eyes open again. Roll on to my back and look around.

Win.

He's sitting on a chair a few feet from the bed. His head is leaning back, resting against the wall. He looks like crap. Maybe even worse than I probably look. I try sitting up, then reconsider, fall back down on to the bed, and that's enough to get Win's attention. He jumps up and rushes to my side.

"How are you feeling?" He picks up a glass of water on the bedside table and kneels down to hand it to me. His knuckles are white as I reach back.

I shake my head slowly and drink. I start with a sip, then down the entire glass.

"Do you want a painkiller? Advil? Aspirin?"

"No." My voice sounds like shit.

Flashes of last night skip through my mind. Someone helping me to the toilet, being sick, someone holding my hair back, cooing me through the dizziness and fog and gently rubbing my back getting me through it. Realization dawns on me: it was Win.

"Thank you."

Win smiles. "Water's free, Princess. You can have all the water you want."

"Not the water." My eyes tear up. "For everything. Thank you for coming."

I lean back against the pillows and try to compose myself before he notices. The bed is the most comfortable thing I've ever laid on,

203

luxurious to say the least. I look around the room trying to take it all in. The blinds are closed but there's a ring of sunlight around the edges. It's daytime so I've been here for hours. It feels like it could be maybe days but I'm betting hours.

"I will always be here, Princess. Don't you know I will always come for you?"

"I know." I smile. It's a weak smile but it's all I can manage in the moment. "That's the only thing I'm sure of right now."

"He's going to pay. I promise you, Lil D will pay for what he did." He runs a hand down my cheek then across my jawline. "You need to sleep some more. Text when you wake up and I'll come back. If you're feeling strong enough, come down and find me."

"Sleeping more sounds good."

Win stands up. He leans over me and kisses my forehead.

"I'll be checking on you." He turns to leave the room.

I pick up my phone from the table and the brightness hurts my eyes. There's a ton of missed calls from Maya, Jessie, and Val. My heart rate picks up as I scroll through the missed calls and messages from the night before. Apparently I managed to type out a garbled text that freaked them out. It got worse the longer I didn't reply until Jessie's last message.

Jessie: Win texted us and said he's with you. Please call when you're awake. We love you, Princess.

I'm about to reply to the group when I notice one from John.

John: How are you? R u okay?

I burst into tears. It happens so fast that I can't stop it. They come fast and hard. I'm right back at the mansion. In the bathroom, drugged and incapacitated and terrified. There were moments when I thought I might die. When I was certain that something terrible was going to happen and I had no escape route. I fully realize that no one else picked up my calls but I know they were busy—at work, with family—but John was simply ignoring me. Ignored my mother. He could have been back at the house faster than Win's security but we fought and he didn't want to deal with me.

The phone buzzes, a call coming through, and it's John. I take a deep breath in through my nose and try to stifle my tears as I answer.

"I can't talk right now."

"Are you okay? Val called and told me what happened. Fuck. Princess, this is so fucked up."

"I can't do this now. I'm tired. I'm done with this."

"C'mon, you can't be mad at me. This wasn't my fault."

"My mom called you. Why didn't you pick up?"

"I don't know." There's defeat in his voice. "I guess I thought she was calling to yell at me."

"When has my mother ever yelled at you?"

"I . . . Never." He paused. "Look, the fight triggered old, heightened emotions. We were back to the Riley thing again and I was fed up so I left. Your mom called and I figured it was about that. But I didn't know you were in trouble and the text was unclear. I swear, if I knew, I would have been right there. I didn't mean to leave you in a dangerous spot."

"You never mean to, John. You just do it."

"You can't be mad at me for not knowing."

"Like I said, John, I'm not mad." It's true. I wasn't mad. My voice was no longer hoarse or craggy. I felt calm. Safe. "I'm done."

There's a long pause—so long that I wonder if he's walked away, again—before he speaks.

"Princess. I'm sorry. I don't know what to say."

"You don't need to say anything else. I think we've said it all. I love you. It's not the kind of love like before or that I thought would always be there but I do love you. And despite everything and all this shit, I actually hope that you stay in my life for a long time. Not as my boyfriend but hopefully, eventually, we could be friends. But that might take a while." There's been so much back and forth lately with my heart but I know this decision is final, and right. "Goodbye, John."

"Princess—"

I tap End Call before he can say anything else. There's nothing left for me to do except roll back onto my side and cry. Deep, gut-wrenching sobs like I haven't done in years. It's a painful thing to let go. To release someone you love and admit that that person, that relationship, no longer exists.

20

Win's house is big but not overwhelming. Once in a while, you end up in places that are all hallways and extra rooms that seem designed to confuse you. I tease Val a lot about wealthy families having more rooms than they know what to do with and Val usually responds by laughing, "You're not wrong." Win's house, though, feels different. It's elegant and well designed, like it's right out of *Architectural Digest*. As I walk down the stairs I hear voices, so I head in that direction.

Win sits at the head of the table with Maya, Val, and Jessie. As soon as I see them my eyes well up and they run towards me.

"Are you okay?" Maya wraps her arms around me and pulls me into a tight hug.

"We're so sorry for missing your call." Jessie is next with the hug. "I was at the library and had my phone on silent. I'll never do that again."

"Here's hoping that I never have that kind of emergency again."

"That asshole!" Val says. She holds my face with both hands. "How are you feeling?"

"I'm okay. I woke up pretty confused and feeling like crap but I'm okay now."

"Honest?"

"Honest." I hold a hand up like I am swearing an oath. "Other than a slight headache, I'm okay."

I cried myself to sleep after talking to John, but it wasn't all about him. Everything was flooding in and overwhelming me. My body was spent, my mind a jumble. I woke up a few times through the night, confused and still feeling distraught. I turned on the television to keep me company before I officially got myself out of bed and *TMZ* was on. Lil D's house was being raided by the police. It was said that they received a tip that he was in possession of illegal substances.

"The doctor who was here said this is normal after being drugged." Win looks better than he did earlier but still ragged. "She said you could take Advil for the pain."

"I saw a report that Lil D's house was raided."

The girls responded with a chorus of *thank god* and *best news* and I hear Win muttering. I can't make it all out but it sounds something like *nothing will ever be enough*. I realize who was the source that sent the police to the mansion.

The moment is broken when his phone rings.

"Excuse me, ladies. Duty calls." He gives my arm a quick squeeze as he walks out of the room.

"Can we eat now?" Maya sits back down. "I'm starving."

"Can you tell us what happened?" Jessie sits across from me at the table. "But we understand if you don't want to relive it."

I take them through the night from the moment I walked through the door until I closed my eyes on the bathroom floor. Then I told them about calling John. "It was a lot. Everything rose to the surface and I didn't hold anything back."

"You're not feeling bad about it now, are you?"

"No. I was maybe a bit harsh, but I spoke the truth. At that point, I was going to lay it all out there. Then I was furious that he left, which maybe wasn't fair considering how much pressure I was putting on him. It just seemed like further proof that he wasn't in it for the long haul. Or if things got tough or inconvenient, he'd just leave. And I think I was also just really fucking sad that it was over. Finally. Nothing more to hold on to or convince myself it was worth saving. I had to finally admit that the person I was in love with is gone. And I'm not the same person either. I was holding on to something that was already over."

"Sooooooo . . . It's done?" Val rips apart a croissant as she speaks. "You and John are over?"

"Yes. Done." I wave a hand in front of me. "We are over."

"Well, huzzah to that one!" Maya raises her cup of coffee in a toast.

"He called back later. We talked."

"Second round of the fight?"

"Not really." I push my plate forward so I can lean on the table. "There isn't anything left to fight for. It was John doing the usual apology tour. This time, though, I didn't waste time on it because none of it mattered. The words don't hold any weight anymore. I never thought I'd say this and it would be true, but I don't want to be with John. Genuinely. I hope someday we'll be friends but that's not going to be for a while. Because none of this changes the fact that he could have been something else. He could have answered my mom's call. He chose not to be there."

"How do you feel about this decision?"

"I feel good about it . . . relieved. A little sad, maybe a bit angry that

I wasted time taking him back and more time considering taking him back, but I feel good overall. I have no doubt it is the right decision."

"Was Riley still there? After John left and everything else happened?"

"Yes. She was there." I take a moment to think it through and pull those images back up. "It's a bit foggy. I saw her just as I felt like I was going under and I still didn't understand what was happening. There was a group of girls there, the ones who posted those selfies of us—they thought I was drunk. I remember there was a lot of pointing and laughing and it felt like slow motion."

"They thought you were drunk so they laughed?" Val sat back in her chair gobsmacked. "A woman by herself at a party and clearly fucked up and they laughed. Didn't offer to help."

I shook my head. "You probably aren't going to like the next part of this story, then."

"What did she do?" Maya did not look pleased.

"I don't know exactly. I don't have a clear memory of it. But I did see her with that group of girls laughing and asked for her help and she brushed me off. She's clearly capable of being manipulative and mean but could she really be this cruel?"

"Are you trying to convince us or yourself?"

"It's entirely possible that I don't want it to be true. But I am turning a new corner here and I don't want to carry that one around. That anyone would turn their back and laugh. She was petty but this was life and death."

I don't want it to be true but my gut is telling me otherwise.

21

I feel almost back to myself but still so exhausted. Part of it is physical—first the drugs, then sleeping them off for many hours. The doctor said I'm likely to feel the effects for a day or two as my body recovers. But the exhaustion is about so much more. I've always had plenty of energy, a get-up-and-go attitude about almost everything—ready to hustle, get the job done—but I don't feel like I have the strength to tackle any of it. This isn't a heartache moment when I want sweets and ice cream and rom-coms with the girls. This time, the outside world feels like entirely too much and one more reason to stay hidden in Win's house.

He's been locked away in his office for the last hour. He was so cute and almost flustered before he went in, saying he had to get a few things off his plate and wouldn't leave me alone for long.

"But you can text or call or knock on the door if you need me."

"I'm okay." I put my hand on his arm. He feels so solid and reassuring. "I should probably get going soon anyway."

"Are you sure? Maybe you should give it a bit more time. Make sure you've fully recovered."

He was being so protective but still trying to give me space. He wasn't demanding I do one thing or the other but was being obvious all the same.

"Trying to keep an eye on me?"

"Yes. I let you out of my sight and this happened."

"You didn't cause any of this to happen." Did he honestly blame himself? That's ridiculous. "Win, you're the reason I got out of there safely. I'm okay because of you."

He shakes his head a few times, takes a deep breath. "I don't know what I would do if anything happened to you, Princess. I don't even want to think about it."

I think about how Win looked when I woke up earlier. Dark circles under his eyes, hair a mess, clothes rumpled from sitting by my bedside for so long. I'd never seen that look before from him and didn't even know anything could shake him or set him off. We'd had so many talks these past weeks about his life and business and that he prided himself on always having a level head in negotiations. Never losing your cool in moments of stress often meant having the edge in closing deals. But he had looked anything but cool and collected while waiting beside me. When I finally woke up, the change in his expression was incredible. Suddenly bright and animated. Relieved.

His reaction was so different from John's. John, who could have helped in a number of ways. He could have stayed at the party with me. Could have answered the phone and come back to get me. He called me to check in, said he was worried, but he also wanted to reiterate that none of this was his fault. I needed to understand *his* feelings and how hard all of this was for *him*. Win thought that he didn't do enough. The man who picked up his phone right away, sent his security to rescue me, called the authorities to raid the mansion, gave me a safe place to rest, called a doctor, brought my friends in to see me . . . felt guilty because it had happened at all. Seeing this contrast side-by-side was both heartbreaking and exhilarating. How had I put so much faith in John for so long when he clearly couldn't see me past his own ego?

"I'm safe and probably alive because of you. Who knows what would have happened if it wasn't for you. There's no way I can thank you enough."

"I don't want thanks." His voice is low, his eyes steady. "That's not what I want."

My heart speeds up and my mind races. What does he want? He cares—he's proven that over and over—but does he want me? I want to wrap my arms around his neck. Press myself close to him and feel safe. Protected. But I don't want to push him or make him uncomfortable. Take advantage of his kindness.

"Go to work, Win." I know I sound abrupt but hopefully not rude. "Don't worry about me."

"That's impossible. Today, at least." He smiles. "Maybe I can manage it tomorrow." The look on his face tells me that is unlikely. "I won't be long. Don't leave until I get back. Promise?"

I draw an X over my heart. "I promise."

For the briefest of seconds, I think maybe he's going to kiss me but he steps away and heads to his office.

Now, I wander around his house. Make a cup of tea. His chef offers to make me something else to eat but I decline. I don't want to put anyone out. They are all being so generous but I worry I'm distracting them from their regular routine. They aren't used to having other people hanging around the house. Hell, even Win isn't here half the time.

With my tea in hand, I wander into the living room. There is an expensive-looking stereo system and a wall of vinyl on shelves. There is no way I can go through all of them, or even reach the top shelf without a ladder, so I pick a record out at random. Nina Simone's *Pastel Blues*. Picked by chance but the perfect choice. I put the record on and curl up on an armchair to close my eyes and listen, let Nina's voice surround me.

My moment is cut short by my ringing phone and I jump. Kimi. My moment of peace quickly ends and I feel my anger rise again. I don't really want to talk to her but it has to happen at some point.

"Princess, are you okay?"

Kimi sounds stressed, maybe frightened. Did she see this as a wake-up call or is she worried that there are other repercussions?

"I am now." What happened wasn't her fault but she did push me to do the song and to go to the party. When I expressed concerns about any of it, she insisted all this was in my best interest. That collaborating with Lil D was good for me. It was *not*.

"Wayne and I are on speakerphone."

"Princess, I'm so glad to hear your voice. We were so worried."

I'm not sure how much it helps to be worried after the fact but I try to keep my cool, to remember Win's negotiation tactics.

"We have the whole team working on this. You weren't there when the raid happened and your name will be kept out of all the reports."

"Good. Because I don't need my name dragged through the mud or associated with him considering I'm the victim."

"We know, Princess." Wayne sounds almost distraught. "I can't believe any of this happened. We're going to work to make this right."

"Exactly how?"

"First off, the label agreed that the song with Lil D won't be released. Consider it permanently shelved."

They claim they are the ones to secure that decision but who knows. Not completely trusting Kimi and Wayne is a new thing. I have no way of verifying what they say is true.

"Good. I don't think I could listen to that song now. Let alone perform it anywhere."

"They've decided to go with 'Never Mine' next."

"Really? I go through all this and then they decide to go back to the original plan?" I hold back a laugh of disbelief.

"We've got their agreement on the song, and we'll get it out soon." Kimi's got her best *just go along with it, Princess* exasperated voice going.

"Good." I take another deep breath. Stay cool. Stay calm. "What about the cosmetics line? I refuse to let it go out as is. The product formula was changed. Was that you?"

"It doesn't matter now. We'll resend the PR packages."

They're not answering my question, which tells me everything I need to know. "Nothing goes out until I approve the product and am sufficiently reassured this won't happen again. I'm not happy with how any of this has gone down. Not only what happened at the mansion. That was seriously fucked up and needs to be dealt with but I mean overall how my project is being run, being managed."

"Princess." Wayne tries for both soothing and sympathetic but I only hear condescending. "Everything with the label and the cosmetics are bumps in the road. Something that every artist goes through. Labels often panic if a song or record doesn't get the numbers they predicted. Everyone goes through it at some point."

"I understand how the industry works and that the label wants to make money. Maybe there's an exec or two who believes in me, but for the most part I'm numbers and dollar signs to them. But it's supposed to be different with you. I respect you as managers and have been trusting *you* to have my best interests at heart as far as my career is concerned, but it really feels like you're ignoring me as a person. You're not taking me seriously. Not taking my opinion seriously. I trusted you to fight for me with the label and it feels like you rolled over as soon as there was any pushback. You approached John before me and got him on board with switching out the songs. Made a deal with him. Where was I in the conversation? The deal for me was recording a song as a supporting player for Lil D, and I'm angry about it for very obvious reasons."

"It sounds harsh but this is how it works. Compromises happen. Sometimes it feels like it's not a fair shake but other times will feel like a win. You just need to be patient," he says.

"So my only option is to keep letting this happen until the label decides I'm worthy of making decisions about my own career?"

"No. We gain traction with each move. You have to trust us, Princess. We know what we're doing."

But that's the problem, isn't it? I'm not sure I do trust them anymore.

"Listen, we'll let you rest and we can talk more later," says Kimi, always trying to placate me.

"Sure. We can talk later."

I hang up and regret that I don't have an old-school landline phone. It would be so satisfying to slam the handset down with a loud thud.

The needle lifts as the side finishes. I could get up to flip it over but I don't think even Nina Simone could calm me now.

My phone rings again. My mom.

"Hey." I want to break into a million pieces instantly.

"Oh, honey, it's so good to hear your voice. How are you feeling?"

"I'm good." My eyes well up with tears. "Thank you for everything. I was so scared. Sorry I didn't call earlier. I slept for a long time, then the girls were here. Think I'm just starting to get my bearings back."

But maybe not? It feels good to hear her voice but I feel scattered. Anxious.

"Win's been keeping me up to date. He told me what the doctor said and that the girls were there with you."

Knowing how attentive Win was to my mom sends chills though my whole body. Just when I think he can't do anything more, he proves himself to be the most reliable, thoughtful person. He's been my constant for so long but I somehow didn't see it until now. Despite having a demanding and consuming business, Win still manages to care for all the pieces of my life and doesn't consider it a burden.

"Win's a great guy." My voice catches in my throat. "Really special."

"I see that. It seems like there's a lot more to him and possibly this story than you let on."

"It's complicated."

And that might be the most underrated comment of the year.

"It doesn't sound complicated to me."

"He's a friend. A very rare and very good friend." I don't hide things from my mother but I also don't reveal all. She knows about John and our back and forth and I didn't want her to think I was being a flirt or not honest if I told her about my growing feelings for Win while still, technically, working things out with John. "We've been talking a lot more lately, spending some time together, and, well, I don't know how else to say it. Things are complicated."

"Yes, you've said." Was my mother laughing at me? That definitely sounded like a stifled laugh. "I think there are many people who talk a good game. They say they love you, they promise things, they beg for forgiveness because they've changed. But I suggest you to think about those people in your life who show you they love you through their actions. Who prove it."

I take a moment to think about what my mom is saying. It's true, I've heard *I love you* plenty of times without any follow-through. So many promises that were discarded almost as soon as they were said. From John but also from Wayne and Kimi. It was something else entirely to have someone rush to my side, or my rescue, simply because I needed them. Because they wanted to be there. Maybe it took me so long to recognize it because I was always waiting for the words. What did I value more? Words without meaning or action without reward? Win was there for me because he wanted to be, not because he wanted something from me or I had promised anything.

"Are you saying Win loves me, Mom?"

My heart was racing so fast I could practically feel it in my throat. I'm not sure if this is excitement or fear or if there's any difference at this point.

"I don't know." She laughs. "Are you blind? Is the sky not blue?"

"Thank you, Mom. I wish you weren't so far away." I'm feeling a slight panic coming on. "I'd really like to hug you right now."

"Well, you'll have to give me an extra big one next time I see you."

We say *I love you* a few more times, then hang up.

I need to process everything that Mom said. Everything I'm feeling about management and my career. And Win. He's shown me how much he cares and I think he's almost said it a few times. Suddenly, I have no doubt. I know what Mom said is true. What Win hasn't said it but has proven it many times. He cares about me. Maybe even loves me. And for the first time, thinking about Win doesn't calm me. It fucking terrifies me.

This house is beautiful, but it's not mine. It isn't alienating and cold like Lil D's place but it's Win's space. His house, things, staff. I like it, but it's not mine. I haven't earned it. Maybe I haven't earned a place beside Win either. I love him. I know I do and it's not just because he's been my rescuer so often. First of all, I'm not looking for someone to rescue me. I appreciate what Win has done for me but that's not what attracts me to him. He lifts me up, listens, supports me, makes me laugh, believes in me, and makes me horny as hell. But he's established and I'm still getting started. I don't want to be subsumed by him. I don't want to lose myself because it would be so easy to lose myself in this world and with Win. It was different with John. We were the scrappy underdogs together. Would anyone look at me if I'm with Win? Would they think that I've earned my place or that it was given to me the same way Riley was handed hers?

And I know, without a doubt, that trying this and then losing Win would break me. I'm already too invested, too caught up. I don't feel tired anymore but this isn't a positive energy. It's an *I need to run* kind of energy. It wasn't that long ago when I had my record release and I felt on top of the world. How did everything go wrong so quickly? I'm not feeling so resilient right now. Am I still meant to do this? Or is Hollywood not for me anymore?

22

I am still sitting in the living room, my tea gone cold, when Win finds me. He pops his head around the corner and smiles.

"There you are."

"Here I am."

I'm happy to see him. So happy. I actually have a physical reaction to the sight of him. Pulse quickens, temperature goes up a notch. I'm used to seeing Win in suits and dress shirts so it's almost jarring to see him in a T-shirt and sweats. Looks like maybe they've been ironed but definitely on the casual side. He's dressed for home and privacy and he's letting me into this world. Welcoming me with open arms.

It's so easy to imagine us being in this house together. Sharing morning coffee, eating breakfast. Lounging in the living room, listening to music. I could even set up my painting area in the corner where the light is perfect. There's a garden out back that's green and lush and looks so serene. Everything about this place screams comfort. I often walk into a new place and think about all the ways I would redesign

DIAMONDS, DECEPTION & DESTINY

it—even if I like what's already there, it's a fun exercise—but there's nothing in this room that I would change.

There's nothing about Win that I would change either. The trouble is, I feel like a mess. Untethered. I'm a goal-oriented person and I've always had a target in mind. I work with milestones—songs, albums, shows, ventures—and I've marked each step and achievement. But at the core, it's always been the music. I knew the first time I got on stage as a kid. The pride I felt with the first song I wrote. How every song after that felt like I was going deeper, connecting, becoming more me. Always steps in the right direction, sticking to the course. Learning who I am as an artist means learning more about myself. Growing. But I feel so off track right now. So conflicted by what I'm supposed to do next.

"What are you thinking about?" Win sits on the couch. Leans forward with elbows on his knees. His upper arm muscles flex and my mouth waters.

"I might need to get out of LA for a while." I sigh.

"I thought you might be feeling that way." He tries for a sly smile but it's more goofy because he's clearly a bit excited. "Because we're going to Mexico."

"What?!" I think I might have squealed as I jump up. "When?"

"Right now." He looks happy. Pleased to see me so excited.

Win sent me photos of his place in Mexico during one of our late-night text sessions. We were talking about our favorite places we've been and why. I have a few. A beach in Hawaii, the backyard of the house where I grew up in Guam, the first professional studio I recorded in because it meant I was on my way to achieving my dreams. It took some prodding to get Win to admit to having a favorite place. He kept saying he was on the road so much that it was one office, boardroom, or hotel after another.

221

Eventually he admitted to having an attachment to his record collection—which is honestly so sweet—and his place in Mexico because it was one of the first things he bought when he started making his own money. "It's a beautiful place with a lot of privacy and beach access. Over the years, I've done renovations and added some square footage but I kind of like that it feels a bit rustic." I know from photos that it's an incredible place. It's rustic in the sense that it's not over-the-top posh but no one would look at it and think "cabin in the woods," especially with the infinity pool.

"We can leave as soon as you're ready." He stands and puts his hands on my shoulders. "You don't need to pack. Everything is arranged and they'll have the place stocked for you. If we stay down there longer, we can get more of whatever we need. There's lots of good shopping nearby too."

I freeze and feel the panic start to set in again.

"I can't go." I almost can't believe I've said it. The words were out of my mouth before I was even aware of thinking them. "Mexico sounds great. I really love the idea of spending time down there at your place but I can't do it."

This. There's a part of my brain thinking *I can't do this* but I'm not sure which *this* I am trying to avoid.

"Okay, yeah, of course." He looks disappointed but tries to keep his expression neutral. "We don't have to leave right away. Is there anything you need to clear up before we go?"

"My entire life?" I try to sound light-hearted but there's no way he believes it. Win knows me too well. He's too observant.

"Mexico is meant to be a getaway to give you some time to reboot. Get away from all this stress, but of course, no pressure."

"I understand." Why do I feel like crying? I really don't want to cry right now and make all this harder. "And I appreciate what you're trying to do but I really need to clear my head and get some perspective.

Everything that happened at the party was awful but that was just the cherry on top of so much more going on."

"In Mexico, you'd have all the time you want and all the space you need. But it's also not going anywhere, we can go any time."

"I know." I step away so he's no longer touching me. I like it too much. "Win, I know you'll do everything for me. You'll do whatever it is you think I need. And the truth is, you'll probably be right about it. You listen so well, pay attention to everything, and sometimes it feels like you have a better handle on me than I do. But I need to figure it out on my own."

He looks into my eyes and it feels like he's peering into my soul. Cutting through the layers and protective shield to figure out what's going on.

"It's been a lot for you lately and I only wanted to make sure you had time to recover."

"Me too." I take another couple of steps back like I'm trying to put some space between us. "But I need to do it on my own. It sounds perfect, Win, but I can't." I need to stand my ground. Win makes promises that I know he'll keep. If he says he'll leave me space and time to think, that's exactly what he'll do. "But it's your place, you giving me space, you taking care of me."

"And that's a bad thing." He looks hurt. "You don't want me to take care of you."

"Actually, I love the idea of you taking care of me." I chuckle but can also feel the tears coming on. "I love how well you know me and that you are always there for me. Not just in a crisis but to listen to my stories and about my day. I've said it before but I mean it a thousand times more now. You see me and that's the greatest feeling."

"It's okay, Princess, you don't have to explain." Seeing his defeat kills me.

"It's because I'm not sure who I am right now!" I raise my arms in frustration, my emotions getting the best of me and with Win I can't hide the truth as it spills out. It's an automatic reaction. "I moved here to be a musician. I knew I'd have to hustle and I like the hustle but it's all business right now and negotiations and compromises. Everything is *do this one thing now and we'll give you something later* but that's not a guarantee. Promises made are not promises kept. Everyone is out for themselves, which sure, this business is cutthroat, but this is too hard. I'm doing my best and it feels like I've been failing every step of the way. I thought I had a management team I could trust but that relationship feels so fraught and frayed right now. I know I can trust them to help me grow my business and execute my vision but I'm not sure if I can trust them to protect my creative integrity, to protect me as a person. Then there's the whole John disaster, which is done but at the same time my creative self is so tied to him that I'm not even sure what I'm capable of. It feels like my entire life has shattered and I can't gather the pieces fast enough to save myself."

"That song, your biggest hit, was all you." Win takes a step towards me and I take another one back. He holds his hands up like he's surrendering. "Not John. Not Kimi and Wayne. Not the record label. You."

"But that feels so far away. It almost doesn't feel like me. Am I the same person who wrote it?"

Win shakes his head. He can't fathom what I'm saying.

"Of course you're the same person. Remember, I see you. I know you."

"That's what I need to rediscover." Tears start and I can't be bothered to blink them away. "I need to find me again. I need to be alone. Like truly alone and not have you or my mom or the girls hovering nearby to protect me."

DIAMONDS, DECEPTION & DESTINY

"I don't hover." He holds a finger up in mock defiance, a smirk on his face. "Take that back."

"Okay, you don't hover. But you want to take care of me when I need to take care of myself. I need to fix this on my own. Decide if I still want to be a part of the music industry, if this is a life I want to fight for anymore."

Win drops his head and takes a moment to collect his thoughts. I hate that this is hurting him. I want to be in his arms. I don't want to think or worry about any of this anymore and just hide away with him. Win finally lifts his head.

"I told you before that I'll wait for you."

"Win, whatever happens with me and music, I need you to know how much I want to be with you. I tried to push it away but being with you, everything about you, is all I think about sometimes. Which is another reason why I need to get away and clear my head. But you shouldn't wait for me. That's not fair to you."

"Don't tell me what to do." There's a small twinkle in his eye that makes me laugh despite my tears.

I step to him and raise myself onto my toes to kiss his cheek. He blinks a few times while looking at me.

"What's that for?"

"For saving me." I put a hand on his cheek. His late afternoon stubble feels slightly scratchy. "Not just from the party. For giving me the strength to try this on my own. Believing in me."

His hand cups my jaw, his thumb gently brushing my cheek. He leans down and kisses my mouth. It is a soft and perfect kiss.

"What's that for?" I ask.

He smiles that smile that threatens to break me in two.

"For saving *me*."

23

"Can you play it back again?" I pull my legs up onto the chair with me and wrap my arms around my knees. I close my eyes and bend my head forward as I listen. I love being in Malibu in the summer. I've never done it like this alone, but I think it'll become part of my creative process. Beautiful sunsets, cold refreshing air, time to myself. Just what I needed after almost dying at Lil D's. The song starts with my acoustic guitar for a few bars then my voice. We kept the recording pure with no filters or tricks. It's just my voice and my guitar filling the room. It's the third time we've gone in to record the track and it's getting fuller, richer, with every new version. When the drums come in, my head starts bobbing. The song picks up and more instruments come in. By the end, it's an up-tempo, energetic dance track.

"I think you could still pull in a few more musicians." Harlow slides the mix down with one hand. "We could get some guitar players in fast enough."

"No." I shake my head. "Not for this one. Maybe horns, though."

DIAMONDS, DECEPTION & DESTINY

"Horns are easy enough too." Harlow turns in her chair and types a quick message on her laptop.

"Wow!" I laugh. "That's all it takes and a horn section will suddenly appear?"

"It is if you've got a great studio coordinator who takes care of everything."

"Does everyone get this treatment?"

Harlow laughs as she turns back, then pulls herself closer to the mixing board. "We make most pay through the nose for these services. You get the Princess deal."

I'm so glad that I am working with Harlow. She makes this entire experience so much better. I definitely don't feel alone or like I'm stumbling through the process with her at my side. She's been working as an engineer in the studio since it opened in the '90s. She's been entertaining me all week with stories of the antics of various artists during recording sessions. Lots of stories about drugs and musicians trying to bring prostitutes in, fist fights, someone who vomited and barely missed the mixing board. It was all so far removed from my experience in studios—definitely this week—but it makes me laugh.

It's a bit unusual to work out of a studio space without a producer of any kind—plus I'm using it on off-hours because I booked so last minute—so I assume Harlow's been given this assignment because no one else wanted it. She was all business when I got there and didn't seem that interested in what I was doing. She called herself a lifer and seemed way more into the gear than the music. It probably didn't help that I didn't really know either. I arrived with a stack of notebooks and a few ideas I wanted to try. I've been jotting down ideas, poems, and sketches since I was a teenager. Every song that I've written started out in one of these journals. John and I used to go through them while in

227

the studio to find the perfect line, the thing we needed for whatever we were working on. But there was still plenty in there that John didn't latch on to or wasn't interested in. A few ideas that had been rattling around inside my head for years.

Part of my plan in coming up to Malibu was to see if any of them could grow into something bigger if given the chance. So, coming up with ideas was slow that first day and I was nervous. Then I did a take of a song—well, part of a song—giving it my all. When I was done, I looked at Harlow through the recording booth glass and she was staring at me with wide eyes. I got a smile and a thumbs-up and Harlow has been my champion ever since. By the third day, she was pulling in other players from different sessions and getting them to add to my songs. I thought she might try to take over and act like my producer because that's the way these things usually work but she didn't. She offered suggestions and we often talked things through but there was never any doubt that I was in the lead. It was weird at first, almost tentative, but I got the hang of it pretty quickly. I'd always given up so much space to John and others, thinking they had the answers, and it turns out I have plenty of answers all on my own.

I've been up in Malibu for a little more than a week. I called Kimi on my way back from Win's and told her I needed to get away. Needed some studio time and an Airbnb in Malibu. She tried to argue, saying I needed to get to work promoting the song and the cosmetics PR relaunch since we were already behind schedule. I held my ground, though.

"I need this. I need a reset. You owe me this one."

She couldn't dispute that. Instead, her assistant sent me a message with all the necessary info by the time I'd thrown a few things into a bag.

DIAMONDS, DECEPTION & DESTINY

It wasn't until I got up here that I realized the random assortment of things I'd grabbed. Mostly sweats and comfortable clothes but also a few dresses and shoes, a couple of purses I hadn't used in I don't even know how long, and a hat I bought on a whim and never wore. Basically, anything that was easy to grab from my closet or dresser. I usually spent a lot of time coordinating my outfits so this collection was enough to make me laugh. It didn't really matter, though, since I wasn't planning on going out. I was here to give myself the time and space to work on things and try some new music.

I've never had this much time alone. Vacations were always with friends. Or I was always practicing, rehearsing, learning. Being around people can be a real energy source for me and a comfort. Not parties and events so much as friends, family, the chosen few. But here I've been sleeping alone, waking up alone, eating alone. I exercise. I go for morning walks. My Airbnb is near Zuma Beach so I sometimes take my coffee down to watch the surfers. Write in my journal and think about the day ahead. By the time I get to the studio my mind is all fired up and ready to go. One day scaffolds on top of the last. I have no idea what I'm building, but it's getting stronger and higher every day.

My phone lights up with a text notification.

Maya: Do you want to try for dinner tomorrow night? What time are you done?

Princess: I could meet at 8.

Maya: 👍 We'll make a reso.

Damn, I love my friends. They've been so good about regular check-ins and seeing how the week is going. I didn't just disappear when I went up the coast. I wanted to remove as many obstacles as I could and devote myself to the process. I wanted to get back to the roots, the basics, of why I make music so that meant taking more alone

229

time than normal. I didn't want them to think I was ignoring them, especially since they were still worried about me after the party, so I let them know that I might be harder to reach. They were supportive and understanding, which wasn't a surprise at all. They sent *thinking of you* and *love you* texts and didn't get upset if I was slow in responding.

When I'm not at the studio, I am usually in the house going through the notebooks, writing, and making notes for the next day. Harlow gives me a rough mix at the end of each day and I pore over all the songs. This part has never really been my thing. I always left the mixing and adding bits to John. I offered suggestions and gave my opinion but this was something he lead, then brought back to me. I really thought I'd only manage to mash a few tracks together so I'd have a decent enough mix to listen to, but apparently I picked up a lot more from John than expected. I've watched him move tracks around, add sounds, clean up my takes thousands of times. I miss the back and forth we had, and I really did love hearing what he'd come up with, but exploring this on my own is opening up something new for me. I'm having fun. Enjoying the process as much as the final product. I'm not writing or recording and trying for the next big hit. I'm letting myself try things I normally wouldn't, experimenting with being open and vulnerable with others.

Win is the inspiration for many of them. I was trying to deny it for the first few days, then Harlow pointed out how some songs—ahem, Win songs—felt more accessible and I decided to lean into it. What the hell did it matter now? I knew how I felt about him, and that I might not even be in the space to write these songs if it wasn't for him so why pretend? Whether or not anything happens with me, he's a supportive and inspirational person in my life and that deserves a few songs.

Or a dozen.

Win and I have been texting, too, though it's been more surface level and less frequent since I've been trying to give myself some space. I'll update him with all the details when the time is right, but for now it feels a bit like quitting smoking. I pick up my phone constantly looking for messages. Everything that happens, every song that plays, every meal I eat, every joke I hear, I want to text him. I want to tell him all about Harlow, how I have made a new friend. How she's been sitting at mixing boards for years, recorded hundreds, maybe thousands of bands and artists, and she is still impressed by my songs. She talks to me like an equal, someone who deserves to be at the soundboard with her and doesn't act like she is doing me a favor by just being in the same room as me. I realize more and more that's how people have treated me. They want to sign me to their record label, book me on shows, collaborate on products, and it's always that I should be grateful I'm getting any of their time. I know I'm not the only one and I know that's not something I can change but I can find a way to live and work within it that doesn't crush me. And it's Win's voice that I hear when I need reminding.

That song, your biggest hit, was all you. Not John. Not Kimi and Wayne. Not the record label. You.

I want him in my life—honestly can't imagine not having him in my life—but I'm not sure how that can work. Because at this point, I have no idea how to take Win in small doses. I want to consume him whole. Although he hasn't said the words, I'm fairly certain he feels the same. But I want to have more equal footing. I don't want to be a burden for him in any way. Win deserves an equal counterpart. Win lifts me up, makes me feel powerful and invincible, and I want to do the same for him.

He sends me morning and evening texts, quick *thinking of you* texts. I sent him a picture of Harlow and me in the studio. He understood that all was well and I was happy even though Harlow refused to smile for the camera. He told me he was going out of town for a few days and I somehow missed him even though we weren't together anyway.

"You okay?"

I blink a few times and look over at Harlow. One eyebrow is raised as she watches me. I realize I've probably been staring off into space.

"All good." I sit up straight in my chair. Both feet firmly back on the floor. "Just thinking about those horns. And what to do next."

"Right." Harlow gives me a slow nod. We've only known each other a week but she's already pretty good at reading me. "And here I was assuming you were thinking about that person you refuse to talk about."

"There's no person."

"I've heard all the songs, Princess." Harlow laughs. "There's definitely a person."

The door opens and the studio coordinator pops her head in. "Hey. I can get you two trumpets and a baritone sax player tomorrow morning. Good?"

I look over at Harlow but she's looking at me, waiting for me to say the word. Do I know the word? I do a quick mental survey of horns, sounds, my song, then turn back to the coordinator.

"Sounds perfect."

"Got it."

The door closes and the coordinator is gone.

Harlow picks up her coffee mug and leans back in her chair. She's relaxed and waiting for me to announce the next move.

"Did you go to school for this?" I wave my hand in a small circle indicating the room. "To learn how to record and mix?"

DIAMONDS, DECEPTION & DESTINY

"Nah." She shakes her head. "I had a boyfriend in high school in a rock band. They were recording an EP at this low-rent studio in Hollywood. The place had next to nothing, including no one to help set up or record. Since I was hanging around anyway, because it was first love and we couldn't bear to be apart even for a minute, I ended up assisting. Set up drums and mics, learned how to engineer, I'd make myself fit into whatever the producer needed. And I loved it. I started hanging out more, helping wherever I could, and eventually I got paid to figure things out."

"What happened to the boyfriend?"

"I married him."

"Really?" I don't know why this surprises me but it does.

"Really. He's a lawyer now and hasn't played the guitar in years but no one's perfect." Harlow smiles and winks. "The shit studio didn't last, though, which is good since it also barely paid. When this place opened up, the owner offered me the gig and I've been here ever since."

"You learned on the job?"

"Mostly. But also had good mentors. The crappy studio had Chuck, he was a good boss. He let me come around and record whoever I wanted. Same with here. They made the big money on famous bands and artists but I could bring in whoever I wanted overnight. I have no idea how many artists I recorded between midnight and eight in the morning. Now I can't imagine working past ten. Back then, I worked several days straight and only needed a smallish amount of drugs to keep me going."

"And your husband didn't mind?"

"That was a long time ago. Maybe he wasn't crazy about it. I wasn't either. But you work in waves. Sometimes I'm the one going nonstop, sometimes it's him. When the kids were young, we had to set up a whole schedule to make it work but we did."

"You've got kids?"

"Three. All adults now and we'll have our first grandbaby coming in a couple of months."

"I don't understand how you can juggle it all. Or how one or both of you doesn't feel neglected. Or like the other person isn't giving a hundred percent."

"No one can give one hundred percent all the time. That's a ridiculous thing to expect of someone else. We're both one hundred percent committed to each other, our kids, our lives together, but time is fluid. We talk, we tell each other if we need anything more, we listen. And we forgive each other if one of us gets too far down the work hole."

I grimace at the phrase *work hole* and Harlow laughs.

"We make it work because we both want it to work."

I rock my chair back and forth, giving myself a second to think, burning off my quick jolt of nervous energy.

"My ex and I worked together until recently. It was some of the favorite times of my life. We created really special songs and it was a good partnership but work and ambitions got in the way a lot." My voice trails off and I fail to mention all the other fucked-up stuff that went down but I think Harlow understands. "In the end, we weren't choosing each other, you know? And I think I let myself get lost in it. I've realized it's too easy to get lost in someone else. I want to make sure I completely know who I am before I try something like that again."

"Knowing yourself is overrated." Harlow holds up her hand like she's cutting me off even though I didn't speak. "An exaggeration, of course. But sure, be aware and reflective and all that shit. But also let yourself get lost in the weeds and trust that someone else will pull you out. Or that the person who knows you best will say, 'Babe, you need to shake it off right now.' You don't have to do all this alone. You don't have to do any of it alone. If you want, that's all good. And it's good to know that you can do it alone. But don't use isolation as an excuse because you're afraid of needing someone."

"Okay, I see your point. But I think I'll feel secure, like I can pull my own weight, if I'm more established." I almost add another *you know*? Because there's nothing that says certainty and self-assured as much as ending every sentence with *you know*?

"Like I said, this business, maybe all businesses but definitely this one, is all ups and downs. I've had people in here that were the hottest shit a decade ago and are down to almost nothing now. Only difference is it's harder to maintain that 'we're gonna conquer the world' spirit when the world has already tried to crush you a few times."

"Is this a pep talk? Because it's not feeling very peppy."

"Hang on. I've got a point." She sips her coffee then sits up straight in her chair. "There are no guarantees, no promises of longevity, and careers don't work in one direction. Up now, down later. People think the tough times are when you start out then everything improves, but I've watched plenty on top of the world and plenty who lost their damn minds. That level of success can drive you crazy in a completely different way. You need someone to support you when you're up as much as when you're down. To keep you steady and remind you who you are. Who loves you for being you, whether you're up or down. Someone who wants to learn and grow with you. Lets you learn and grow."

"That's . . ." I don't know what to say. "You know, I'm not paying you more for the therapy sessions."

Harlow lets out a bark of a laugh that makes me laugh too.

"Well, if I ever sell this place, I'll look into therapy as my next career."

"Wait, you own this place?" I stare at her in surprise. "You said the owner hired you when this place opened."

"Yeah, and I bought it from him fifteen years ago. Did you think I was a really bossy engineer demanding the studio hire a horn section?"

"Kind of." I shrug. "But why are you working with me? There must be bigger acts here needing your attention."

"Because I like this part of the job. Working with new talent. Seeing what's up and coming." Harlow puts her cup down again and pulls her chair back up to the board. "And you're going places, Princess. I've got no doubt about that."

I smile again because I can feel my confidence returning with every new song and every conversation. Because I'm excited about everything we're doing. Because I miss Win and I know he misses me. Because I've made a new friend.

"Then let's get back to it." I push my chair back and stand. "Let's do another take; I want to add a few more things. I'd like my vocals to pop a bit more when we get to the last third."

"You got it, boss." Harlow starts hitting buttons. "Ready whenever you are."

I walk into the booth and put my headphones on. I smile yet again because I know exactly how I want this song to sound and exactly who this song is for.

24

Our waiter clears away the last of our dishes and leaves dessert menus for us. I love Nobu's desserts but there's no way I can eat another bite. Even a cup of coffee feels like it might push me over the edge. Maya and Val have come up to Malibu for dinner and we've spent the last hour eating and talking. It hasn't been that long since we've seen each other or had a long chat, but this feels like we're catching up after summer camp. So at this point, I'm feeling pretty satisfied all around.

"We will never let you live this down." Val laughs and shakes her head.

"You're making too big a deal out of it." Maya scowls at us. "It's a couple of hook-ups."

"Hook-ups that include dinner one night and hanging out at his place on another."

"Hook-up, hanging out. Same thing."

"You watched a movie! That's more than a hook-up."

Maya rolls her eyes at Val's relentless teasing while I laugh. Maya is endlessly devoted to her friends still she refuses to admit there may be any emotional attachment to someone she's sleeping with. I've often wondered if she mostly keeps her exploits to a one and done so she can avoid anything resembling emotion at all costs.

"Okay, fine!" She holds a hand up like she's directing traffic. "I am willing to concede that some interactions between myself and this gentleman have been date-ish but that's as far as I will go."

Val and I break down in giggles and Maya joins us.

"Will there be more dates?" I pat a hand under my eyes to make sure my makeup didn't run with all the laughing and near tears.

"We may have something planned for tomorrow night that some may consider a date-like activity." Maya is full-on laughing now too. "Look, I honestly don't want to make a big deal out of it. We're having a lot of fun together and we both agree that there's more fun to be had. So we're going to have more fun. That's it."

"How much fun?" Val leans forward with one eyebrow raised.

"So. Much. Fucking. Fun."

In typical fashion, Maya, who is reserved and careful about admitting any emotional connection, has no issues in describing every physical act they've engaged in so far. She also doesn't bother lowering her voice or worrying if anyone might be listening in. I feel like I have an open mind but I do occasionally feel the need to cover my eyes in embarrassment. I don't need to know every position or how well parts do or don't fit together. Val and I don't need to ask any questions because Maya requires no encouragement. She is happy to tell all.

"I might need your expert advice." Val does a quick shoulder-check to see who might hear. She is definitely not as bold or brazen as Maya. "This can't go beyond this table either. Tripp knows I tell you both everything but it's still a private thing so lips are sealed, okay?"

Maya and I both pledge our loyalty.

"Is it something bad?" I do not want Val to hit another snag, especially since things seem to have cooled down with her family.

"No!" She gives my hand a quick squeeze. "It's all good. Maybe too good . . ."

"The floor is yours." I pass her an imaginary microphone.

"Well . . . it's my damn jaw."

Maya and I share a look of confusion before I urge, "Do explain."

"It gets so tired when I'm—"

"Giving head?" Maya blurts.

"That's the worst."

"Yes, exactly."

Val and I respond simultaneously.

"Let me tell you a little secret. Men are simple. Easy to please and easy to distract. If you need to give yourself a second to breathe so your jaw doesn't fall off, you just twist, pull, and juggle. It looks a little something like this." Maya fake snatches the imaginary microphone attempting to perform the act.

"Conceptually it makes sense but I'm still not seeing the vision." Valerie squints at Maya.

"Hold, please." Maya takes her table napkin and rolls it into a very large, very long, very thick, very questionable cylindrical shape and mimes her hand sliding up and down and twisting, while cupping the base all at the same time.

I burst out in laughter and my stomach cramps like never before. Valerie *ohs* and *ahs* as she very seriously takes her phone out to write these notes down.

If I were on the outside looking in, we look like complete psychopaths.

"I admire your determination, my sexy godmothers, but for the love of God, please stop giving the napkin a handjob now. You're going to get us banned from this place!"

"Fair enough." Maya relinquishes the dick napkin unfazed.

"Thanks for that." I laugh. "I might never get that image out of my head."

"I would suggest you file it for later." Maya winks. "You never know when you'll need it."

"Have you talked to Win?" Val's voice is suddenly serious. Concerned. "Or have you gone cold turkey?"

I almost choke on my drink, caught off guard.

"We talk." I feel my cheeks warm up. They are probably tinged with pink. "Well, text. We haven't facetimed or talked on the phone but we've had a few quick texts. I've been trying to give myself some breathing room even though that's the last thing I want from Win. But I'm a big girl and a self-care reset is what's been needed."

"Have you talked any more about everything?" Val looks almost hopeful.

"No. They're mostly *good morning* or *how was your day?* Just texts letting each other know that we're thinking about each other but nothing major."

"I think he's being careful."

"I think we both are. Have you talked to him?" I look at Maya and suddenly feel anxious for more information. I promised myself I wouldn't ask her but it's different if she offers. Right?

"Not much. He's contacted me a couple of times to ask if you are okay. He also offered to pay for this dinner."

"Of course he did." I laugh.

"I don't know him well enough to say with any certainty but I think the guy feels stuck. I bet it's been years since he didn't get exactly what he wanted when he wanted it. He's rich and powerful and gorgeous. A dangerous and irresistible combination."

"He can't expect me to just fall into his arms!"

"Of course he can expect that to happen. He's crazy about you and no one says no to that guy. But he's trying to do right by you."

"How are you feeling about everything?" Val asks.

I let out a sigh and shrug my shoulders. "I don't know. Good? Confused?"

"Well, case closed." Maya gives me the ultimate Maya look. "That's the most definitive answer you've ever provided."

"I know. I sound like I'm all over the place with it. But I actually don't feel confused about how I feel. I want to be with Win. I'm not going to say I love him because it's way too soon to say something like that and also I think it's something I should say to him first. And I know that he feels the same about me. I have no doubts. But that doesn't mean that we should be together. It's the timing that has me messed up. Is now the right time for this to happen?"

"Is there a wrong time to be with someone you care about?" Val asks.

"I think John and I proved that more than once. We work perfectly on paper and it worked in real life for a while. But it's not something that can or should happen now."

"Have you talked to John at all?"

"Nope." I feel no pain or remorse in saying it. I am merely stating a fact. "We're done. I want us to be friends eventually and maybe continue work together but I need time away from him. He needs to grow up and get his priorities straight."

"That might take a while." Maya sips her wine. She's looks happy that she can finally openly voice her dislike of John, not that she had an issue doing it before. "That man is almost thirty and he acts like he's not even old enough to legally drink."

"He's not quite that bad but point taken." For a few seconds I feel almost wistful about John but I shake it off. "If he ever gets his shit together, he'd make a great boyfriend or husband for someone. Not me because that door is sealed shut. But it will work for someone else."

"And what if that person is Riley?" Maya has that devil's advocate look about her. "How will you feel about it then?"

"Honestly? If that's the choice he makes then they deserve each other."

"I thought you and Riley were trying to be friends again?" Val leans back in her chair, crosses her legs under the table.

"I'd say I'm more trying not to have an enemy." I pause as Maya and Val laugh. "I really wanted to find the person I first met but I'm not sure she exists anymore. Or maybe she never existed. I don't want to stir things up again and I'm perfectly happy playing nice for the cameras, but I don't trust her."

"Maybe you need to play her game."

"Playing the game has never been my style. I think that's why I've had such a rough ride."

"I'm not saying to use people but take advantage of things. Make the most of the cards you're dealt. Specifically, maximize the connections Riley offers you, if you can use them. You said she offered to hook you up with Stephanie to work on your launch."

"Sure, but Kimi said we couldn't afford Stephanie. We're already paying more to get the formula right again."

"And that's where Riley comes in." Maya holds up her glass in a salute. "Riley wants your help shilling her perfume or whatever the hell

DIAMONDS, DECEPTION & DESTINY

else she has going so see if you can use that to your advantage. Use a favor to get a favor."

"How would that work?"

"Don't ask me. I'm not a business negotiator." Maya leans back again and smiles. "Too bad you don't know someone who's a business genius and master negotiator. That might really help you right now."

Val and Maya both take a few minutes to mock me for being too nice and possibly naïve. If it came from someone else—cough, cough, Riley—that would feel like an insult. Like it would be further proof of my status as an outsider. But I know their teasing is loving and that they have a point. I often am a bit slow on the uptake when it comes to taking advantage of a situation. Playing nice is definitely my default position.

Our waiter returns with the check and we all pull out our purses. Val looks at the price and laughs.

"Now I'm a bit pissed you didn't let Win pay. I knew that second bottle would be a mistake."

"Oh, I would have said yes but I knew Miss I Need Space wouldn't want it."

"We all make our own money. We can cover a night out." I put my purse on the table to pull out my card.

"Hey, is that new? Adorable."

"No, I've had it forever but it's been a while since I used it." I reach into the inside pocket for my card but find something else. I pull it out slowly.

"What the hell is that?!"

The delicate chain, the straight bar with small and perfectly cut stones, the engraved musical note on the back.

"It's the necklace Win gave me on our blind date." I hold the pendant in the palm of my hand, turning it towards the light. It sparkles just like I remember. "That must have been the last night I used this purse."

"And you forgot about the necklace?"

Is that possible? Could I have forgotten all about it? The date was long, lingering. We both said we had to get up early the next day but we couldn't stop talking. I can certainly remember that I didn't want the night to end. He drove me home and I wondered if he wanted to kiss me but pushed that idea aside. I was still reeling from my breakup with John and not in a place for anything to happen. I also remember I was exhausted and practically fell asleep before undressing. The next morning I was up early to do press for my record release and the cleaning service came in while I was out. Everything was tucked away when I got home and life went into high gear.

"How in the hell did I forget?"

"That was a crazy time." Val holds out her hand and I pass her the necklace. She looks at it and nods a few times. Clearly she approves.

"And then everything only got crazier." Maya holds out her hand for her turn with the necklace.

That was the beginning of everything getting hectic and great, then things starting to unravel. And Win was with me the entire way. When my career was on the rise and everyone wanted to catch a ride or when things got shaky, Win was there. He always stayed at whatever distance or proximity that I needed. He watched; he cared. Made it look like he was in control but always let me lead the way. When I said I needed time to think, he told me to do whatever I needed to do. His support never wavered. He was always my solid ground.

"Are you doing okay?" Maya looks at me with a small smile. She knows my mind is spinning.

"I'm okay. Good. I'm good."

They're both looking at me and laughing. It takes me a few seconds to realize I'm laughing too.

"Would you guys mind waiting around for me to pack so I can ride back to the city with you?"

"Sure. No problem." Maya exchanges a quick look with Val. "I can drop you off at your place. That's easy enough."

There's never going to be a perfect time. There'll always be one more thing. One more job to do or trip to make. My career will likely be unpredictable with time, success, direction. My time in Malibu has shown me that I can face whatever obstacles come up, that I know what I'm doing and I can learn more. I can do this on my own but I don't want to. I can be creative on my own or when collaborating. I can adapt and grow and learn. And I know that I want to wake up every day and see Win. And I want to end every day telling him what's happened and hearing about him. I don't want the quick texts. I want the details. The big and the little. All of it.

"I need to go somewhere first." I know my smile is wide and I feel a warmth starting in my chest and spreading out. "Hopefully, it's somewhere I can stop for a while."

25

In my mind, I pictured something closer to the ending of a rom-com. Banging on Win's front door late at night, calling out that I needed to talk to him. Maybe it would even start to rain to add to the mood. The reality, though, is that I can't get anywhere near his front door because of security. I have to buzz in at the gate to talk to the guard on duty. I think he's new because he doesn't know my name but does say he'd check to see if Win is awake and accepting visitors. So not the grand romantic gesture that I'd hoped for, but it's a start.

The guard probably wonders if I am a stalker or a crazy ex. From his point of view on the security camera, a woman wearing a short sparkly dress and pulling a small suitcase arrived on premises at 10 p.m. demanding to see his boss. I'd been so excited and nervous on the car ride down that Maya and Val took turns holding my hand and laughing. They also offered me some prosecco to calm my nerves, but I knew more alcohol wasn't the answer. I needed as clear a head as possible. I didn't want to be under any type of influence when I made my case. I wanted

DIAMONDS, DECEPTION & DESTINY

to be able to say all the things I wanted to say. I jumped when the gate's motor started and it slid open. I took a deep breath, attempting to calm my nerves again, then started walking up his driveway.

Win flings open the front door as I am about to knock. I know he's been in bed because his hair is askew. He's wearing a black T-shirt, gray sweats, and no shoes. He looks startled but like he's trying to keep it contained. That now-familiar warmth spreads throughout my body again and I don't even try to keep my smile in check. He's happy to see me and that's all the encouragement I need to keep going.

"Hey."

"Hey, yourself." He steps back so I can enter the house. The lights in the foyer are low; all the rooms I can see are dark. There's always staff somewhere nearby but it feels like we are completely on our own. "This is a surprise. A good one. I hope."

"Do you think I showed up at your house at night with a suitcase to tell you I never want to see you again?" I cocked my head to look at him. God, he's handsome.

"Or that you wanted me to know that you're leaving town for good this time."

He's not kidding about that one. I can see in his eyes that he's genuinely concerned I'll leave Los Angeles, that I want to remove myself from this life. From him. I shake my head a few times while biting my bottom lip. He's standing too far away, still looking a bit shell-shocked, but I can't seem to make myself move either.

"I wasn't running away when I went to Malibu."

"I know. You needed time. *Need* time."

His Adam's apple rises and falls as he swallows. There's a slight twitch in his eye as he watches me. He's nervous. I definitely didn't expect Win to be nervous. The second half of my romantic fantasy

247

was Win sweeping me up into his arms at first sight and swinging me around *Notebook*-style. (Yes, there's a lot of rain in this fantasy.) But he's being careful. Gauging my reactions. Checking to see if I'm skittish and ready for flight.

"Do you know Tarot cards?"

Win laughs. I've caught him off guard. He puts his hands on hips—slender, perfect hips—and shakes his head.

"I know the hits. Devil. Lovers. Fool."

"Do you know what the Hanged Man is?" I smile when he shakes his head again. "I got into the Tarot stuff when I first came to LA. It was a good way to calm my mind when things were a bit crazy. Tarot doesn't tell you your future as much as tell you where you are and maybe what you need to do or focus on. Anyway." I'm suddenly feeling nervous but there's no stopping now. I thought plenty about what I wanted to say to Win and I am already wildly off book. "The Tarot works in cycles, so it starts with the Fool and ends with the World and the Hanged Man is right in the middle. The image is usually some version of a guy hanging upside down from a branch or something. When you first look at it, it looks like the guy is in trouble because it's obviously a bad predicament to be in. Except the guy doesn't look too stressed. The card is there to remind you that sometimes you need to shift your perspective and look at things from a different angle. Or do something to shake things up so you aren't always doing the same thing, making the same assumptions, letting past experience cloud your judgment."

Win is listening. Once again, he is giving me the space to express and explain myself. Why didn't I see all this earlier?

"I've had tunnel vision about what I needed to do with my career, my life in general, because I've had to forge all this on my own. I trusted

DIAMONDS, DECEPTION & DESTINY

John and I don't think that was a mistake. Not at first, anyway. But I kept going with that tunnel vision because I didn't know how to see outside it. I'd been doing it for so long I thought I had to keep going. Keep trying."

"Sunk-cost fallacy." Win's voice is low, almost grumbly as if he hasn't spoken in a long time. "Economics term meaning you think you have to stick with something because you've already invested so much time and money."

"But sticking with it doesn't guarantee a good return on your investment. It just means you wasted more time and money."

He gives me the smallest of smiles and my heart nearly bursts out of my chest.

"I want you to know that I didn't spend all my time in Malibu thinking about you." I clasp my hands in front of me. "I worked on songs and went through old journals. Found lots of things that I liked but forgot all about. Picked up a lot of threads and let myself explore, see where things might take me. I ran the sessions and people listened to me. Made a new friend, even." I laugh. "I know I wasn't gone that long but apparently I just needed to give myself a little bit of time to see what I already knew. To step back and let myself see myself for the first time in a long time. I'm not the same kid who arrived here from Guam. Or the same one who went into the studio with John. Or the one who let herself be swindled by Riley. Or maybe even not the same person who wrote the song about you. So much has happened and I understand so much more. I realized I have a hell of a lot to learn about a lot of things but I know that I want to learn them with you. Or at least with you in very close proximity."

His smile gets wider. "How close?"

"Very."

Win takes one step, then two. He looks down and finally notices my necklace. Reaches out and takes the pendant in his hand.

"This reminds me of our first date."

"The blind date?" I laugh.

"Not a blind date." He lets go of the necklace and brushes hair back from my forehead. Tucks the strands behind my ear. "Eye-opening."

"How so? I mean, it was a good night, but what was eye-opening about it?"

"It changed everything. I knew I was into you, but that night proved I was a goner. There was no coming back."

"What was the bet? The one you lost."

"It wasn't exactly a bet. It was more of a slight push from a friend to take a risk in showing you how I feel."

"Oh." I thought that night was just a weird coincidence and I try to recall the date looking for these clues.

"It was Maya actually. She suggested it but I wasn't sure how you'd feel. She was sure there was something there and said she 'bet' if we went out to dinner, the feelings would have a chance to show themselves and they'd be mutual."

I'm still in a bit of shock as he continues to explain.

"That night, I feel like there was something in the air. An energy. But I wasn't sure how you felt. I've felt a strong pull to you from the first time I heard you sing. I pushed the feelings away. I never believed in love at first sight, but it was a done deal the first time we talked. I've never felt such an immediate connection."

"I'm sorry that it took me so long to understand. To admit all this too."

"I told you I'd wait for you." His hand traces my cheek, then my jawline. "All I care about is you being here now. That's all that matters."

DIAMONDS, DECEPTION & DESTINY

I kiss him first because I can't wait a second longer. And because he's made all the first moves up until now and that's not how I want things to go in the future. He needs to know that I want him as much as he wants me and I want him a fuck of a lot.

Win returns my kiss with hungry passion, gripping my waist and pulling me even closer to him. Our bodies are connected at every point—lips to lips, chest to chest, hip to hip—and the way he's grinding into me makes me moan into his mouth. I need more of him. Closer. Harder. He pulls back his eyes hungrily to scan my body from head to toe. I've lost control of my body—I whine for him and he slowly brings his lips back to mine. Softly kissing me. Dragging his tongue over my lips in the most delicious way. I wish he was on his knees making that same motion over that low part of me that is desperately aching for him.

My hands rake through his hair, gripping and pulling at his roots and he responds by doing the same. I like when he pulls my hair. I want him to pull harder, so I do it to him and he mirrors my action. We stumble over each other making our way to the living room and I push him down onto the couch, pillows falling to the ground. I mount him and he takes off my shirt, kissing my stomach, and I lean over him giving my neck to his warm mouth. He sucks, teasing a hickey, and I reach below his belt to feel for the hardness, positioning him so I can feel his length.

Win groans the most beautiful sound I've ever heard and I help him pull his shirt off, revealing a perfectly sculpted body. He grips my back and stands with ease, walking us down the hallway.

"Bedroom," he gasps.

"Hurry," I plead and he bites my lower lip.

We're a messy tangle of bodies and clothes ripping off and leaving a trail of sex clues until we make it to his bedroom with only our last bits on, my panties and his boxers. We're standing at the base of the king bed, my knees against the edge and he bows down. Win's teeth graze the edge of my panties, pulling them down, and I am dripping for him. He puts his mouth to me and I collapse onto the sheets, spreading wide open for him.

"*Fuck*." He is godly.

"You taste so sweet, baby." He nips my inner thigh and I pull him on top, my hips rolling up towards him.

"I need you. *Now*." I'm getting greedy

"Patience, sweetheart." He chuckles back.

Positioning himself between my legs, he gently pushes, easing himself into me, and I let out a sound I've never made before. This is ecstasy. His hips grind into me and the pace quickens.

"*Harder. Harder. Harder*," I beg.

He pins my arms down on either side of my head.

"You are so tight." Hearing him is going to make me climax.

"I'm almost there," I say breathlessly.

"Me too." His smile is devious, completely sending me over the edge.

I feel him spill into me and bliss consumes every part of my being. This is what I want for the rest of my life. Win is what I want.

We're obsessed. We barely get any sleep, bringing each other to climax over and over again. I never want this night to end.

Waking up beside Win is better than anything I imagined. He's asleep on the pillow beside me, rumpled and sexy. Perfect. I'm still groggy, maybe a bit exhausted, but also still tingling. I want to tuck into him, to feel his warmth, but don't want to disturb his sleep. He needs his rest after last night's performance.

"Are you watching me sleep?" Win opens one eye to look at me. "I can feel you staring."

"I like watching you."

"I'm glad. I like you watching me." He pulls me in close and I drape my legs over his hips. "I like everything about you."

"What do we do now?"

"Sleep?"

"No. I think I'm done with sleep now." I laugh.

"Hmmm. I wonder what else we could get up to in bed. We're going to have to brainstorm some ideas." He rolls me onto my back. "Let me start."

The kiss is incredible. Long, slow, and sultry. He pulls back to look at me and smiles.

"I love you, Princess. I never thought I would feel this way about anyone and I've definitely never had the urge to say it to anyone." He kisses me again. "But, goddamn, I love you."

I laugh and wrap all my limbs around him. Hold him tight like I might never let him go.

"I love you too. So much." I put a hand on his cheek. There's morning stubble and I love that too. "I feel so happy right now and it freaks me out. I don't want this feeling to go away."

"We'll do everything to make sure that doesn't happen. What do you need to believe this is a forever moment?"

"I believe you! Honest. I think the rest of it just takes time. We need to go back out into the real world and figure out how the rest of it works. How we work there."

"Does that worry you?"

"I'm worried that it will complicate things. We work well together when texting and calling each other despite busy schedules. We work in restaurants that you've booked out and private rooms. We definitely work inside this house and there's no question that this"—I wave my hand around indicating his bed and bedroom—"*this* is where the magic happens." He laughs and I feel pleased. "But we have to leave this room sometime. Don't pout! You'll need to have a meeting at some point. You probably are already late for one now. I need to deal with the record label and Kimi and Wayne."

"What are you thinking about there? Have you talked to them much while you were in Malibu?"

"Some. I told them the recording was going well, said we have to have a proper sitdown when I get back. I don't want to stop working with them. Not yet, anyways. They've made some mistakes but they've been a good team for me. I need to hear how they plan on making changes and I'll decide from there. And the London shows are still on in the New Year. I'm glad I pushed the rehearsals until much later this fall."

"Do you want me to come with you?"

"Yes." I give him a quick squeeze with my thighs. "But no. I'd like to prep with you and get a few tips but I need to do it on my own. I also need to talk about the cosmetics line with them. That whole thing was a royal fuck-up and we need a new plan."

"What are you thinking?"

"This might sound crazy but Riley gave me a good idea. She recommended Stephanie Lorne and seemed to be willing to pull in a favor or two to get me a deal."

"Stephanie? I know her. She's good."

"She's the best. I really think I need to push on this one a bit more to get it back on track."

DIAMONDS, DECEPTION & DESTINY

"I can put in a good word for you too. If you think it would help. But I don't want to overstep. This is your thing and I'm here to support in any way I can."

"You are incredible. Once again, why did it take me so long to be here?"

"As long as you're sure this is where you want to be, then I don't think we need to ask that question anymore."

I squirm underneath him, in part because I feel a surge of energy but also because I love hearing his groan.

"I feel so exposed sometimes when you look at me."

"Is it because you're naked?" He kisses my neck, the collarbone.

"I feel naked with you when I'm fully clothed. Sometimes it feels like you're the first person to look at me and not only see what I can do for you. You don't see marketing and record charts or dollar signs. You see me."

He moves down my body, kissing along the way.

"I see every inch. I want to know every inch. Intimately."

I have no idea what time it is and I don't care because right now it feels like we have all the time in the world.

255

EPILOGUE

One month later

"Princess! Princess! Over here."

The photographers shout my name as cameras click and flashes go off. Win holds my hand as he leads me onto the red carpet. They're calling his name, too, trying to get him to smile for a shot but he only has eyes for me. He holds on to my hand and I know he has no intention of letting go. Maybe not ever.

The past few weeks have been a blur. After that first morning, Win whisked me off to Mexico with the excuse that we needed a bit more prep time before facing the real world. It was incredible. Days upon days of not worrying about anything. There was even a closet full of clothes and bikinis. His private chef kept us fed with gourmet foods. I'm not sure how he managed it, but Win actually pushed work aside and there were no meetings or emergency phone calls to tend to. There was just us. We spent time on the beach, wandering around the nearest town, relaxing like I haven't done in years. There was a full gym and even trainers at our disposal, but we didn't need them. We had other ways to exercise and work out any tension or stress that might be building.

My mom was ecstatic about this development. There was a lot of *I told you so* and *I knew it* coming from her end. I just laughed and said, "Yes, Mom. You were right. I should never have doubted you."

The girls were pestering me with questions, but I didn't provide too many details while away. They kept asking if we were official now and I only promised to fill them in when we got home.

Princess: I just really want to be here right now. Be in the now and enjoy it.

They understood and tried to be chill about it but I knew they were chomping at the bit for more information.

When we got back, I invited everyone over to Win's and even Jessie came down from San Francisco. It was a fun dinner with everyone asking questions and putting Win on the spot. He wasn't bothered by any of it, though. He didn't mind being grilled because he knew it meant my friends had my back.

"Don't ever make her cry." Maya held up a finger and gave Win a stern look. "Because I'll find a way to kick your ass, bodyguard or no bodyguard. I'm tougher than I look."

"Never." Win laughed and held up his arms in surrender. "Tears of joy maybe, but I will never break her heart."

There are no guarantees in this life, but I believe him. Whatever happens with Win and me, I know he will do everything in his power to ensure I don't get hurt. I am his priority and that blows my mind.

I had my meeting with Kimi and Wayne and let them know the plan with Stephanie. I'd already contacted her, and she was looking forward to working together. I'm sure some of it was the challenge of fixing the fuck-up that already happened, but she also seemed interested in working together. I told them we would re-launch in six months and when they tried to argue with me, to tell me that they knew better, I pulled out the terrible lip gloss and made them both use it.

"Riley says such great things about you. This will be fun," Stephanie said the other day when we talked on the phone.

I'm surprised that Riley had positive things to say, but I'm grateful for the recommendation. Since John and I imploded and everything went wrong, Riley's been riding high. Perhaps she's only being nice to me because I'm having some trouble professionally right now and maybe the other shoe will drop, but I'll take it. I told Stephanie that Win also had good things to say about her business and she was somewhat vague in her response.

"That's so nice of him to say. I should really reconnect with him. It's been a while. We worked together to launch an electrolyte supplement a few years ago. He's amazing. With him on your team, everything should go smoothly."

"Princess! Are you and Win together? Is this a date?"

I look over at him and he smiles. This is our first public event appearance together but we've been around town a bit. We like to do the farmer's markets in the Palisades, I attended some business dinners with him, Win picked me up from a night out with the girls, so there was already some talk. Word was out enough that I got a stream of angry texts from John.

John: Really?? Are you fucking kidding me? That guy?

John: He's a player. He'll use you. Only wants you as arm candy.

John: All he's got is his bank account. He thinks he can buy you!

Princess: I'm not for sale, John. End of story.

Some time passed and Harlow and I have been back in the studio together again, taking our time to explore where I want to go with my next project while the rest of my current music drops. John and I had some songs slated that have started to come out but we've had virtually no contact. Win, of course, offers to take care of things for me, but that's not what I want. The other night he asked if I wanted him to take over the cosmetics line from my management. Or find me new management—knowing how badly Kimi and Wayne messed up this year.

"Oh, babe, no, thank you. 'Never Mine' is doing well, getting the numbers the label wants, and it's been all fine in the studio. But I will call in all the favors"—I make air-quotes with favors—"if things start getting messy."

The last few months have been the hardest of my life. Mending a broken heart. Accepting John's true colors. Reconciling with Riley. Taking control of my life. I feel like I've grown up more in the last few weeks than I have in all my twenty-three years. My drive and instincts have never been wrong. But *trusting* myself, my goals, my drive—that's what got me through. And now I've got him. A true partner. Through the diamond façade, the heartbreaking deceptions, I've paid my dues, and I might have lucked out and found my destiny.

Win steps back while still holding my hand, giving me space to pose for the cameras. After a few moments, he pulls me in close and lightly kisses my neck. His intentions and response to the reporters' questions couldn't be more clear. We don't have to say we're official and in love because actions speak more loudly than words. And we can save all the words for when we are alone.

ACKNOWLEDGMENTS

We made it to book two in the Starlight series! Writing has been a lifeline for me since I was a young girl. I have always kept journals of diary entries, poems, song lyrics, concepts for books, and all kinds of lists. Writing romance novels was a dream of mine that turned into reality a few short years ago when I wrote *Sand, Sequins & Silicone*.

I'm grateful to my Wattpad and Frayed Pages family for their support and guidance throughout this journey. Anna, Deanna, Kathleen, Delaney, Jen, Flavia, Alyssa, and everyone who has helped me in bringing *Diamonds, Deception & Destiny* to life, thank you! I am so grateful to work alongside so many talented creatives.

To everyone who has read, shared, posted, attended book signings and online events, and invested their time into the world of *Sand, Sequins & Silicone* and now *Diamonds, Deception & Destiny*, thank you! Seeing your posts, reviews, theories, and comments on this series is so encouraging and drives me to work harder and make the surprises, twists, and turns even more satisfying. Without your support none of this would be possible. I hope the Starlight series brings you a glittering escape from reality whenever you need it most.

ABOUT THE AUTHOR

Pia Mia was born on the Western Pacific island of Guam and moved to Los Angeles to pursue a career in music. She went on to sign with major music labels and became a multi-platinum recording artist, songwriter, actress, entrepreneur, and creative. *Diamonds, Deception & Destiny* is the second book in the Starlight series following her debut *Sand, Sequins & Silicone*.